'CI

A lot of our Christmas traditions, such as the Christmas tree with its decorations, Christmas cards, and Christmas crackers, were created by the Victorians. We wanted to know what Christmas was like in the Regency period, and the idea of twins separated in their childhood, brought together as adults, and finally sharing a Christmas with the men of their dreams seemed perfect. Each twin has her own story, first ROSABELLE, and then ANNABELLE, but rather than make you wait to link the stories together, we decided to publish both books at Christmas time. Sylvia Andrew has created two marvellously distinct characters for the identical twins, the heroes are charismatic, and the Christmas detail comes cheerfully to life.

We hope you have a wonderful Christmas of your own and that you thoroughly enjoy reading about Rosabelle and Annabelle

~the **Christmas Belles**~

Sylvia Andrew taught modern languages for years, ending up as Vice-Principal of a sixth-form college. She lives in Somerset with two cats, a dog, and a husband who has a very necessary sense of humour, and a stern approach to punctuation. Sylvia has one daughter living in London, and they share a lively interest in the theatre. She describes herself as an 'unrepentant romantic'.

Recent titles by the same author:

ANNABELLE
FRANCESCA
SERAFINA

ROSABELLE

Volume One

Sylvia Andrew

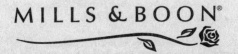
MILLS & BOON®

*MILLS & BOON and MILLS & BOON with the Rose Device
are registered trademarks of the publisher.*

*First published in Great Britain 1998
Harlequin Mills & Boon Limited,
Eton House, 18-24 Paradise Road, Richmond, Surrey TW9 1SR*

© Sylvia Andrew 1998

ISBN 0 263 81258 8

*Set in Times Roman 10½ on 12 pt.
04-9812-77909 C1*

*Printed and bound in Great Britain
by Caledonian International Book Manufacturing Ltd, Glasgow*

Chapter One

London—Christmas 1818

'I don't care what you say, Giles! I have bowed to your opinion enough. This time I shall do what I know to be right—'

The young woman had been standing at the window contemplating the snow-covered scene outside, but now she turned and looked at the man in the centre of the room. Her expression was an uncertain mixture of defiance and a plea for understanding. But her companion remained unmoved.

'A rare event, Rosabelle! Or will you manage to convince yourself yet again that what you wish to do is conveniently what you ought to do?'

There was a short silence while Rosabelle Ordway struggled to remain calm. This was no time for one of those bouts of helpless weeping which had of late become such a hazard to her composure. The gentleman standing before her would have no patience with such weakness. Giles Stanton was a hard, uncompromising man. She drew a deep breath.

'Giles, my sister is alone at Temperley and my father is not in good health. Surely it is not unreasonable for me to want to be with them this Christmas?'

'To say nothing of the fact that it is really rather dull here in London, since convention, if nothing else, demands that you are not seen in Society during your period of mourning!'

'I have no wish to be seen in Society, Giles. I merely wish to spend Christmas at Temperley.'

'Such devotion! Tell me, when did you last visit Temperley?'

She bit her lip and turned away. 'Four years ago.'

'Four years? So not since you married my cousin, and became the rich Mrs Ordway? I do not find your present impatience to see them very convincing.'

'We…we went to see them once… But there were reasons at the time—'

'Of course there were!' he said derisively. 'Why should anyone wish to leave a doting husband, a fond mother-in-law, and such a very comfortable home in order to visit a recluse of a father and a country mouse of a sister? How could a shabby and probably draughty old manor house compare with all this?'

His eyes travelled round the vast white and gold drawing room in which they stood. Rosabelle's eyes followed his. Huge gilt-framed mirrors reflected walls covered in silk, glittering chandeliers, and delicate French furniture. The collections of snuffboxes and other valuable *objets d'art* which had been one of Stephen's passions covered most of the surfaces.

Rosabelle shivered. It was not a room she liked. She looked into the mirror opposite. Dressed in mourning, a wraithlike figure against all this magnificence, she was lost against the tall figure standing at her side. The room did not suit Giles either, she thought. But he dominated it all the same.

'Well?'

'Giles, why do you hate me so? You were away for those four years, so how can you possibly know anything about them?' She tried to speak reasonably, but her voice trembled and started to rise. She clasped her hands firmly together to stop their shaking. She had discovered that Giles despised any display of emotion. But she must get away, she must. Much as she loved Aunt Laura, she herself must have time to recover her strength and spirits. It looked as if she was going to need them.

'An unnecessarily theatrical word, Rosabelle. I do not "hate" you. But I certainly distrust you. Any fool could see why you want to escape from London at the moment. It is now two months since I first met you, and I have yet to observe any sign of genuine regret that my cousin is dead. I could hardly expect that you would stay merely because Aunt Laura depends on you. Life must be very dull for you now that the routs and balls and all the other frivolous pursuits you once delighted in are denied to you. But, for once in your idle life, you will earn your keep.'

'But I still don't understand why you think of me like this! What have I done?'

'Lady Ordway took you in and brought you up as her own daughter—'

'She was my godmother, Giles! When my own mother died—'

'She took you in,' he went on inexorably, 'and you soon found you could wind her round your little finger. She was so captivated that she let you marry her only son—before Stephen reached his majority, even. I am not surprised at your haste—he was always easily led, and you might well have been uncertain that his affection for you would last. But what a blow it must have been when Stephen died before he actually inherited the Ordway fortune!'

Rosabelle was stung into reply. 'But this is madness! I was as young as Stephen. And I certainly had even less knowledge of what I was doing—' She stopped short. She had sworn not to talk of such matters to anyone.

He ignored her words, his voice full of bitterness as he went on, 'You couldn't keep your side of the bargain, could you?'

'Bargain?'

'Yes, Rosabelle. A life of ease and comfort for a girl who had nothing to offer of her own, in return for loyalty and a little affection for my cousin. But you couldn't do it!'

Consciousness of her own shortcomings caused Rosabelle's voice to falter. 'What...what do you mean?'

He nodded. 'You know very well what I mean. Stephen was still a boy—a sweet-natured, delicate, trusting boy. You betrayed and eventually destroyed him. Don't shake your head, Rosabelle. I have proof.'

'You can't have!'

'I may not have been in London, ma'am, but I have my cousin's letters. Your faithless behaviour broke his heart. He is quite explicit.'

'What faithless behaviour? With whom? I can't possibly have broken Stephen's heart!' Rosabelle cried wildly.

'Does the name of Selder mean anything to you? Ah! I see it does.'

'But it wasn't...it's not what you....' Rosabelle fell silent. A great weariness overcame her. What was the point of denying anything? Stephen had always been able to twist facts to suit himself. He had always been so plausible. No one would believe her, except Aunt Laura. And in her present state, the last thing Aunt Laura needed was to be confronted, reminded of the truth about her only son. So she shook her head, but made no effort to defend herself further. 'You are wrong, Giles, so very wrong, though I cannot hope to persuade you of that.' She looked away and said forlornly, 'I…I cannot understand why you wish me to remain here. Would it not be better for everyone if I went to Temperley and stayed there?'

'Oh, no! I am sure that escaping to Temperley would suit you very well for the moment, though what you would live on would be a problem. I can hardly imagine your father would want to support you again after all these years. But no, you will not go to Temperley. You are still needed here. My aunt no longer needs nursing, but she does need constant and sympathetic companionship. What little good there is in you seems to lie in your feeling for your mother-in-law…'

'I love Aunt Laura,' Rosabelle said passionately. 'She was my godmother before she ever became my mother-in-law, and I shall never forget her kindness to me when I was a child.'

'Brave words, Rosabelle! And now you can live up to them,' Giles said calmly. 'If you really mean what you say, you will stay here in London to look after my aunt, until she has fully recovered from the shock of Stephen's death. She will be your first priority, but you will also look after the running of the house. The task is not onerous—you have servants enough for your needs.'

'But you don't like me! You said you didn't trust me!'

'I don't have to like someone to make use of them. And I shall make sure that a careful eye is kept on you.'

'I can't do it, Giles! I cannot live in such an atmosphere of suspicion and dislike, I cannot!' She heard her voice rising once again and she took a deep breath. She must stay calm, she must!

'I think you will find you can. Otherwise...otherwise, my little schemer, I can still refuse to honour my cousin's debts. I need hardly remind you that they are now your debts. Yours and Aunt Laura's. Your husband ran through an astonishing amount of money in his short life. By the time his creditors are finally paid you will be a very poor widow indeed, my dear. So will Aunt Laura, who, I gather, supported you both in your extravagances.'

'You wouldn't! You couldn't! You're bluffing!'

'Are you about to call my bluff? I don't advise it.' The sight of the pathetically slender figure before him, hands clasping and unclasping, dark blue eyes huge in a pale face seemed only to enrage him further. 'Don't try your tricks on me, Rosabelle! Good God, you deserve anything that happens to you! Stephen had more money than anyone should need, and my uncle left Aunt Laura with a very generous jointure. I have spent the last two months trying to establish where it all went, but you have consistently refused to help me.'

'I...I don't know where it went,' she said faintly.

'What? No donations to the poor?' he jeered. 'No contributions to your poverty-stricken family? I had expected a better tale than "I don't know where it went".'

Rosabelle closed her eyes. This was all part of the continuing nightmare of the past few years. The thing to do was to ignore the malice, and concentrate on saving what she could from the situation.

'And...and...if I do stay? Where will you be? Are you going abroad again?'

'Not for long, my dear.' Giles's smile was unpleasantly

grim. 'Don't pin your hopes on my continued absence! I shall be leaving next week for France, but it won't be all that long before I am back. I don't intend to abandon Aunt Laura and the Ordway treasures to your rapacious little hands for longer than I can help.'

Rosabelle fought to control the shaking which was threatening to take over her whole body. She had always found it difficult to cope with disapproval, dislike, hard words. Her life had been governed by the desire to please, a search for love and security, and this man with his harsh voice, his bitter contempt, frightened her as she had not been frightened before—not even with Stephen.

Of course, she was not completely herself. Nursing Aunt Laura on top of what she had been through in the year before had wrecked her nervous system. And now, for two months, ever since Giles Stanton had first come to the house in Upper Brook Street, she had been battling with his prejudices and threats. He had arrived convinced of her guilt, and nothing she could say or do had caused him to change his mind about her.

It was all so unjust. She sat down suddenly and put her hands to her face. She was ill. But where could she go for help or even understanding? She must get away, just for a short time. Panic rose again, constricting the air in her throat. She must be calm! She must keep her head. If Giles would only give her a breathing space!

'Giles!' She took a deep breath. 'Giles, I will look after Aunt Laura—I would have done so without your threats. But…I need a little time to myself first. You need not fear I wish for dissipation or gaiety—I'm only asking to go to Temperley to visit my family.'

Giles felt a sudden surge of impatience. Why didn't the woman say she intended to go and have done? He would have respected her more if she had, though at the

moment it would be damned inconvenient. The whole
business was most unsatisfactory. What his aunt and
Stephen had seen in this pale, nervous creature he would
never know. But, he reminded himself, she must be a
consummate actress. This air of helpless vulnerability
was very well done, and if he hadn't known better it
would have taken him in completely. She had certainly
led his poor cousin a pretty dance. And others, too, if
what Stephen had written was true. Well, young Mrs
Rosabelle Ordway would soon find that she had met her
match at last. Life at Upper Brook Street was going to
be a lot less to her taste! Still, though he had no intention
of changing his present plans to suit her whims, he ought
to let her visit her family some time.

'Giles?'

'You can go for a month later in the year,' he said
abruptly. 'At the moment Aunt Laura needs your help
more than the people at Temperley, and she is as much
your family as they. Besides, for the next three or four
months, until the Duke's move back to England is complete, I might be anywhere. Easter is the earliest I can be
reasonably sure of having time for my own concerns.
Even you will agree that Aunt Laura cannot be left alone
during that time. If she continues to improve you can
arrange to go to Berkshire for Easter.'

'But—'

'That is my final word, Rosabelle. And don't plan to
stay for longer than the month, either. Even though I hope
to be back permanently in England by then, you will have
obligations to fulfil here. If you don't return to time, you
might find your creditors on Temperley's doorstep.'

Rosabelle bowed her head. Where had her old energy
and spirit gone? In the old days she would have found
things to say to him, protested at his cruel treatment of

her. But nowadays she was tongue-tied, nervous, the consciousness of what she had to hide inhibiting all her normal responses. Could she stay in Upper Brook Street till Easter? It appeared that she would have to. Giles was right in one thing—Aunt Laura could not be left alone. And if he was to be away in Paris for most of the time, she would at least have more peace.

'Thank you, Giles,' she said.

'Don't thank me—I'm not doing this to please you. I still intend to see that you pay what you owe to my family.'

Rosabelle escaped from his presence with a sense of profound relief. But outside the door to her godmother's room she stopped and took several deep, calming breaths. Four months! Four long months to Easter. How could she bear it? However, all thought of escape left her as she trod softly into the dimly lit room. How could she think of abandoning her godmother while she was looking so pale and old? Of course she must stay with her till she had recovered. Lady Ordway's eyes opened, and she said sleepily, 'Is that you, Stephen?'

Rosabelle picked up the glass on the table by the bed. 'No, Aunt Laura. Stephen can't come at the moment. It's Rosabelle. Shall I hold you up so that you can have a drink of this?'

'Rosabelle!' The sick woman's face lit up with a smile. 'What time is it?'

'Two o'clock. And it's snowing again.'

'Two o'clock? That's late.'

'You've been asleep all morning.'

'I thought you were Stephen.' Lady Ordway's face changed, and she turned her head into the pillows. 'How silly of me. Stephen's dead. How long is it now? Six months?'

'Seven, Aunt Laura,' said Rosabelle quietly.

'Is Giles still here?'

'I think he's just about to go. Do you wish to see him?'

'Not at the moment. He will soon have to go back to finish his work in Paris, I know. And he still has so much to do for the estate—dealing with the lawyers and…and all the rest. It's all his now, of course. He was to inherit if Stephen didn't have a child. And Stephen didn't.'

'No.' Rosabelle's voice was still quiet, but there was pain and revulsion in it. There had never been the remotest possibility that she and Stephen would have a child.

'I'm sorry, I shouldn't have said that. I'm sorry, I'm sorry—' Lady Ordway was getting very agitated. Her hands were plucking at the quilt and tears were rolling down her cheeks.

Rosabelle stretched to still those hands. 'Have some more of your drink.'

Lady Ordway sipped a little, then lay back. 'I…I forget, Rosabelle. I'm a stupid old woman.'

Rosabelle kissed her godmother's cheek. 'You're sick. Things will be better soon, you'll see.'

'Giles was always a kind boy. Very fond of my poor Stephen. I'm sure if he had been here Stephen would not…would not…'

Rosabelle put her finger to her godmother's lips. 'Don't talk of it, Aunt Laura. It upsets us both.'

'I should never have made you marry my son. I just hoped… You were always such a happy little soul—and so beautiful. I thought it might save him… And look at you now.' She took Rosabelle's hand. 'You've done your best to keep it from me, but I still have eyes. You're so pale and thin, and your nerves are in shreds, like mine. I did that to you, Rosabelle. Can you forgive me?'

'Of course I can! I love you, Godmama.'

They sat in silence for a while. Then Lady Ordway said, 'I've been thinking. Giles will soon have things under control—you should pay a visit to Temperley.'

'I…I can't at the moment. You said yourself—Giles has to be away quite a lot. He says I can go at Easter, if you are well enough.'

'Then I shall make sure I am! You know, lying here, thinking of what I can say to Giles, and realising how much I have to hide—all this has brought me to my senses. I was wilfully, wickedly blind—and though I loved you, I tried to use you. Now I want you to be young again. I want to hear you laugh as you used to. I think you should spend some time at Temperley—say, three months. Spend the summer there, perhaps, as you did in the old days. I shall miss you, but I'll manage.'

'I shan't stay away as long as that! Giles has given me a month.'

'It isn't enough!'

'It will have to be. Giles is quite…adamant.'

'He always was a little arrogant. It comes of being in command in the army. He's with the Duke, you know,' said Lady Ordway with a touch of pride. 'The Duke of Wellington. He always has been—fighting in Spain, then France. Then, after the war, the Duke took him on his staff. He's very used to having things his own way.'

'So I've noticed,' said Rosabelle drily. Lady Ordway looked at her with a smile.

'Well, if you need longer, you must take it.'

'I can't! He would never allow it. And it just isn't in me to defy him, Godmama.''

'Really? We must think of something, then.' She gave Rosabelle a small grin. 'You could always send Annabelle back in your place. She's your identical twin, and heaven knows, you played enough tricks on me when you were children. Giles would never know the difference.'

'It would certainly serve him right—he is something of a bully. But I know you can't be serious.' Rosabelle sighed. 'No, I shall do as he says.'

'He has never married, though he must be well over thirty now—he was a good bit older than…than Stephen.' A shadow fell over her face again, and Rosabelle held the glass once more to her lips, until it was drained. Lady Ordway sank back against the pillows. 'Giles is basically a good man, Rosabelle dear. And he was always fond of me, too. We're safe in his hands, in spite of his domineering ways.'

'I'm sure we are, Aunt Laura,' said Rosabelle, putting as much conviction into her voice as she could manage.

A week later Giles Stanton had gone back to Paris. Rosabelle sat in solitary state in the dining room while the servants brought her course after course, very little of which she touched. They had decorated and dressed the table with greenery and fruit, but the room was cheerless. Christmas Day! She wondered what her sister Annabelle was doing today. Christmas was always an important day for countryfolk, and Temperley would be looking its best—tables piled high with food, rooms decorated with masses of holly and ivy and the rest, and… She sighed. There would be ordinary, uncomplicated, cheerful company, with laughter, and song, and…life.

She surveyed the dismal formality of the room she was in, and a wave of nostalgia swept over her. She wished passionately that she could go back to Temperley, to her childhood, to a time when the world had been bright with promise… Oh, if only she could have gone to Temperley for Christmas! Rosabelle sat up straighter and made an effort to pull herself together. There was no question of going to Temperley at the moment. She had written to tell Annabelle so. But Giles had promised she could go at Easter and she must just survive till then!

Chapter Two

'Miss Belle, Miss Belle! Mr Winbolt is here.' Becky met Annabelle at the bottom of the stairs. 'I've put him in the little parlour.'

'Why didn't you tell him I wasn't here?'

'I couldn't do that! Now come upstairs again and change into your decent dress. I'll do your hair, too. He can wait a minute or two—I gave him a glass of wine and some biscuits.' She clucked and shushed a protesting Annabelle upstairs.

Becky Bostock had come to Temperley as a kitchen maid, long before Annabelle had been born. Now she was the housekeeper, rosy of face and ample in figure, and though she treated the young mistress of the house with suitable respect when others were present, neither of them ever forgot that Becky had been nurse, guide and companion to the lonely little girl throughout her childhood. It had not been easy—Annabelle had always been a sturdily independent child, determined to go her own way. Her mother had died before she was six, and her father preferred his own company to that of his daughter. If Becky had not been there to guide her, scolding for her wilful ways, and comforting her when she suffered the consequences, the child might well have become unmanageable.

Now Annabelle had grown up and was managing the Temperley estate in place of her father, but Becky had remained Annabelle's chief support and confidante. The arrival of Philip Winbolt in the neighbourhood—young, rich and unmarried—had stirred Becky's romantic heart, but it had left Annabelle totally unmoved.

'You know what will happen, Becky!' she said resentfully, as Becky helped her with her dress. 'He'll ask to see Papa, and I'll tell him Papa is not in the best of health and cannot see him. I'll ask if I can be of any help, then he'll look concerned and hum and haw, and say something about females and business…'

'Hold yourself still, Miss Belle, till I get this hook done up. There! You know Mr Winbolt never says anything of the sort!'

'He may not say it, but it's perfectly plain that he thinks it! Three times he has called, and he still hasn't grasped the fact that Papa is indifferent to neighbours, estate business—indeed, anything but his books! If Mr Winbolt wants anything done, then I'm the one he has to talk to, single female or not! I expect he's come to tell me that the fence is down again in Four Acre field—as if I didn't know! If I were a man he'd lose his temper and tell me to get on with having it mended. But because I'm a young lady he thinks he can't. I have no patience with him. He's an idiot.'

'You're not fair to Mr Winbolt, Miss Belle. You never have been from the moment he arrived.'

'Well, his uncle was so much more of a man,' said

Annabelle impatiently. 'And less of a tailor's dummy! My hair is well enough, Becky—leave it! I can't hope to compete with Mr Winbolt's exquisite neatness.'

'There, that's better! There's no harm in looking tidy, Miss Belle.'

'Old Joseph never bothered, and he managed perfectly well! He never worried about propriety, either. If he felt like swearing at me he did—not that it made a difference. The fences on the estate are so old they're forever breaking. The whole lot need renewing. But Joseph Winbolt said what he thought, then simply had them mended, instead of paying morning calls and talking about it. Oh, I do miss him, Becky!'

'He was a good friend to you, that's sure.'

'He was. And this Winbolt is so different from his uncle! I suppose that's why I'm hard on him. But I find his excessively good manners very tiresome.'

'There's nothing wrong with good manners, Miss Belle! We could do with a few more round here, if you ask me. And I think you're wrong. I think Mr Winbolt makes the fencing and such an excuse to see you. He's quite taken with you—anyone can see he is. You'd better be nice to him—he'd be a feather in any girl's cap.'

'Becky, I know you're anxious to see me married off, but I swear to you this is the last man I would choose for a husband! He's far too gentlemanly for my taste— I've no desire for a doormat.'

'In my opinion, that's another mistake you're making, young lady. It's true that Mr Winbolt is a proper gentleman—I wouldn't disagree with you there. But he's no doormat. He may not shout and bluster the way Mr Joseph used to, but he gets things done just the same. He has a way of looking…'

'Oh, pooh, Becky! He's a doormat!'

Annabelle's voice was clear and carrying. By this time they were coming downstairs again, and it was slightly disconcerting to see that the parlour door was half open. It was very possible that the gentleman warming himself by the fire had heard this last remark. Annabelle's colour rose a trifle as she entered the room, but she remained calm as he took her outstretched hand and bowed over it.

She eyed him critically. Nothing could be faulted about his attire. He had removed his many-caped overcoat to reveal a beautifully cut tobacco-brown coat, immaculate buff breeches, and boots which had obviously been highly polished before he had ridden through the mud to Temperley. Above his intricately tied cravat his face wore a polite smile, with nothing to show that he had heard her comment. She concluded that he had probably been too busy admiring his reflection in the mirror.

'Mr Winbolt, what can I do for you now?' asked Annabelle somewhat less than graciously.

He considered her before replying. She had an uncomfortable feeling that somewhere at the back of his eyes lurked a slight smile. Then he spoke and she was sure she must have been wrong.

'I came to enquire after your father. Jardine says he is no better?'

'I'm afraid he isn't.'

'Is there anything I or my sister could do?'

'Thank you. You are very kind, but I really cannot think of anything at the moment. He never looks for company, not even mine, so that of a comparative stranger—' Annabelle stopped short. Had that sounded rude? 'I mean, sir—'

'Don't worry, Miss Kelland. I know what you mean. I am sure you will let us know if and when anything occurs to you. But I also came to tell you that Emily and I will be spending Christmas in town with my grandfather, so we shall be away for a few weeks.'

'Oh! Oh, how pleasant! For you, I mean. The…the neighbourhood will miss you, I am sure.'

'I doubt it, Miss Kelland. We have not yet found our feet, so to speak, among our neighbours. Six weeks is hardly long enough to establish a wide circle of acquaintances, and my uncle had the happy knack of offending most of them. We have only just started to have callers.'

Was he laughing at her? Surely not! His face was perfectly serious. But when would he get to the business of the broken fence? 'Well, sir, I must wish you and your sister a happy time in London. Well…' she paused. 'Is that all?'

'I think so. Er…may I finish my glass of wine? Perhaps you would drink a toast with me?'

Annabelle blushed scarlet with mortification. She had been guilty of gross discourtesy. 'Oh, forgive me!' she stammered. 'Pray be seated, Mr Winbolt. Another biscuit?'

He smiled, filled a second glass from the decanter Becky had placed on a small table, and handed it to her. 'Thank you, but I can't stay long—I have a great deal to do. If I can't be of help to you, I'll drink up and be gone.'

His smile was sweet, his manner gentle, but Annabelle rather thought she might just have been put in her place. The feeling was not welcome. She gave the traditional toast to Christmas in a stiff little voice, then, for the life of her, could not think of another thing to say. She waited in silence while he donned his overcoat, and then escorted him to the door.

She cut short his courteously expressed farewells and

asked impatiently, 'Aren't you going to ask about the fence in Four Acre field?'

'It's mended, Miss Kelland. Goodbye.' She was still standing at the door staring when he rode off.

'Well? Do you think he heard you?' Becky's voice was anxious.

'Heard what?'

'Heard you call him a doormat, of course.'

'Of course he didn't. He's much too much of a gentleman to listen. You can stop being so excited, Becky. Mr Winbolt and his sister are going to London. They'll be away till after Christmas,' said Annabelle dismissively.

She would not have been so complacent if she had witnessed the scene between brother and sister at the Winbolt home.

'How did you get on, Philip?'

Mr Winbolt looked at his sister with a rueful smile. 'She thinks I'm a doormat,' he said.

'*You?* A doormat? She's mad.'

'No, just unused to polite ways. And for the life of me, I cannot behave differently, though I know it irritates her.'

'I should think not, indeed! You'd do better to abandon any ambition in that lady's direction—if she could be so described.'

'She's so lovely, Emily! I know she behaves like a termagant, but only think of the life she has led—brought up by servants, running wild, no training in the ways of polite society... But there's a sweetness about her nature—I know there is. And though she is so lovely she is not in the slightest vain.'

'I agree with you there. Miss Kelland is far too careless with her appearance.'

He went over and took her hand. 'You're very censorious, Emily. Do you not like Miss Kelland? She isn't easy to know, I agree.'

'I confess I would like her more if she was kinder to you! For myself I like her well enough. There's a directness about her which is appealing. But I cannot feel that she is right for you, Philip.'

'In what way?'

She hesitated a moment, then said, 'You are far from being a doormat, but you do like a more peaceful life than Miss Kelland would be likely to give you.'

'I'd like you to explain that, if you don't mind!'

'She has an air of independence about her which would come into conflict with that highly developed sense of responsibility of yours for those you love. I am sure she would resent your desire to cherish and protect us.'

'Do I really stifle you? Am I over-protective?' he asked with a rueful smile.

'Of course not! You are the dearest of men and most women would feel themselves fortunate indeed to win your favour.' She went to him and hugged him. 'If Miss Kelland is your choice I shall welcome her into the family with all my heart, Philip. But I have great hopes of our visit to London. Five weeks might help you to change your mind about her.'

'I'm not sure I shall satisfy you, Emily. I doubt I will find a more beautiful girl in the whole of London!'

'But perhaps a more suitable one? Oh, Philip, don't look like that—I only want to see you happy—you deserve it so much. Let's talk of something else. Do you intend to set off early on Friday and make a push to arrive in Arlington Street before nightfall? Or shall we take a more leisurely pace and stay with the Verrinders on the way? What are the chances of snow, do you think?'

'Has John come back with the post yet, Becky?'

Annabelle stood by the window gazing at the whirling flakes of snow. The Winbolts had departed for their Christmas festivities, and in the household at Temperley life was going on as quietly as usual. Mr Kelland had decided to get up, and now spent some time each day in the large chair by the fire in his bedchamber. He was still weak, however, and no more sociable than usual.

Christmas was drawing very near. Annabelle had distributed small gifts to all the servants on December 6th, and now preparations for their modest Christmas were well on their way—parcels for the poor, food for the villagers for Christmas Day. Every day Annabelle stood like this, gazing out at the weather; every day she asked the same question and received the same reply.

'Just this minute, Miss Belle. But there weren't anything from London.'

'Oh, why doesn't Rosa write? I wrote over two weeks ago, and still no answer! It is too bad of her! And now it wants only three days to Christmas.'

'Perhaps the mail has been held up by the snow? John had a terrible time getting to the receiving office—and the stage was held up for an hour at Hounslow.'

'You may be right. But I doubt it. My sister doesn't seem to want to see us any more.' Annabelle cast a glance outside—the snow was falling more heavily than ever. 'And if she leaves it any later she won't be able to get here at all.'

'Aye, it looks as if we're going to have proper snow this year, and no mistake. A real Christmas.'

'A real Christmas? What is that?' asked Annabelle moodily. 'When have we ever had a real Christmas?'

'Shame on you! Why, we have the waits coming round every year, and we've always set a good table for anyone who wanted to feed themselves here. Your father has never denied the poor their Christmas feast.'

'I'm sure my father is happy for us to fulfil his duties as a landowner at any time of the year, and especially at Christmas. But it's always been a joyless occasion for all that.'

'It weren't always so, Miss Belle. When your mother was alive there was so much fun and laughter, such preparations, such feasts and games. And the house used to look lovely, it did, all polished and decorated.'

Becky's familiar, rosy face was so concerned that Annabelle abandoned her position by the window and drew Becky to the fire. 'Tell me about it,' she said.

They sat by the fire, as they had so many times before over the years, seeking comfort in each other's company. And Becky once again described the scenes of revelry and mirth which had filled the old house twenty or thirty years before.

'There'd be an expedition to go out and gather long strands of ivy, and great branches of holly and fir. Then we'd wind them up and down the oak staircase, and round the candlesticks and along the mantelpieces. And there'd be mistletoe as well...'

'And I'll swear you were kissed a good few times under it, Becky!'

'Well, I won't say as I wasn't in the old days,' said Becky with a reminiscent smile. 'But after my John came on the scene there wasn't anyone else who dared!'

'Does he kiss you under the mistletoe now, Becky?'

'Get away with you! Over thirty years married, and the

children all grown! A fine to do that'd be! But I was saying there was mistletoe and apples and spiced oranges tucked in everywhere. My, we were kept busy! Baking and roasting—venison, mutton, beef—'

'And goose?'

'If there was one left over from Michaelmas, Miss Belle. The snow never kept folks away—they used to come from all over and stay till it thawed, or till Twelfth Night was over. Your mother used to make everyone dress up—Punch, and Punch's wife, King Cole, Red Riding Hood, Columbine. And she made names up for them, too—Johnny Piecrust, Mrs Croaker, Prince Toploft, Jimmy Rusty Trusty and the like. My goodness, they had some fun! Snapdragon and Bullet Pudding and Hunt the Slipper and I don't know what besides. The servants used to be invited in to watch the plays and charades the company put on, and many's the laugh I've had at their antics.'

'And now you and I eat in the kitchen, entertaining the people from the village…' said Annabelle gloomily with a return to her former mood.

'For some of them it's the only decent food they get all winter, miss. It's a good old custom. Don't you forget it.'

'Yes, but I'd like just once to have fun at Christmas, Becky! Or fun at any time, if it comes to it. The sort of fun Rosabelle has had in London, with parties and balls and concerts!'

'It hasn't been all that happy for her in the last seven or eight months, though! You've no call to envy your sister at the moment, Miss Belle.'

'No,' said Annabelle in a subdued voice.

Becky looked at her downcast face, and went on, 'You were both not six years old when your mother died. Little

mites—both as pretty as a picture, and as like as two
peas. Both called after your mama, God rest her. Rosanna
Kelland. ''They're both so beautiful, Becky,'' she said.
''I'm going to put a 'belle' for beautiful on their names—
Rosabelle and Annabelle.'' You were always such an in-
dependent little thing, but even when she was so young
Miss Rosabelle looked…lost, as if she was always look-
ing to be loved, always wanting to be cuddled, bless her.
I suppose Lady Ordway chose the one she thought
needed her most. And Miss Rosabelle was her godchild.'

'She was the lucky one—my own godmother died
when I was ten, and all she left me was a hideous silver
epergne. Where is it now, Becky?'

'In the attic. There wasn't room for it in the dining
room.'

'The attic is the best place for it!' Annabelle returned
to her original theme. 'Then Rosabelle became Lady
Ordway's real daughter in the end—by marriage, at least.
I wonder what Stephen was really like.' They sat in silence looking at the fire for a while, then Annabelle
added, 'It's strange that Rosabelle has not been to see us
for such a long time—only once since she married, and
not at all since Stephen died. She always seemed to enjoy
herself when she was a girl and spent the summer with
us.'

'I expect she's led a busy life in London. And Mr
Ordway was such a rich young gentleman, brought up in
the city and all. The country didn't seem to be at all to
his taste.' The two women carefully avoided looking at
each other. Stephen Ordway's visit had not been a success. 'Miss Rosabelle wouldn't have wanted to cross
him.'

'But why doesn't she come now, when I asked her to?
I told her Papa wasn't well. And it's Christmas! Lady

Ordway could surely spare her for a little while. Rosabelle must have some feeling for us, she never seemed to blame Papa for giving her away.'

'No... but—'

'What?'

'Well, I've always thought that being taken away like that did something to Miss Rosabelle. There was no doubt that Lady Ordway loved the little girl, it weren't that, but...taking the child away from her home—and especially from you, her twin. You were so close, it must have given her a shock. She was always less sure of herself than you, Miss Belle, but I think she got worse after that.'

'I have this curious feeling, Becky—that Rosabelle isn't happy.'

'Of course she isn't! It's not a year since she lost her husband.'

'No, it's deeper than that. Rosabelle hasn't been happy for a long time. But she never says anything when she writes to us. Oh, I wish she would come!'

'She'll come if she can, my dear. She wouldn't stay away without good cause after she read your letter.'

'But what if the snow lies?'

'Now stop fretting and do something useful—have you been to see your father in the last hour?'

'No, I shall go now. But he doesn't need anyone, you know, Becky. Not for company.'

'I know, my dear. But you ought to stay with him for a little while.'

As Annabelle mounted the wide oak staircase to her father's bedroom, she tried to imagine what it would be like as Becky had described it, wound with holly and ivy, and scented with spiced fruits and dried herbs. The for-

lorn silence of the hall and landing would give way to
the rustle of taffeta and silk and the sound of hurried
footsteps and suppressed laughter. There would be a fra-
grance of lavender and perfumes from the bedrooms,
honey and beeswax, apples and spices, mingling with the
aroma of roast meat and baking from other parts of the
house…she could almost smell it all.

She reached the top of the stairs, then turned and ex-
ecuted a deep curtsy to some imaginary tall, dark-haired
beau, coming in through the door to be King of the
Revels to her Queen for the twelve days of Christmas.
He might even escort her to a neighbouring ball in a
handsome carriage drawn by four perfectly matched
horses…. But no one came up the stairs to meet her, no
hand reached out to raise her, no admiring voice complimented her on her magnificent costume. The hall was
empty and she was alone on the stairs.

Annabelle sighed, then laughed as she looked down at
her simple house dress and practical shoes. No imagination could turn her into a fairy princess! The twelve
days of Christmas would pass as quietly as any other
twelve days of the year. A walk in the snow, visits to
church, calls on the sick—those were her entertainments.
She knocked on the door of her father's bedchamber. It
was opened by his manservant.

'Is my father awake, Walters?'

'Yes, miss. But I'm not sure…'

'Nonsense. If he's awake, then I'll see him. You go
downstairs for a while—I'm sure you need a break.' She
walked past the gloomy, elderly man who had been with
her father for as long as she could remember, and advanced to the fire. 'Papa! How are you?'

'No better than I was an hour ago, Annabelle. And no

worse either. You can pour me a glass of water, since you've seen fit to dismiss Walters.'

Annabelle poured some water into the glass and passed it to him.

'Put the other candleholder nearer my chair. And fetch me the commentary on Donne I was reading yesterday.'

'But Dr Jardine said—'

'I know what he said. Fetch the commentary, there's a good girl.'

Annabelle sighed and brought the well-worn book from the bedside. Her father sat up with some difficulty, brusquely rejecting her offer of help. He opened his book and became absorbed.

'There is still no word from Rosabelle, Papa.'

'Hmm? Well, it doesn't matter. Close the door carefully when you go out, Annabelle. The draught is most unpleasant if you don't. And tell Walters not to be too long.'

Annabelle looked at him in some exasperation, then silently left the room, taking pains to close the door behind her. Becky and the others said her father had been a great charmer in his youth, but his daughters had never seen anything of it.

Mr Kelland had withdrawn from the world after his wife, Rosanna, had died, just five years after giving birth to a longed-for son. The child had been born before the twins, Rosabelle and Annabelle, were a year old, and the mother's constitution had not been equal to the strain. She was never really well again and in the end, in spite of her indomitable spirit, she had simply faded away.

Henry Kelland had been distraught, he seemed not to know how to survive without his wife's gaiety and verve. The idea of bringing up three children, all under the age of six, seemed to overwhelm him, and Lady Ordway's offer to take one of the girls had seemed heaven-sent. So the twins had been separated—Rosabelle had gone to London, and Annabelle had been retained as a companion for the little boy. A useless exercise, as it turned out, for he, delicate from birth, had died before he was seven. Since then Mr Kelland had lived as a recluse, interested only in his books, attended silently by his manservant, and ignoring when he could the demands of the outside world.

Annabelle was left very much to herself, and when the various governesses and tutors finally departed no one suggested that she should see something of society. So she gradually taught herself, with Becky's help, to run the household and oversee the management of the estate, and sometimes it seemed to her that, except for a few short weeks each summer, she had never known what it was to be a child—carefree, without the burden of responsibilities.

Rosabelle, younger by twenty minutes and slightly less robust, would have gone under had she been subjected to such treatment. Her nature needed constant love and encouragement if it were to blossom. Her intelligence and sense of humour were as keen as Annabelle's, but quieter and more easily suppressed. Her imagination was as lively, but often dominated by fear of failure: failure to please, failure to conform to her godmother's standards, failure to make Lady Ordway proud of her.

The happiest times either twin knew were the summers spent together on the estate at Temperley. For three months of each year Rosabelle had been delivered to her family home and left in Becky's care to enjoy the companionship of her sister and the freedom and fresh air of the country. And during this time the twins renewed the bonds of their birth, trying, albeit unconsciously, to make up for the separation which circumstances had forced on them. Becky watched with pride in them both as the sedate, grave little visitor from London turned into a laughing, carefree girl, and her own reckless, impetuous charge learned to match the grace and control of her sister.

But the summer visits came to an end the year before Rosabelle married, and since then Temperley had seen her only once, in the company of her husband. It had not been a happy occasion, and had never been repeated.

Three days later Annabelle stood gazing gloomily out at dark skies heavy with the threat of yet more snow. Christmas was nearly over. She had attended the midnight service in the church nearby on Christmas Eve, and Mr Kelland had surprised everyone by coming with her to morning service that day. He had returned to his room immediately after, however. In spite of the weather, the Christmas parcels had all been distributed to the poor of the parish, and numbers of villagers and tenants had trudged in to give them the season's greetings, and to enjoy the traditional meal in the huge kitchen. Now they had all gone, and the house had resumed its normal silence.

Rosabelle had not, after all, come. When the long-awaited letter had finally arrived its message was disappointing. Rosabelle was deeply sorry—she only wished she could come to Temperley for Christmas. But there were too many difficulties in the way. Aunt Laura had still not recovered from Stephen's death and Giles Stanton, Stephen's heir, needed her presence in London for the moment. She had every hope that she would be coming to join them all at Easter.

'So that is that!' Annabelle had said to Becky. 'But this letter is too short and too uninformative. If there were

not so much to do, and if I were able to leave Papa, I
would post off to London to find out exactly what is
going on. But I can't.'

'You can't anyway, Miss Belle. I think most of the
roads are blocked now. It's just as well Miss Rosabelle
isn't coming, if you ask me. She could easily have got
stuck on the way. We must just look forward to Easter.
The weather will be much better then.'

After Christmas the weather remained harsh. Winter
lasted well into March, and the biting north-easterly
winds continued even beyond that. Annabelle put aside
her disappointment over Rosabelle's non-appearance, and
taught herself to look forward instead to Easter. She went
about her normal business in spite of the snow and wind,
seeing to the estate, calling on her father's tenants and
dependents. Mr Winbolt called several times after returning from his Christmas visit to London, but even his op-
timistic nature was wilting slightly in the chilly atmosphere of Annabelle's indifference—much to Becky's
regret.

'I don't understand you, Miss Belle—you couldn't ask
for a nicer, more gentlemanly gentleman. And it's not as
if you were snowed under with offers.'

'I keep telling you, Becky! I couldn't bear to be tied
to Mr Winbolt! I'm sure he would cosset me to death!'

'Well, what's wrong with that, I'd like to know?'

'It would stifle me. I like to fight my own battles.'

And an episode at the end of March illustrated just
how much Annabelle's passion for independence was offended by Mr Winbolt's sense of chivalry.

At the time Annabelle was delivering a basket of eggs
to one of her father's pensioners, a former servant who

had married and now lived in a cottage at the edge of the village. Jenny's choice of husband had not been wise—he was a lazy good-for-nothing who spent a great deal of his time and wages in the Dog and Duck. His wife and children would have come off poorly except for the charity of friends and neighbours. Annabelle tried to avoid Sam Carter for he was almost always drunk and very often abusive. But on this occasion she was unlucky.

When she got to the Carters' cottage he was standing in the doorway, and refused to move. The thought of accepting her charity seemed to enrage him and he snatched the basket away and threatened to throw it to the ground. His manner was ugly, but Annabelle was perfectly prepared to do battle. As she well knew, Samuel Carter's blustering manner was mostly show, and a firmly worded request to return the basket was almost certain to succeed.

However, before she could utter it, Mr Winbolt, who was riding by at the time, leapt from his horse and strode over. Before either Annabelle or Carter knew what was happening, the basket was safely removed, and Carter was being held in the hardest grip he had ever experienced.

Chapter Three

'Why aren't you at work, Carter?' asked Mr Winbolt curtly. Carter cowered and mumbled something about not feeling up to it.

'Go and dowse your head in the water butt, man! Go on!' Mr Winbolt gave Carter an almighty shove in the direction of the water butt, then turned to Annabelle. 'I hope he didn't hurt you, Miss Kelland.'

'Not at all. I am well used to Sam Carter's ways, sir.' The lady's tone was cold. 'I assure you, he would not have carried out his threat. He knows me too well for that.'

'He's drunk, however. And men in liquor are not always aware of what they are doing. You should be all right now—the cold water has sobered him up a little, and I shall see that he goes back to work.'

'You are very kind.' If anything the lady's voice was even colder. 'I am sure Carter's wife would be glad to see him go back to the farm. They need the money. But I do assure you, Mr Winbolt, your help was unnecessary. I am perfectly able to deal with Sam Carter and his ilk, drunk or sober.'

Mr Winbolt seemed about to disagree. Then he glanced

at the small crowd which had gathered, hesitated, then merely nodded his head. He regarded Annabelle with some amusement.

'I am relieved to hear it, Miss Kelland, but if you should need my help with Carter—or anyone else—at any time in the future I shall be ready to oblige. And I hope,' he continued, raising his voice a little, 'that Sam Carter knows as much!'

There were visible signs of approbation among the villagers round about. Respectful as they were of Miss Annabelle's authority, it was clear that they regarded the gentleman's intervention as natural and right. Annabelle was furious, but dared not show it. She gave the briefest of curtsies and turned into the cottage. Mr Winbolt stopped a passing wagon, arranged for Carter to be taken back to the fields, then continued on his way.

Annabelle received little sympathy when she gave an account of the incident at Temperley. Her father stirred uncomfortably, then said, 'John Bostock should have been with you.'

'Papa! I couldn't possibly have John nursemaiding me whenever I go to the village. What would they all think? I've been dealing with Sam Carter for years! You know he is harmless.'

'Not this time, apparently. Winbolt was right to intervene.'

'I would rather call it interfering! And I can manage perfectly well without it.'

'If you say so, my dear. Has the post arrived? I'm expecting a set of dictionaries.'

Becky's first words were, 'There, I knew it! I've always said John ought to be with you when you go into the village. Or that you have a groom of your own. It's not right.'

'Becky! Not you too! John can't be spared, and we cannot afford another groom just to dance attendance on me. The whole notion is ridiculous!' Annabelle stormed. 'I don't know what has come over you all. We were all perfectly satisfied till Mr Winbolt came along with his stupid London ways! I wish he would leave us alone!'

The Winbolts departed for London soon after, and Annabelle was left in peace as she wished. Mr Kelland had suffered a chill after his Christmas excursion to church, so he announced, with his doctor's full approval, that he would not leave his bedchamber until the weather became warmer, ordered a new supply of books from London, and spent his days in front of his fire, or resting on his bed. He was, if anything, even less sociable than usual. Annabelle visited him several times a day, but she was never made welcome.

Rosabelle had written regularly, but though her letters were usually straightforward enough, Annabelle suspected that some of them at least had been written and rewritten until all feeling had been removed from them. The planned visit at Easter was still in place, but, though Easter was now only a week away, they had heard nothing. Annabelle was growing anxious—Rosabelle must come, she must! She could not bear to wait any longer before seeing for herself what sort of state her twin was in.

Just a few days later Annabelle was on her way to her father's bedchamber, when she heard a strange sound from outside. She stopped and listened, but all she could hear was the wind whistling wildly through the chimney pots. She went on her way.

'Did you hear anything just now, Walters?' she asked as the manservant admitted her.

'I heard the wind, Miss Kelland. It comes through the windows. The draught is not at all what one would ask for an invalid, but though we have asked Bostock to mend them, he hasn't yet shown his face.'

Annabelle ignored this. Walters, jealous of the Bostocks' influence in the running of the house, seldom lost an opportunity to criticise them. 'That's not what I meant,' she said as she went over to her father. 'How are you, Papa?'

'Quite well,' he said absently. 'Have you any more candles? Walters asked the girl to bring some, but she hasn't appeared yet.'

'I'll look for her and tell her to bring them straight away. There's still some life left in these, isn't there?'

'A little. It's irritating if they run out. Thank you. You could pass me that dictionary, if you would.'

'I wonder if Rosa will come, Papa. Don't you?'

'I don't venture into useless speculation, Anna. You'd better find that girl. A dozen candles should do. And you might try to fasten those curtains more securely—Walters doesn't seem to know how.'

Annabelle sighed. Walters didn't want to learn, she thought, as she went over to fasten the heavy curtains. But what she saw from the window chased all thought of curtains and candles right out of her mind, and caused her to exclaim with joy. A handsome travelling coach was coming up the drive. 'Papa! Papa! It's Rosa! She's come, after all!'

Shouts from the coachman and grooms could be heard, as the coach came to a halt. Annabelle flew down the stairs and pulled the huge oak door wide open.

'Becky, Martha, John, quickly, quickly! Mrs Ordway

is here! Why didn't you write to let us know, you silly thing?'

She ran out to the elegant carriage, heedless of the icy wind, and stood impatiently waiting for her sister to emerge. It seemed to take an age, and when she did appear, she looked so fragile that a breath could have carried her away, let alone the present tempest. Annabelle heard Becky beside her murmur, 'Lord save us!' Then they moved forward and the sisters were laughing and crying and hugging each other as the servants bustled in and out with luggage and rugs, the wind catching Rosabelle's blue fur-trimmed travelling cloak and blowing it about like a banner.

They took Rosabelle into the kitchen, for she was shivering with cold, and it was the warmest room in the house. Becky hurried round muttering about beds and fires and warming pans, while Martha heated some milk for the traveller. John could be heard outside, telling the coachman and grooms where they could put the horses for the night.

'Shall I take your cloak, ma'am?' Martha asked as she brought the milk. 'The warmth of the fire will reach you better.'

'That's right,' said Becky, bustling up. 'Hang it up carefully, lass, then go and fetch the bottle of brandy from the cupboard in the dining room. A drop of cheer wouldn't come amiss for Mrs Ordway.' Annabelle sat on the floor beside her sister, rubbing the blue hands and gazing anxiously into the white face.

Rosabelle smiled at her sister. 'Oh, it's lovely to be here! Don't look so worried, Annabelle. We were held up at Maidenhead Thicket—there had been a landslip. I had to get out and wait while they got the carriage round on the road again. It was so cold! I had hot bricks and rugs when I set out, but they had lost some of their heat by then. I shall soon thaw out. How is Papa?'

'He's reasonably well—I was with him when I saw you arrive. Oh, Lord! That reminds me! Martha! Martha, get one of the girls to take a dozen candles up to the master's room. She's to tell him that Miss Rosa has arrived, and that I'll bring her to see him soon.' She turned to Rosa. 'I'm so happy you've come at last!'

As Annabelle brought her sister up to date on the state of affairs at Temperley, she examined her covertly. Rosabelle was bone thin, and her skin was transparent. The hands wrapped round the cup of milk must be warmer now, but they were still trembling. Something was very wrong—Rosabelle was sadly altered since she had last seen her.

Surely the loss of her husband alone could not have caused this transformation? Or was love a stronger force than she had imagined? Never having been in love herself she found it difficult to judge. The mystery surrounding Rosabelle was growing, and Annabelle resolved to fathom it before her twin returned to Upper Brook Street. But for the moment she needed love and attention and that she should have in abundance.

'There now, Mrs Ordway, your bed's made up in the room next to Miss Belle's—'

Becky stopped short as the twins smiled. 'Which Miss Belle, Becky?' they chorussed.

This was an old joke. Becky had over the years shortened Annabelle to 'Miss Belle', but whenever Rosabelle was visiting both twins quickly learned to answer to this, and Becky was forced to use their full names.

Before Becky could reply, Rosabelle said, 'Please, Becky, please call me Miss Rosa, as you did in the old days. I'd like it so much better. ''Mrs Ordway'' sounds so strange coming from you.'

'You and Miss *Anna* used to plague the life out of me in the old days, but I dare swear you've learned more sense since then. And, to be honest, it's not so difficult at the moment to tell which of you is which. Whatever have you been doing to yourself, Miss Rosa?'

Rosabelle's eyes dropped to her cup of milk. 'It's a long story, Becky.'

Becky's sharp eyes regarded her for a second, then she said briskly, 'Well, never mind it now! Suppose you paid a visit to your papa, and then went to bed? I'll bring you something to eat if you desire it, but what you need most is a good rest after that journey. Don't you agree, Miss B—Miss Anna?'

'I do indeed. I'll take you up to Papa now, Rosa, if you're ready.'

After a short and entirely typical interview with her father, the gist of which was that Mr Kelland was glad to see his second daughter, but not if she was going to disturb his peace too frequently, Rosabelle was happy to let Becky undress her and help her to bed.

'Another day tomorrow, my dear.' Rosabelle smiled sleepily at the familiar words. She hardly heard Annabelle's whispered goodnight before falling into the first undisturbed sleep she had had for many months.

'What are we to do?' asked Annabelle as she and Becky descended the stairs. 'Should I send for Dr Jardine tomorrow?'

Becky frowned. 'She's very pale and thin. And I don't like those shadows under her eyes, and that's a fact.'

'It may just be that she is overtired—she was telling me that Lady Ordway is still an invalid. I expect she has been spending a great deal of time with her. Shall we see what a few days' rest and good, wholesome food will do?'

'Maybe you're right—do you know when they want her back in London?'

'I don't care when they want her back! She's not going back before she is absolutely fit again, however long it takes. They must just do without her.'

Rosabelle stayed in bed for the next couple of days. A fire was kept going in the pretty little bedchamber, and the door to Annabelle's room was kept wide open all the time. Though she maintained each day that she was feeling considerably better, Annabelle was still undecided whether to call Dr Jardine or not.

Rosabelle slept heavily for the first day and a half, only waking to take a sip of water and a spoonful of Martha's broth. But then her sleep became more restless and Annabelle often woke in the night to hear desperate protests, followed by heartbreaking sobs coming from the next room. When she went to comfort her sister, Rosabelle would cling to her fearfully, even in her sleep, refusing to let her go.

On the third day after her arrival Rosabelle seemed to recover some of her spirits, and announced that she would get up. Becky and Annabelle had decided that they would make a particular effort this year to make Easter as joyful an occasion as they could, and the kitchen was redolent with spices for Easter cakes and Easter biscuits. Annabelle spent hours decorating the traditional Easter eggs, and raided the garden and copses round about to fill the house with daffodils and fresh catkins.

So Rosabelle came down to a warm fire in the small parlour, the fresh scent of flowers in the hall and a delicious smell of baking from the kitchen. The dining room was deemed to be too large and too cold, and a small table had been set up in the parlour, which also had its vase of flowers—late snowdrops, celandines and wild daffodils.

Between them Annabelle and Becky had wrought marvels, for time had been very short. Their efforts were well rewarded. Rosabelle's smiles grew more frequent, her cheeks acquired a little colour, her rest was less disturbed.

On Easter Sunday, as the bells rang out over the countryside, she startled Annabelle by announcing that she would accompany them to church.

'But, dearest—'

'It's only a short walk, Anna. I shall be well wrapped up. And look! The sun is shining. Please. I should like to.'

The weather suddenly cooperated with Annabelle. The wind dropped round to the west, the sun shone more frequently, and the temperature rose. The buds on the trees and flowers in the garden, which had been held back by the inclement weather, began to swell. Rosabelle was hesitant at first, but then she seemed to grow stronger and happier with every day that passed and Becky looked on with delight as the sisters laughed and argued, came back with pink cheeks from walks which grew longer each day, and played silly games with great energy in the evening.

Though Dr Jardine came to see their father, no one suggested that he should look at Rosabelle. Her sister waited patiently for any sign that Rosabelle was ready to confide in her, but none came. Rosabelle seemed to be determined to put London and all its associations behind her.

* * *

For a while all went well, then, towards the end of April, there was a sudden and dramatic reversal. Rosabelle grew quiet, started losing her appetite again, and was soon well on the way to her former nervous state. Annabelle sensed the turmoil in her sister's mind, but was at a loss to account for it. Eventually when she found Rosabelle sitting in her bedroom, gazing out at a landscape full of blossom with an expression of deep despair on her face, she decided not to wait any longer. She demanded to know what was wrong.

Rosabelle started to speak, then stopped. 'Nothing, Anna. Nothing you could do anything about. I must just face it again myself.' She gave a long, shuddering sigh. 'I just…I would like… It's hard, Anna.'

'What is? And what do you have to face? My dearest Rosa, whatever it is, you needn't face it alone! There are two of us, remember.'

'No. You can't help. No one can. I have to go back.' The low voice was lifeless, but when Annabelle looked at her sister's hands they were twisting the handkerchief that she held round and round her fingers.

'To London? But this is rubbish! I thought you could stay till the summer?'

'They're sending the carriage for me in one week. Exactly one calendar month from the day I left London. He's very exact. I expect it comes from being in the army… He said I had to return when he sent the carriage.'

'Who is ''he''?'

'Giles Stanton—Stephen's cousin. He was Stephen's heir.'

'Why haven't I heard of him before?'

'He's been away in Europe for most of the past ten years. He came home only a few months ago.'

'But what has he to say to what you might or might

not do? Rosa, it's clear that you are not yourself. Why do you take any note of what Giles Stanton says?'

'You don't understand, Anna. I have to take note. Stephen…left a lot of debts. Somehow or other he got hold of some of Aunt Laura's money, too, and spent that. I expect he would have paid everything off, if he had lived to inherit all the rest. But he didn't, and now Giles is…in charge.'

'Stephen was over twenty-one when he died, surely?'

'Yes, but under the terms of his father's will Stephen had either to have a son, or wait till he was twenty-five, before he could inherit.'

'I see! I didn't realise… Wasn't that…rather strange?'

'Yes,' said Rosabelle briefly. 'But there were reasons… Anyway, the result of it is that Aunt Laura and I will be practically penniless unless Giles clears Stephen's debts.'

'Mr Ordway is, however, honour bound to see that you and Lady Ordway are secure!'

'Not…not legally.'

'Perhaps not, but any man of feeling—'

'That's just it! He has no feeling.' Rosabelle's voice rose slightly and her fingers were now tearing the delicate handkerchief to shreds. 'He dislikes me, he thinks I'm a parasite.' She looked down. 'And perhaps I have been, all these years. Aunt Laura was always so kind, so loving. Perhaps I did let her spoil me. Then when she was so insistent that I should marry Stephen I felt it was the least I could do… It was never for the money…'

'Is that what Giles Stanton thinks? What a pleasant man he is, to be sure! But, Rosa…are you saying that you didn't love Stephen?'

'I…I loved him because he was Aunt Laura's son. It…it seemed the right thing to do. He was kind enough to me....when I was little. But—' Rosabelle came to a sudden stop, her lips firmly closed. Then she added, 'I must go back when Giles sends for me. He is going away to France again soon, and he needs me in London. So I have to go next week. I...I just don't feel... It hasn't been long enough to...'

Annabelle gently removed the remnants of the handkerchief and held her sister's hands. 'You mustn't go back till you are fit, Rosa. This Giles Stanton will surely understand that. You must write and tell him.'

Rosabelle shook her head. 'Giles Stanton wouldn't believe a word I said.'

'But *why?*'

'Stephen told him dreadful things about me.'

'Rosa—?'

'And that's all I can tell you. I've given my word not to talk about Stephen, and I've already said more than I should. No, I have to go back and there's an end!'

There was a silence. Annabelle didn't know what to say. The picture of Rosabelle's life in London was so different from what she had imagined.

'Then I shall get Papa to write to Mr Stanton. He would if I refused to leave him alone till he did. Mr Stanton must listen to reason.'

'I tell you, he won't! He made me promise that I would return to Upper Brook Street when the carriage comes to fetch me, and look after Aunt Laura, and run the house for him, while he's away. Otherwise he'll refuse to pay Aunt Laura's debts—'

'He's a monster!' said Annabelle, really shocked. 'He can't mean it!'

'I don't really think he would hurt Aunt Laura. He's fond of her. But I can't risk it! And when he jeers at me in his horridly sarcastic voice, and accuses me of being unfaithful to Stephen…I don't know how to answer him. To tell you the truth…I'm frightened of him.'

'The man is clearly out of his wits.'

'Out of his wits or not, he now has complete control of the Ordway fortune. Aunt Laura and I will live in penury, unless he agrees to pay Stephen's debts.'

Annabelle frowned as she considered her sister. 'You know, Rosa, you've allowed all this business to get you down. It can't have been easy—losing Stephen, Aunt Laura ill, and now these debts. But you are not usually so…so spineless.'

'Is that what you think me? I suppose I am. But, Anna, I've never had your…your enjoyment of a fight. I like to be friends, to be at peace with those around me. And…and…' Rosabelle's voice trembled. 'In recent years there seems to have been nothing but unhappiness.'

'Why didn't you tell us this sooner? Or come earlier?'

'I couldn't leave Aunt Laura. And then after Christmas Giles went away to France and things were better for a while. Aunt Laura and I were on our own, and the house was peaceful. Waiting till Easter to get away didn't seem so impossible. But then Giles came back again and started working on Stephen's papers. He found some diaries. It was much worse again after that. Stephen was ill. He hardly knew what he was writing, he ranted and rambled, and sometimes you can hardly make out what he has written. But Giles is sure he understands it all. He only sees what he wants to see, of course. Anna, I swear I gave Stephen no cause to hate me—you believe that, don't you?'

'Of course I do!'

'Giles doesn't. It ought to be easy to convince him, but I just can't do it. I keep thinking of what he could do to Aunt Laura, and then I get in a panic and can't think straight. If only I felt better about going back!'

'You shan't go back!' said Annabelle decisively. 'Not until you are ready, at least. It is clear to me that you need time to build up your strength and spirits. I know—' she held up her hand as Rosabelle tried to speak. 'You feel you can't leave Aunt Laura. But tell me, Rosa, what will happen if you collapse—as I think you will unless you are given time to recuperate? No, you must stay at Temperley until you are fit. I shall get Papa to write to Giles Stanton tonight.'

'No! You mustn't! Giles is so determined to believe the worst of me, Anna. Indeed, I wouldn't put it past him to stop the payment of Stephen's debts out of sheer malice, and the bills are already overdue. He was so angry with me the day before I came away that he almost stopped me coming. I tell you, I had to give him my word that I would return when the carriage came for me.' Rosabelle grew even paler. 'He said he would tell my creditors where I am if I didn't. Or that he might even come himself to fetch me.'

'I wish he may! I would enjoy telling him what I thought.'

Rosabelle shook her head. 'Aunt Laura needs me, and Giles has the power to make her life a misery. I must go. That's the end of the matter, Anna.'

Her face was gentle but obstinate. Annabelle could see that her twin was determined to submit to Giles Stanton's ruling, and nothing anyone said would persuade her otherwise. It was because of Lady Ordway, of course. Even in her present state of health Rosabelle would have challenged Giles Stanton's threats if they had been directed solely at her. But her sister had always been devoted to Lady Ordway—apparently to the extent of tying herself for life to someone she clearly had not loved, merely to please her godmother. Giles Stanton's callous use of Stephen's debts to threaten Lady Ordway was the lever which was forcing Rosabelle back to London. The man deserved to be punished!

If only they could find a way of letting Rosa stay at Temperley without harming Lady Ordway… Quite out of the blue an idea came to her—an idea so audacious that she rejected it immediately. It would be *impossible!*…wouldn't it?

Over the next few days, as Rosabelle grew more and more miserable, the idea kept coming back to Annabelle, like an importunate gnat. What was the use of being an identical twin if you couldn't use it to good effect? In the past they had often played tricks on Becky and the others for their own amusement. Now some active good could come out of it. Eventually the idea no longer seemed so out of the question, and she decided to try it out on Rosabelle. Her twin stared at her as if she had gone mad.

'*You* go to London in my place? Don't be absurd! Aunt Laura suggested something the same, but she was only joking. It's impossible, Anna! We couldn't carry it off.'

'We've done it before.'

'But never for so long. Giles would be bound to suspect.'

'Giles Stanton has never seen me. No one ever believes how alike we are until they see us together—you know that! In any case, if he dislikes you as much as you say, he probably wouldn't even see that much of me. From what Lady Ordway writes, he is to be away for a month—perhaps we could change over again before he

comes back! And, Rosa, didn't you say that Lady
Ordway even had the same idea?'

'Yes, but I can't believe she meant it.'

'I think she did. Why should she mention it otherwise?
I am sure it would be perfectly possible! Think, Rosa!
You could have another month or so—the summer,
even—down here with Becky, and no one else to cause
you the slightest worry. We should have to tell Papa, but
he wouldn't object, I am sure.'

'It would be wonderful!' Rosabelle's face was full of
longing. 'But no! I can't let you do it.'

'Why ever not? The more I think of it, the more I like
the notion.'

'But you don't know the servants, the house, your way
about London…'

'You could coach me. We have a little time before the
tumbril comes.'

Rosabelle chuckled. 'Anna! Things may be bad, but
Giles wouldn't submit you to the guillotine!'

'Well, then, what have we to lose?'

'What about your neighbours? Mr Winbolt's nephew?
And his sister?'

'It couldn't have worked out better—they are away
again, spending Easter with their grandfather. You'll
meet them very little before we change back. And you
can always make some excuse. Since I hardly ever pay
calls, I haven't seen much of Emily Winbolt at all. Philip
Winbolt has visited us several times, but Papa has always
pleaded illness as an excuse for not receiving him, and I
haven't wasted time on entertaining him. Rosa, this is the
best idea I've had for a long time. You must let me put
it into practice.'

'Let me think it over. I cannot deny that it's very
tempting…'

* * *

One week later the twins stood in the little parlour and gazed at one another. Rosabelle was no longer the pathetic creature who had so shocked Becky and her sister on her arrival. The twins were once more almost indistinguishable one from the other. Identical dark blue eyes were surrounded by the same absurdly long lashes. Identical dark golden curls surrounded the same delicately modelled faces, though one head was half hidden by the hood of a travelling cloak. There was not a tenth of an inch difference in the height of the two slender figures. Each face even had the same half-excited, half-apprehensive expression. They were saying their farewells, for the Ordway carriage had come as arranged and was now waiting at the door.

'There's still time to change your mind, Anna.'

'What, and waste all those hours spent learning the geography and customs of the Ordway mansion—not to mention the streets of London? What a foolish suggestion! Besides, I am determined to enjoy myself—I wouldn't miss it for all the money in the Bank of England.'

Rosabelle was still anxious. 'You have my note for Aunt Laura?'

'Safely tucked inside my reticule. She shall have it as soon as I see her.'

'No, no! You must make sure she is strong enough first. I know she suggested we should change places, but she may not quite have thought we should actually do it. Take care of her, Anna! Make sure she understands why we have done this—I wouldn't hurt her for the world. And remember to call her Aunt Laura!'

'Rosa, I shall do everything necessary. Stop worrying, my dearest girl. You will best prove your devotion to Lady Ordway by getting fit enough to look after her yourself, and acquiring the strength of mind to stand up to Giles Stanton. Though by the time I have done with him he may well be more human.'

'Don't upset him, Anna! Please!'

'Of course, I shan't upset him,' said Annabelle reassuringly. 'I shall be the soul of discretion, I swear. You may trust me—I have learned a great deal from dealing with Papa, you know. I must go—we mustn't keep the horses standing. Don't come out with me—we don't want the Ordway servants to see us together, but tell me the names of the men out there.' They went to the window.

'I'm not sure of their names—they're all newly engaged. The one on the left is Roberts, I think, but they won't think it strange if you don't remember them.'

'Who is the man waiting by the door?'

'He's important. That's Goss.'

'Giles Stanton's man? The one who was a sergeant in the army?'

'Well remembered! Giles must have sent him to make certain that I do go back, as promised.'

'How charming of him!'

Rosabelle hesitated, then suddenly took Annabelle's arm and said in a rapid undertone, 'Anna, I gave my word to Aunt Laura that I wouldn't tell anyone about Stephen, but I can't let you go without warning you! He…he had some strange friends. Don't take any risks—especially if you come across a man called…called Selder.'

'I shan't take any risks at all. Don't worry so, Rosa! I can't imagine Stephen's friends will bother anyone after all this time.'

'But you will take care?'

Annabelle took her sister's worried face between her hands and kissed her. Then she said slowly and clearly, 'I shall take every precaution not to receive any of

Stephen's friends, I will remember to call Lady Ordway
"Aunt Laura", and I shall treat Giles Stanton with great
respect—for as long as I can manage it! Now will you
stop worrying? I shall soon lose all patience with you,
Rosa! Come, you can see me to the door, but no further.
And you can take care to call me *Rosabelle* in public!'

'There you are!' Becky bustled up as they emerged
from the parlour and made their way to the front door.
'Have you everything you need, Miss Belle?'

It was what was needed for this fraught moment. The
twins looked at one another and smiled as they chorussed.
'Which Miss Belle, Becky?'

Becky frowned severely as she looked at the Ordway
grooms, waiting just outside the door. She said, gazing
hard at Annabelle as she spoke, 'Why, Miss *Rosabelle*,
of course!'

The figure in blue embraced first her sister, then Becky
and allowed herself to be assisted into the coach. The
grooms leapt up, the driver cracked his whip and the
carriage trundled down the drive. Annabelle Kelland was
on her way to London.

Chapter Four

Rosabelle sighed and turned back towards the parlour. She suddenly felt exhausted. The last week had been exhilarating but hard. Equipping Annabelle with what she needed to carry out her impersonation had taken every bit of their joint ingenuity. They had chanted and memorised, tested and re-tested, joked and laughed, had even come close to quarrelling once or twice, but in the end they had agreed that Annabelle had as much information as Rosabelle could impart, and Annabelle could absorb in the time given to them. She hoped it would be enough.

There were dark areas in her life regarding Stephen which she had not discussed with her sister, but they had remained undisturbed for some time now. And she had put Annabelle on her guard. In fact, the situation seemed to be under control...as long as Annabelle kept her head and didn't provoke Giles. She shook herself. She now had a month—perhaps more—to forget the tensions of the house in Upper Brook Street and learn to relax. That was the whole purpose of this daring escapade.

The small household soon learned to accept 'Miss Belle', and indeed it was hard for most of them to re-

member which Miss Belle it was, so alike were the girls.
The present Miss Belle had a gentler air, perhaps, a more
ladylike manner, but not so that a casual observer would
notice, and Temperley's secret was well guarded by
Annabelle's loyal band of servants. There had not been
time for Rosa to learn about life at Temperley, so she
spent a great deal of her time working with Becky and
John in order to acquire the routines of the house.

Her father remained in his room. Mr Kelland's condition was pronounced not life-threatening, but his weakness, allied with his indifference to the world, made it
most unlikely he would leave his bedchamber in the fore-
seeable future. He had been told of the switch between
the twins, but it had not seemed to mean much to him.

Life at Temperley carried on in its quiet, uneventful
way—the best possible treatment for Rosa's shattered
nervous system. John brought news from the village that
the Winbolts had accepted an invitation from some
friends in Surrey, and were not expected back for another
few weeks. Rosa breathed a sigh of relief. Anna had been
dismissive about Philip Winbolt, but nonetheless it would
have been a strain meeting him. Becky seemed to think
he was more wideawake than he appeared.

May ran the rest of its course and the countryside
started to show signs of summer. Rosa went out most
days, walking or riding. She took to performing
Annabelle's duties with the people on the estate, gaining
more confidence with every day that passed. Fresh air,
peace and Becky's loving care had wrought wonders.
Rosa's step had a spring to it, the shadows under her
eyes had vanished and her cheeks had lost their hollows.
She was now slender, rather than thin, and the fragile,

transparent look which had so shocked Annabelle, had quite gone.

She began to believe that in a little while—quite soon, in fact—she would be able to cope once again with life in London. The thought was not a happy one. She had discovered that life in the country suited her far better than city life, and Upper Brook Street was a poor exchange for Temperley. However, it was her clear duty to look after Aunt Laura, and she prepared herself gamely for the changeover.

One day, leaving her horse tethered to a tree, she walked along the banks of the river which marked the boundary of the Kelland estate. After a while she came to a spot where the view was so beautiful, that she left the path and stepped down on to the river bank to admire it. Willows, bending their slender branches to trail and sway in the water closed the vista on either side. In the foreground, a family of swans made their stately way upstream in slow, rhythmic strokes. And beyond, on the other side of the valley, the green slopes of the Downs rose serenely to an azure blue sky. She stood lost to the world, breathing in the scented air, feasting her eyes on the idyllic scene.

'Miss Kelland! How very pleasant to find you here. I was on my way to call on you when I saw your horse. But—take care! You'll be in the river.'

Rosabelle had swirled round to find a perfect stranger standing on the bank behind her. With a cry of alarm she had taken a step back, stumbling over the skirt of her riding habit. If he had not caught her she would have fallen.

'I'm sorry to have startled you. I didn't think… Please forgive me!'

He assisted her up to the path, but released her im-

mediately when she took a step away from him. Now she
could see that he was quite the handsomest man she had
ever met, with regular features, grey eyes and blond hair
cut in a Brutus crop.

'Miss Kelland? Are you quite well?' He was regarding
her with such an expression of concern that she forced
herself to respond.

'Perfectly well, thank you. The…the sun was in my
eyes. Thank you for rescuing me.' Who could he be? He
obviously knew Annabelle. Was…was this Philip
Winbolt? The doormat? She rejected the idea immediately, it was impossible! But who on earth could he be?
Annabelle had not mentioned any other newcomers. He
was looking at her as if waiting for her to say something.
She must speak.

'I…wasn't expecting to see you here.' That was safe
enough. But he still appeared to be waiting! 'Temperley
has not seen you for such a long time.' That was safe,
too. She had been home for nearly two months, and this
man had not called in all that time.

'I dare not hope you've missed me! Emily and I have
been visiting friends and relations, but I confess I am
more glad than I can say to be back at Shearings.'

It *must* be the doormat! The Winbolts had owned
Shearings Hall for as long as anyone could remember,
and Annabelle had called Mr Winbolt's sister 'Emily'.
Oh, how could Annabelle have been so blind? She decided to risk his name.

'Mr Winbolt…' That seemed to go down well. He had
smiled. She said more confidently, 'Mr Winbolt, did you
say you were on the way to Temperley?'

'Yes, I did.'

'Shall we ride together?' A flicker of pleased surprise
crossed his handsome face.

'Of course, Miss Kelland—I should like nothing better.'

Stupid, stupid Rosabelle! Of course! Annabelle would have been far less gracious. But she could hardly withdraw the invitation now. Think, Rosabelle, think! Annabelle had said something about fences... She set off along the path.

'I thought we could look at…at some of the fences on the way,' she said in a cooler tone, throwing the words over her shoulder. 'I believe you wanted them seen to?'

'Ah, yes. The fences. Shall we not leave John Bostock to deal with it?' He drew ahead to hand her over the stile. 'I confess I am still in holiday mood, Miss Kelland.'

There was a quirk to the corner of his mouth, and the grey eyes were dancing as he stood on the other side of the stile and looked up at her. She found the humour in them irresistible, and laughed. Mr Winbolt stopped short, gazing at her in wonder. Then he took a deep breath and helped her down to the ground. He appeared to forget that he still had hold of her hand as they set off along the road to the horses, and Rosabelle gently removed it.

Her mind was working furiously, but she was also conscious of a feeling of exhilaration such as she had never before experienced. It was clear that Mr Winbolt was more interested in 'Miss Kelland' than her sister had revealed. Annabelle had been somewhat scornful of the gentleman. Had her attitude been a screen to hide her real feelings? Rosabelle was inclined to think not—her sister had been too casual. But how had she come to underestimate Mr Winbolt so? This was no weakling—the hand which had grasped hers was firm, the voice, though perfectly polite, had an assured ring to it.

'Is your groom near at hand?' he said, looking around.

'I haven't one with me.' When he showed surprise she

added, 'I've known Temperley and its surroundings all
my life. I can manage perfectly well without one. He is
better occupied working for John Bostock on the farm.'

'You could still have a fall,' he said gently. Then he
held up a hand and said, 'But I know your independent
spirit too well to say any more. Will you permit me to
help you mount?'

Rosabelle nodded and in a few minutes they set off
back to Temperley. She wondered nervously how she
would fare in this unexpected test, and tried to remember
what Annabelle had said about the Winbolts. After a minute or two Mr Winbolt broke in on her thoughts.

'You seem somewhat abstracted. I hope your father is
not worse? I saw Dr Jardine in the village yesterday. He
seemed to be of the opinion that Mr Kelland's condition
was stable.'

Rosabelle seized on this unexceptional topic of conversation. 'You are kind to be so concerned, sir. Papa is
as well as he is likely ever to be again. He has always
been happiest when left to himself, and though his illness
is undoubtedly genuine, it provides him with the best
possible excuse to be unsociable.'

'So you have said—more than once,' he murmured.
'And I have to confess that I thought it a ruse to keep
me at arm's length.'

'Oh, no! I am sure it wasn't!'

'You sound as if you no longer remember, Miss
Kelland?'

Once again Rosabelle castigated herself for her stupid-
ity. Her deception wouldn't last long at this rate. What
had Annabelle said? She blushed and stammered, 'I
meant that…that I intended no such thing—' She stopped
short. Heavens, she was now sounding as if she didn't
wish to keep him at arm's length! What a tangle she was

getting in! She took a deep breath and said stiffly, 'I think you are aware that Papa is fairly indifferent to us all—family and acquaintance alike. Whatever my own feelings in the matter, there was no ruse attached to what I told you. You misunderstood, Mr Winbolt.'

He looked at her flustered face and shook his head ruefully. 'I apologise. I won't tease you any more. It's a bad habit I have, and a frequent source of annoyance to my sister.' There was a short pause. The horses ambled gently along, neither rider making any attempt to hurry them. The day was delightful—bright without being unduly hot, and the countryside was still freshly green and alive with the movement of small animals going about their business.

'But...' He stopped.

'But what?'

'I seem to have made it impossible for myself to find out whether you still object to my calling at Temperley. Now that I can no longer claim that I have come to call on your father.'

'Oh. I...I...' Rosabelle was filled with conflicting feelings. On the one hand she knew she should not encourage Mr Winbolt—Annabelle would not thank her for it. On the other... It was a long time since she had met anyone whom she found more agreeable. She compromised. 'In the country, Mr Winbolt,' she said primly, 'neighbours call on one another out of simple courtesy, with no particular significance attached to it.'

'Of course,' he said gravely. His face was serious, but she had the impression that he was amused. However, he seemed content to leave the question, for he went on, 'When I last saw you you were still uncertain whether your sister would be able to join you for Easter. Did she come?'

'What? Oh, yes! We had a very pleasant time. Quiet, you know. She...she is a widow.'

'Is she much older than you?'

So he didn't know that the Kellands were twins! So much the better. 'No, not very much,' she said, crossing her fingers and telling her conscience, which was distinctly uneasy, that twenty minutes was indeed not very much.

'Does she resemble you? I should like to have met her.'

Poor Rosabelle was becoming somewhat desperate. 'We are a...a little alike, yes, Mr Winbolt,' she stammered, thanking her lucky stars that Mr Winbolt had never met Rosabelle Ordway before. Had he seen the twins side by side, her present impersonation would soon have been discovered, for nothing much would escape this gentleman's sharp eyes, she was sure. How could Annabelle have been so wrong about him? She must get off the subject of the Kellands as soon as possible. It was too nerve-racking. 'Er...how is your own sister? Did she enjoy her stay in London?'

'We spent the Easter holiday with my grandfather in Arlington Street. I can't say we had a lively time there— he is an old man, Miss Kelland, and tires easily, but we are both very fond of him. We always spend Christmas and Easter with him. Afterwards we spent time with friends in Reigate, and that was more to Emily's taste. She is a sociable creature—we both are. I'm sure she enjoyed herself, but, like me, she is glad to be back at Shearings. Emily loves the countryside round here as much as I do. We hope to have some friends to visit us in the near future, and I should very much like you to make their acquaintance. Dare I hope you would come to Shearings again? My sister would be delighted to welcome you there.' When Rosabelle hesitated he added, 'Just as a matter of neighbourly courtesy, Miss Kelland. With no particular significance attached to it.'

She glanced at him sharply. How dare he quote her own words back to her! But he was regarding her with such a quizzical look in his eyes, inviting her to share in the joke, that she was hard put to it not to laugh again. She would not laugh, she would not! It was too dangerous. He was watching the telltale quiver at the corner of her mouth with great interest, to see what she would do. But when she suppressed it he smiled, as if he guessed what an effort it had been. What was there about this man? She had known him for less than half an hour, but he was already a danger to her peace of mind—and not just because he might see through her charade, either! With immense relief Rosabelle saw that they were at the gate to Temperley.

'Thank you for your company, Mr Winbolt. Pray give my regards to your sister. I hope to meet her quite soon. Goodbye.' She held out her hand in unmistakeable dismissal. He bent his head over it.

'I have enjoyed our ride together, Miss Kelland. But we still have much to discuss. May I call on you tomorrow?'

'What have we to discuss?'

'Why, the fences, Miss Kelland. Had you forgotten?'

'I thought you had decided to leave the fences to John Bostock, sir,' Rosabelle said, unable to decide whether she was pleased or sorry that he was being so persistent.

'That was today when I was in holiday mood. Tomorrow is another matter altogether. Seriously, Miss Kelland, I do need to clear up the matter of our boundaries. I'm sure John Bostock and my man can sort out the larger part, but there are one or two places where we need to come to some sort of agreement. I would have preferred to talk to your father, but you have always given me to understand that he leaves such decisions to you. May I come about eleven o'clock?'

'Of course. I shall expect you then. Goodbye, Mr Winbolt.'

Rosabelle rode up the drive at a good pace. If she was to learn about Temperley's boundaries before eleven o'clock the next morning she would have to begin at once. She rode straight round to the stables, where she hoped to find John Bostock. He was nowhere to be seen. She waited impatiently while the stable lad looked for him, then dismounted and ran into the kitchen.

'Becky! Becky, tell me quickly. Where's John?'

'My John, Miss Belle? He's gone to Reading Market.'

'Oh, confound it!'

'Miss Rosabelle!' said Becky, scandalised.

'I'm sorry, Becky, but it's so urgent! And you mustn't call me Rosabelle.'

'I'm not surprised I did,' said Becky austerely. 'Such language. But what's amiss?'

'Philip Winbolt is coming here tomorrow to catechise me on the boundary fences! That's what is amiss. And I haven't the faintest notion about any of it.'

'Dearie me! What time is he coming?'

'Eleven o'clock. I shall have to pretend I am unwell, that's all. Five minutes talking about fences—no, not even five!—would expose me for the fraud I am.'

'Now don't get in a fret, Miss Belle. The maps and all the other details are in the library. We'll go and get them out first of all. John should be back before long and he can spend some time with you then. And tomorrow you've got till eleven.'

'All the time in the world,' said Rosabelle hollowly. 'I still think it would be better if you told him I was prostrate. Indeed, it will probably be perfectly true.'

'Come, Miss Belle. If Mr Winbolt wants to talk to you about these fences you've got to face him sooner or later—I don't suppose he'll wait till Miss Annabelle gets back. Think of her! She could well be ashamed of you, the way you're going on. You're not ill now, young lady.'

Becky sailed off towards the library, Rosabelle meekly following. Annabelle proved to have been a methodical and efficient worker. The plans were kept in clearly marked folders, and the areas of dispute in the past were outlined in red. Rosabelle carried them carefully into the little parlour and laid them on the table by the window. Becky helped her to change out of her riding things and she was soon absorbed in the plans of the Temperley estate.

The names of the fields and woods were already familiar to her from her childhood summers. She and Annabelle had roamed freely through every corner of the estate and picture after picture unrolled in her mind's eye as she studied the documents. Dead Man's Spinney, Potter's Pit, Four Acre field, South field, Boundary field, Thomson's Wood and the rest—all known, all loved.

It came as a surprise to her when Becky interrupted her with the news that John was back.

'So you can have a bite to eat, and then the two of you can study the things together. Though he's not much of a scholar, my John, he knows the grounds like the back of his hand, and he's helped Miss Belle a lot in the past.'

After supper they worked till the light faded, and then

fetched some candles and worked some more. It soon
appeared that there were only two areas which might still
be in question. John scratched his grey head.

'Though I don't understand what he wants to talk
about, Miss Belle, I really don't. The other Miss Belle—'
he looked sideways at Rosabelle and she nodded. 'The
other Miss Belle sorted it all out with old Mr Winbolt
and the lawyers…it must have been early in the autumn
last year—a month or two before the old gentleman died.'

'All the same, we'd better make sure that I know what
I'm talking about, John.'

So Rosabelle toiled till her eyes couldn't stay open,
and she got up early the next day and went back to the
plans, and worked some more. When the time came for
Mr Winbolt's call, her eyes were sore and her head was
aching but she was fairly certain that she had mastered
the history and layout of the Temperley estate.

'Mr Winbolt, ma'am.' Becky ushered Rosabelle's new
acquaintance into the parlour with dignity.

'Thank you, Becky. Perhaps you'd fetch some refresh-
ment. What will you take, Mr Winbolt?'

There was a very slight pause, then her guest said politely, 'The Canary wine you…offered me before
Christmas was excellent, Miss Kelland. But a glass of
wine of whatever sort would be very welcome.'

'The Canary wine, Becky—and some of those delicious macaroons Martha was making yesterday. I hope
your sister is well, Mr Winbolt…'

Becky left the room and came back a couple of
minutes later with the refreshments. Her face was impassive, but Rosabelle could tell she was perturbed, and
wondered what she had done wrong. She tried to catch
Becky's eye as the housekeeper placed the tray on the

side table, but failed. Becky went out, and Rosabelle, mentally shrugging her shoulders, turned to Mr Winbolt.

'You see, I have all the necessary papers ready for you. Let me show you.' She took him to the table and opened up the large map of the estate. 'I understand the difficulty lies here—' she stretched out her arm and pointed '—and here.'

She became aware that Mr Winbolt was standing very close, and felt slightly breathless.

'Where did you say it was exactly, Miss Kelland? Here?'

His arm brushed hers as his finger touched the spot on the map. He seemed to have come even closer. She moved round the corner of the table, and looked hard at the places on the map, waiting for her pulse rate to slow down a little.

Then she said firmly, 'I am surprised that you do not seem to know where it is, Mr Winbolt! I believe the matter has already been discussed by the lawyers. Before your uncle died.'

'Ah!' He smiled at her apologetically. 'You have found me out.'

'Am I to infer, sir, that you knew this yesterday?' asked Rosabelle, with commendable restraint.

'No, no! I was told about it by my agent this very morning. I went to see him before coming here—something I should have done before even mentioning the matter to you. It was careless of me and I am truly sorry, Miss Kelland. I could have saved you the work of getting these documents out.'

Rosabelle resisted a strong impulse to throw the map at him. If he only knew what his 'carelessness' had cost her! Getting the documents out indeed! That was nothing, nothing at all, compared with the real work she had done

since speaking to him the previous day! The whole of
the evening before and half the morning spent slaving to
master details which he was now dismissing so light-
heartedly as unnecessary! It was too much!

She was about to say so when she suddenly saw the
pitfall before her. She could not possibly vent her wrath
on him, or on anyone else! It would have to be suppressed. The real Annabelle would not have had all that
work—she would have had all the details at her fingertips
without reference to any maps or documents!

Something of her struggle to contain her feelings must
have reached him for he went on, 'I am truly sorry. But
why didn't you tell me yesterday that it had all been dealt
with? I thought when you mentioned fences…'

'I was thinking of the broken fences, Mr Winbolt,'
Rosabelle said with an undeniable snap in her voice.

'They are all mended. You know they are.'

This took her by surprise. 'I do?' Then she pulled herself together and said firmly, 'I mean, I do! Of…of
course I do! But…but it is all very vexing!' As soon as
these words left her lips Rosabelle regretted them. She
knew exactly what she meant by them, but she hoped Mr
Winbolt did not.

She was lucky—Mr Winbolt merely looked anxious as
he said, 'I have made you angry again, and we were
dealing with one other so well, too. How can I make up
for it? You…you wouldn't consider coming out for a
ride? It's too lovely a day to spend indoors, and I enjoyed
our short meeting yesterday so much.' She hesitated and
he went on, 'Be generous, Miss Kelland. Forgive my
thoughtlessness and come. Will you? Or do you think it
too hot?'

Rosabelle was fully conscious that she should refuse
this invitation. Her sister would never have accepted it,

she knew. Annabelle would not welcome a closer acquaintance with the Winbolts. And every moment spent in this man's company threatened the safety of their charade. Most important of all, she was more strongly attracted to him than anyone else she had ever met. It was all too disturbing!

Even if he felt the same attraction, nothing but disappointment could come of it, for her time at Temperley was already drawing to a close. No, not only for Annabelle's sake, but also for her own happiness and perhaps even his, she should not go with him. She opened her mouth to refuse him, and, when their eyes met, she said weakly, 'Thank you. I should like to. I shall only take a moment to change.' Then calling Becky she went upstairs.

'You shouldn't do it, Miss Rosabelle,' said Becky when they were safely in her bedchamber. 'There's bound to be trouble. I shouldn't be surprised if Mr Winbolt is a touch suspicious already. You certainly had him puzzled.'

'Yes! Why? What did I do just now in the parlour? You were frowning.'

'You made him welcome, that's all. The best Canary, Martha's macaroons, enquiries about his sister, one of your best smiles...'

'I didn't smile! Or if I did it was a conventional smile of welcome. Not in the least a...a best smile, Becky!'

'If you say so...but it looked very like one to me. Miss Annabelle wouldn't hardly have given him the time of day. No wonder he was a bit taken aback.'

'I cannot understand why Anna was so determined to dislike him. To my mind he is charming.'

'And no fool, either, Miss Belle,' said Becky, her voice heavy with warning. 'What's going to happen when Miss

Annabelle comes back, that's what I'd like to know. What will he think then? Going for rides day after day, entertaining him in the parlour—you'd best be more careful in future! There! It's a bit loose, but I've pulled the string as tight as I can. You're still a touch thinner than Miss Annabelle.'

In spite of her strictures Becky looked with pride at her charge when she had finished dressing her. On the whole Annabelle paid little attention to her appearance, but her old riding habit, which Rosabelle normally wore when she went out by herself, had recently been replaced with a new one, and today Rosabelle had donned it for the first time. Its lines were simple, all the fullness of the skirt being gathered to the back, and the severity of the cut, the slate-blue colour of its fine wool cloth, its tiny white ruff at the collar were immeasurably flattering—a perfect foil for Rosabelle's slender lines and her delicate colouring.

As Rosabelle stood there, in the middle of Annabelle's bedroom, dressed in Annabelle's clothes, Becky knew that it would be impossible for anyone who didn't know the twins as she knew them to tell the difference. But the signs were there for those who knew what to look for. Life had treated the Kelland twins very differently, and it showed. Annabelle had an air of decision, impatience almost, trained as she had been to run Temperley efficiently and well. She had a kind heart and a very ready sympathy for those in need of it, but she was as yet unaware of the more complex human emotions.

Rosabelle, as intelligent, as quick of understanding as her sister, had always seemed more lost, more in need of affection, and the years had only served to increase her air of vulnerability. If Mr Philip Winbolt spent very long with Rosabelle he would surely begin to suspect something, though whether he would dream that the Kelland sisters were capable of such a mad escapade was doubtful. But what about Rosabelle herself? She was showing a reckless liking for Mr Winbolt's company. Becky shook her head. There was only one consolation in this dangerous situation—Annabelle was now due to return as soon as a suitable opportunity for the changeover arose. Becky prayed that this would take place before any serious damage was done.

It was another day of brilliant sunshine, with just enough wind to keep it agreeably cool. Rosabelle was resolved not to let Becky's anxieties spoil her pleasure. Let the future take care of itself! The long term prospects for this delightful acquaintance did not look promising, for the time was rapidly approaching when she would have to resume her former life in London. She was chilled at the thought. She had had little enough enjoyment in recent years, and the prospect of life in London was not pleasant. All the more reason, she told herself firmly, to put all thought of the future aside and make the most of the present!

However, if she was to relax enough to enjoy the day then she must direct the conversation into safer channels than those of yesterday.

'Mr Winbolt, I am like you yesterday—in a holiday mood. Shall we…shall we forget any difficulties of our past acquaintance, and begin again? Shall we play a game? That we have never met before?'

'If it means that you will look more kindly on me than you have in the past, I should be delighted.'

'It's only for today, mind!' Rosabelle said hastily.

'Then I shall make the most of it. Miss Kelland, I am enchanted to make your acquaintance. Are you familiar

with the countryside round about? Or may I show you
the beauties of this corner of Berkshire?'

'It is always pleasant to see familiar places through
someone else's eyes, Mr Winbolt. Pray do.' Their eyes
met, and they both burst into laughter. 'Please don't stop!
I know it is a ridiculous pretence, but I am enjoying it
so much,' Rosabelle said as soon as she could speak.

'Then may I take you to the little piece of woodland
by Harden Lane? If you haven't been there recently
there's something you might like to see.'

Chapter Five

They rode along sometimes speaking, sometime in silence, but always with a feeling of companionship. They passed fields scattered with grazing sheep, tall trees echoing with the harsh sounds of rooks busying themselves in their untidy nests, hedges filled with the flutterings of small birds. Rosabelle looked at it all with a smile of contentment on her face, and Philip Winbolt looked at Rosabelle and wondered why he sensed sadness behind the smile. He made an effort to amuse her, and met with success, for soon the sound of her laughter filled the narrow lane. They reached the copse, tethered the horses and walked to the stile a few yards away.

Rosabelle had fallen silent, for she was still conscious of the strange sensation she had experienced when he had put his hands at her waist in helping her to dismount. She was trembling as she climbed over the stile, and would have stumbled had he not grasped her hand firmly and held her till she had regained her balance. He appeared to be a little short of breath, but he said nothing. Nor did he this time hold her hand longer than necessary. Colour rose to her cheeks. What an idiot she was!

'I...I...' Mr Winbolt cleared his throat. 'I wanted to show you these.'

'Oh, how lovely! Oh, thank you!' Rosabelle gazed in rapture at a rare carpet of flowers and ferns, a symphony of green, silver-grey, pale pink, white, mauve and purple. She bent down to touch with gentle fingers, caressing the pale lilac florets, the delicately veined petals, the spotted leaves of an orchid. 'I haven't seen anything like this for years...!' She stopped short. Of course she hadn't—but Annabelle would have! 'Anything quite so beautiful, I mean,' she added hastily. 'I wonder how I came to miss them?'

'It's easily enough done. I only came across them by accident.' His tone was easy, but slightly puzzled, and Rosabelle berated herself inwardly. Yet again she had been careless. If she made many more such mistakes, Mr Winbolt was bound to start suspecting something. Delightful as his company was, the risk of being discovered was always there, however harmless the conversation appeared to be.

'You look unhappy. Does the thought of the flowers depress you, Miss Kelland?'

'Oh no! They are exquisite. The orchids above all— they are such a rare sight.'

He gave her another look. 'I suppose you mean rare in the sense of beautiful? As you must know, such flowers are quite common round here.'

Once again Rosabelle laboured to retrieve the situation. 'Yes, yes! Beautiful. Such fine specimens—such a beautiful setting. The ferns look as if they have been arranged by an artist!' It was no use, the sun was still shining, the countryside looked as beautiful as ever, but her happy confidence had evaporated, and the charm of the day quite vanished.

'What is it, Miss Kelland?'

'N…nothing,' she said nervously. 'Shall we go back?'

'Why, of course, if that is your wish. But…will you not tell me what is wrong?'

'I…I suddenly feel rather tired.'

'Then we must go at once. Do you need my arm?'

'No! That is to say, thank you, but the path is too narrow for that. I can manage, thank you.' She gave him an apologetic smile and started back for the stile.

The ride back to Temperley was not as comfortable as their outward journey. Rosabelle was dejected, making one banal remark after another, confining herself to comments on the farms, the state of the track, the weather, refusing to respond to Mr Winbolt's attempts to amuse her. After a while he gave up, and gave her a selection of politely conventional replies. The silences between them were constrained.

As they drew near to Temperley he said, 'I was about to ask you if my sister could call on you tomorrow. But perhaps you would prefer a rest?'

'Yes,' said Rosabelle, eager to seize on this excuse. 'Yes, I think I need a rest.'

'Could she come later in the week, perhaps?'

'I…I'm not sure…'

He regarded her closely, then said, 'Tell me, Miss Kelland, have you been ill while we were away?'

'Wha…what makes you think so?' Then, fearing that he might find the question strange she added, 'Yes, I was. It wasn't serious, however. I am now fully recovered. Except that I…I tire easily.'

'You should have told me—I should not have taken you so far.'

'No, I enjoyed our ride, Mr Winbolt. Those orchids were a cure for any ills!'

'But not for melancholy, it appears,' he murmured.

'I beg your pardon?'

'Nothing, nothing. I spoke without thinking. Miss Kelland, my sister is not a demanding visitor. I think she might well amuse you. And you would be doing her a very good turn, for she has yet to make any real friends in the neighbourhood. Could she not call—later in the week?'

'I should be delighted to see her,' said Rosabelle weakly.

'On Friday then? In the afternoon?'

'On Friday, Mr Winbolt.'

Becky was full of disapproval when she heard that Miss Winbolt was to call. 'I told you, Miss Belle—no good will come of it, you mark my words.'

'But what was I to do, Becky? In the nicest possible way he made it impossible for me to refuse him without appearing to be very churlish. I'm not quite sure how he managed it, but he did! I simply couldn't say no!'

'I always said that young man knew what he was doing. Miss Annabelle wouldn't have it—she thought he was weak, but I always knew! He wasn't here more than a couple of weeks before the people at Shearings were doing as he said. And it can't have been easy—they were that set on old Mr Winbolt's ways. No, he's a determined young man for all he's so soft-spoken. You…you're not getting too fond of him, are you, Miss Belle?'

'I am as aware of the situation as you are, Becky!' Rosabelle spoke with a touch of hauteur. Becky was a privileged servant, but there were some matters which were not for discussion. 'I will not do anything to compromise Annabelle's position. I know that she will take over in a very short time now. But receiving Miss

Winbolt on a simple afternoon call can surely not commit Annabelle to anything but perfectly normal neighbourliness! In fact, I am surprised at my sister for not showing such a commonplace piece of politeness long before now!'

Becky gazed at Rosabelle in amazement. The twins had always been undivided in their loyalty to each other—they might quarrel among themselves, but they would never criticise one other to an outsider. Miss Rosabelle was right, of course. Miss Annabelle had been remiss. But it was extraordinary that her twin should say so. She tried to defend her mistress.

'Your father was ill, Miss Belle. And visitors were never welcomed here—you know that.'

'Well, it's time Annabelle did something about it! My father's illness was severe at first, but he no longer gives us cause for concern. He will remain what he has always been—a natural recluse. But Temperley should begin to live again, take part in the life of the neighbourhood. As far as I can learn, Annabelle has called on the Winbolts only once, though they arrived in the district some time ago. She is in danger of becoming as much a recluse as my father, Becky!'

Rosabelle's face was flushed and her manner was more spirited than it had been for a long time. She looked more like Annabelle than she had ever done before.

Becky would have spoken, but Rosabelle swept on, 'And I intend to do something about it. I shall receive Miss Winbolt on Friday, and what is more, I shall return the call, too—and pay other calls. When Annabelle returns she will find that a normal social life has been created for her, and she will thank me for it. When I have gone back to London, she will be able to enjoy the company of the Winbolts at parties and go for drives and rides with them in the country, and laugh, and look at flowers, and other…other delightful…delightful pursuits…'

Rosabelle's voice suddenly quavered and she fell silent. There was a pause. Then she repeated quietly, 'Annabelle will thank me for it, I am sure. So look out the best china, Becky and get someone to polish the silver teapot. There must be somewhere in Reading where we can obtain macaroons and cakes…'

'You may safely leave the arrangements to me, Miss Belle,' said Becky, very much on her dignity. 'Temperley will not let you down—and Martha's hand is as light as any pastrycook's in Reading.' But she softened at the despair in Rosabelle's next words.

'Oh, Becky, how soon will Annabelle come, do you think?'

'I don't know, Miss Belle. I should have thought she'd have written to warn us before this. But I don't suppose she knows herself exactly when it will be. It's awkward—I mean she has to wait till she can get away without rousing suspicion.'

'And Colonel Stanton is a naturally suspicious man. But it can't go on much longer.'

'There might be something tomorrow,' said Becky.

There had still been no communication from Annabelle by the time Miss Winbolt's carriage drew up at Temperley's door the following Friday. Becky had set a whole series of preparations in train—the little parlour, which had always been a favourite with the ladies of the house, warm in winter and cool in summer, had been swept and garnished. The ancient woodwork in the hall was shining with beeswax polish and elbow grease, and Rosabelle had filled the alcoves and side tables with roses from the garden and masses of greenery. A delicious smell of baking wafted through from the kitchens.

Miss Winbolt proved to be a sensible looking young woman in her middle twenties. It was clear that the good looks in the family had gone to the brother, though she had the same colouring, but the sister's face wore a similarly pleasant, open expression, and her widely spaced grey eyes were friendly. She looked round as she came in,

'So this is the famous linenfold panelling—how lucky you are to have such a fine feature in your house!' She gave her pelisse, and a small basket to Becky. 'Philip says you have been overdoing it, Miss Kelland. He was quite anxious about you. Are you more yourself after your rest?'

'I feel very well, Miss Winbolt. Your brother is kind, but you must tell him that he need feel no further concern on my part.'

Miss Winbolt's quizzical look reminded Rosabelle strongly of her brother. 'Telling Philip not to be concerned is as fruitless as King Canute's efforts to tell the tide not to come in. Whatever we say or do, his instinct is always to regard himself solely responsible for the welfare of his friends and relations. And to blame himself when things go wrong.'

Rosabelle smiled as she ushered Miss Winbolt into the parlour and said, 'Solely?'

Her visitor laughed. 'I may exaggerate a trifle, but I assure you it is very nearly true.'

'But surely such concern cannot be a fault!'

Miss Winbolt had been arranging herself in the chair Rosabelle had offered her. But she stopped at this and stared. 'Now that is strange! I would have sworn you would be just the sort of person to resent it. Oh, forgive

me, Miss Kelland. That was impertinent. I rattle on too
much. But you surprised me, you see. And I must admit
that I myself have occasionally been forced to demonstrate to Philip that I am more capable than he allows.
But he's a good brother, for all that. He sent you some
strawberries from our own beds, by the way.'

Rosabelle flushed with pleasure, but when she saw
Miss Winbolt's eyes on her she merely said primly, 'How
very kind. Would you like some tea, Miss Winbolt?'

After that slightly awkward beginning the afternoon
went surprisingly well. Philip's sister was direct in her
speech, but her manner was friendly, and she had a highly
developed sense of humour. In spite of her earlier words
she was clearly very fond of her brother, and the phrase
'Philip says' was frequently heard in her conversation.

Except for Lord Winbolt, their grandfather, the
Winbolt brother and sister were the last of an old, highly
respected family. They had inherited Shearings Hall from
an uncle who had never married, and their own parents
were dead. But it was clear that both brother and sister
loved the country, especially that part of Berkshire in
which they now lived.

'Have you ever lived in town, Miss Kelland?'

'Er…no. My sister has made her home in London for
some time. But I have never been there.' Once again
Rosabelle's conscience was uneasy at the lie. This masquerade had been embarked on for the best of reasons,
but it involved a web of deceit which was not at all welcome. But what else could she do? She prepared herself
for further prevarication, but fortunately Miss Winbolt
did not pursue the question of Miss Kelland's sister.

Instead, she went on, 'Up to now, I have never been
able to make up my mind whether I preferred city life to
that of the country, but now I am quite sure. I shall al-

ways be happy to spend time—and lots of money—in London's theatres and shops, but though life there is exciting, it cannot compare with life at Shearings.'

Rosabelle smiled with a touch of wryness. Her recent life in London had fluctuated between extremes of dullness and terror. She had no wish at all to return there. The thought pulled her up short. Had she really no desire to return? Not even to Aunt Laura?

'Miss Kelland?'

Rosabelle came to with a start. 'Oh, forgive me! My wits were wandering. What did you say?'

'I can see I've done just what Philip forbade! I've over-tired you again.'

'No, no, no! I've enjoyed our talk immensely.'

'Then may I ask you to come to Shearings? Quite soon? To tempt you further, I can promise to have all the latest versions of the *Ladies Magazine*, *La Belle Assemblée*, and other fashion journals. Philip is going to London next week and he always finds them for me.'

Following the decision she had expressed so forcibly to Becky a few days before, Rosabelle smiled warmly and said that she would come with pleasure.

Miss Winbolt left shortly afterwards.

'So what is your opinion of Miss Kelland now, Emily?'

The day after Emily's visit to Temperley the Winbolts were walking in the grounds of Shearings, enjoying the air and sunshine. They had taken to doing this quite regularly as the weather grew warmer. On these walks they usually discussed Philip's plans for the grounds and estate, but today the talk was of Temperley and its mistress. Philip was eager to hear Emily's impressions of Miss

Kelland, and because they had had company the night before, this was his earliest opportunity.

'I have to say I may have been wrong about her, Pip. Of course, she has only been to Shearings once since we arrived, and her call then was very brief. The Courtneys were here, too, if you remember. I didn't talk to her for any length of time.'

'I thought you saw enough then to disapprove of her?'

'I didn't disapprove of her! I simply thought she would not be a good choice for you. But now...'

'Yes?'

'You said she had been ill. I think it must have been more serious than she has acknowledged. She is...less forceful than I remember.'

'But she doesn't lack spirit!'

'No. She was just as amusing, just as quick to appreciate my—our—somewhat quirky sense of humour. But her personality has...I don't know how to describe it. Softened? I found her very charming, which is not a word I would have used of her before. Perhaps her sister's visit had something to do with it? Her company manners have certainly improved.'

'Her manners have always been delightful,' said Mr Winbolt, somewhat stiffly.

'Philip! How can you say so? I know you have a partiality for Miss Kelland, which not all my efforts in London and Reigate could weaken, but you are usually prepared to be more honest than this. You've quite often given me a description of her behaviour to you which has shocked me, you know it has. Whatever her opinion of you, good manners alone would forbid some of the things she has said and done in the past. Calling you a doormat indeed!'

'You might be right, though she didn't intend me to

hear that.' Philip laughed, but grew serious again when his sister asked, 'And what about the incident with Sam Carter? From what I hear she was almost rude about it.'

'That was different, I agree. She was remarkably determined to fight her own battle with Carter. And though I am very much more willing than you will admit for a woman to have her independence, I thought she was foolhardy—and surprisingly touchy. But I have to say one thing, Emily.' He stopped.

'We would be doing Miss Kelland a grave injustice if we forgot that the poor girl has had little opportunity to learn to depend on others. As far as I can tell she has been fighting her own battles since she was a child. And when has she had a chance to learn how to behave in company, confined to that house with a hermit for a father?'

'You are right, as usual, dear brother! But your Miss Kelland has recently acquired quite a few graces. So what is it which has brought about this present change? Can it possibly be that your persuasive charm is having an effect at last?'

'Much as I would like to think it, I can hardly believe it to be so. There hasn't been time for it to work! No, I believe the change is due to Mrs Ordway's visit.'

'The sister? She was here at Easter...I suppose you might be right. Someone who resides in London, and has a greater knowledge of the world than your Annabelle, was bound to make every effort to cure her sister's country manners. She appears to have had some success. Although...'

'Although?'

'I am reluctant to say this...but I must. If Mrs Ordway is even more worldly than we think, she might just have

pointed out to her sister the advantages of marriage to a
very rich man.'

'No! How can you suggest such a thing? Miss Kelland
may be everything you say, Emily, but she is no fortune
hunter. I'd swear to that.'

'I'm inclined to agree with you. But she would not be
the first by any means to seek to improve her position in
life by marrying a fortune.'

Emily's tone was bitter and her brother took her hand
and held it comfortingly. Six years before, Emily's considerable fortune had attracted a man who was as charming as he was unscrupulous. Fortunately she had found
him out before actually marrying him, but it had been a
hard lesson, and she had taken a long time to recover.

But Philip said now, 'Dearest Emily, Annabelle
Kelland is not such a one as Harry Colesworth. I know
it.'

They walked in silence for a minute or two, then Emily
asked, 'What about you? What is your opinion of the
lady, now that you have seen her again?'

'I...I...' He laughed at his own lack of words. 'Emily,
she is the loveliest, most desirable creature I have seen
in my life. And I intend to marry her.'

'Such arrogance. How do you know she will have
you?'

'It might take time, but she will have me in the end.'

'I know you too well to have any real doubt about the
outcome. And on yesterday's evidence I think Miss
Kelland might turn out to be just the wife you need, darling Philip. There's a lost look about her which I missed
completely when we first met. I rather think she might
turn out to be a perfect subject for cherishing!'

Meanwhile, unaware of the Winbolts' discussions,
Rosabelle continued to perform Annabelle's duties to the

best of her ability. And, eventually, she inevitably came across Samuel Carter. Carter's son had been off colour for some days, and though Rosabelle was no expert, she was not satisfied with the treatment little Sammy had been receiving. She expressed her doubts to the boy's mother.

'Jenny, I really think you should consult Dr Jardine about little Sammy. I am not sure that Granny Carter's cordial is doing him much good.'

The boy had a fever, though it was not a high one, and Mrs Carter had been dosing him with an evil-smelling, black, viscous liquid, which previous generations of Carters had sworn by for all ills. On this, Rosabelle's second visit, the boy seemed to be, if anything, worse.

'But Miss Belle, the boy's father won't hear of the doctor! He swears by Granny's mixture—they all do! Besides, Miss Belle, we ain't got the money.'

'If Sammy has caught some sort of epidemic fever, then Dr Jardine will be only too pleased to come and check on him—without payment. He's a great believer in stopping these things before they take a hold.'

'Epidemic fever? My Sammy? Oh no, Miss Belle!' Mrs Carter looked as if she might burst into tears.

'Please, Jenny, don't get upset! Sammy doesn't look to me to be seriously ill, but I just think it would be a wise precaution to consult Dr Jardine. Why don't I call on him on my way home? And, I promise you, that if there is anything to pay I shall deal with it.'

After spending some time persuading Jenny Carter to agree, Rosabelle picked her way out of the dark cottage and out into the light. Here she was confronted by Jenny's husband, who stood on the threshold, blocking her way. He was swaying slightly, and there was a strong smell of beer about his person.

Rosabelle was nervous, but said pleasantly, 'Good morning, Carter.'

Samuel was surly. 'Marnin!'

'I'm sorry Sammy is ill—I've arranged with your wife that Dr Jardine should call.'

'There baint no need fer that! Granny's mixture 'll do the trick—the boy'll be foine. 'E don't need doctors and such.'

'I'd like to make sure of that, Carter,' said Rosabelle.

'You'd like to make sure! What call have you to come interferin'? I tell you, we don't need no doctors!'

'You do if there's a question of fever, Mr Carter,' said Rosabelle with determination. 'I'll call on him now on my way home. Please let me pass!'

'Fever!' Carter's face darkened. He stayed where he was. 'There's no fever in my house! Don't you go frightening honest folk with your talk of fever and the loike! We ain't got money fer quacks.'

'There'll be no charge. Now let me pass, if you please!'

'I'm not sure I want to, your ladyship! I told you last toime, we doan't need your charity—'

'Get out of Miss Kelland's path, Carter.' The quiet voice behind him caused Carter to turn round. 'If there's a risk of fever in the village, Dr Jardine must be notified—immediately! Miss Kelland, I'll escort you…if you wish.'

'Thank you!' With a sigh of relief Rosabelle stepped round Carter and took Mr Winbolt's arm with a smile. Then she stopped and turned. 'Don't be hard on Jenny, Carter. She's worried enough. Why don't you go back to the farm and leave her to deal with the child?'

'Why don't you, Carter?' asked Mr Winbolt with a steely look in his eye.

Carter shuffled off with a malevolent glance at Mr Winbolt. Rosabelle's eyes followed him down the street, and she sighed. 'What an unpleasant man he is! Will he go to work, do you think?'

'Unless I'm mistaken he's on his way to the Dog and Duck. But at least he'll be out of his poor wife's way for a while. I…I am relieved to see that you do not seem to be offended at my intervention. When I saw you both, I'm afraid I acted quite instinctively again.'

'Why on earth should you think I would be offended? I was extremely grateful!'

'Good! I'm glad to see you've acquired a little sense.'

'Sense?'

He regarded her with the half-rueful, half-quizzical smile that she was getting to know. 'You seemed to think on a previous occasion that you were invincible, that my help was completely unnecessary. And though I said nothing at the time I'm afraid I disagreed.'

'Oh. Er…this occasion. With…with Sam Carter, was it?'

'Yes. Don't you remember?'

'Yes, I do now,' said Rosabelle quickly. 'Of course I do! But…but Carter was worse today.'

'He was quite drunk last time, too, Miss Kelland. He was capable of anything.'

'I…I had forgotten. Well, perhaps I am feeling less invincible today? Or more favourably inclined to you?' She smiled at him charmingly, willing him to forget the subject. 'Shall we call on Dr Jardine?' There was a slight frown on his handsome face, but it cleared at her smile, and he agreed willingly enough.

* * *

A few days later Rosabelle was once again getting ready to meet the Winbolts, this time at their home. As Becky looked out one of Annabelle's dresses and tried it on her, Rosabelle was delving into what she could remember of Shearings. She had been there as a child but her memories were vague—far vaguer than Annabelle's ought to be, for her twin had frequently visited old Mr Joseph Winbolt before he died. Becky made little effort to help her—she was more interested in making the direst prophecies about what would come of it all.

'I wish you wouldn't do this, Miss Belle! Sooner or later it will all come out, and then we'll be in a mess, without a doubt! Oh, I do wish we'd hear from Miss Annabelle! It must be over a month since she last wrote.'

'And she didn't say anything much to the point then! I wonder if she's afraid someone in Upper Brook Street is reading her letters? I wouldn't put it past Giles Stanton—though he should have been off to France weeks ago.'

'You shouldn't say such things, Miss Belle. Colonel Stanton wouldn't read anyone else's letters, I am sure!'

'Colonel Stanton is capable of anything—anything at all, Becky. And I have noticed that Annabelle is always very careful to write as if she really is me. There is nothing in them to reveal her true identity. She must have a reason for being so cautious. But…are you so anxious to be rid of me?'

Becky shook her head vigorously. 'There's no doubt that your stay here has done wonders for you, and if I could have you both here—openly and without any of this play-acting—I'd be more happy than I could say. But since that cannot be, it's time you went back! High time! No good will come of all this visiting and the like.'

'I've told you, Becky. I'm doing Annabelle a good turn.'

'And yourself no good at all, if I'm any judge.'

Rosabelle's lips set firmly. She was not going to pay any attention to Becky. Let the future take care of itself—that was her motto now. 'Have you nearly finished the dress, Becky?'

Becky was working on one of Annabelle's walking dresses, taking it in where she could. 'It's not so bad now, Miss Belle. You're filling out. Soon I won't have to take anything in at all.'

Rosabelle gave a laugh. 'If Annabelle has been crossing swords with Giles Stanton she might well have lost a few inches herself!' Then she was serious. 'I hope she hasn't provoked him. She may not realise just how ruthless he can be. Oh, I wish we could have a proper letter from her, to learn what is really happening in London! But she has at least let us know that Aunt Laura is improving, and that is very good news indeed. Do make haste, Becky! I don't want to be late.'

'You don't want to seem too eager, neither, Miss Belle. There's no need to fuss. John will get you there in time. There!'

The dress was slipped over Rosabelle's head and Becky fastened the inside tapes and started to hook it up. It was a round dress in white jaconet muslin, plainly cut except for a flounce of scalloped work round the hem. Over it Rosabelle wore a close-fitting spencer in cerulean blue silk, with long, narrow sleeves, puffed at the top and trimmed with rouleaux of satin in the same colour. There was even a very pretty bonnet to go with it—pale straw, trimmed with bands of light blue silk and a bunch of marguerites, and a fetching parasol. Annabelle had looked ravishing in it, and so did her twin.

'There!' said Becky. 'You'll do.'

Rosabelle, impatient to be off, gave Becky a reassuring smile and whisked down the stairs. Becky followed at a more sedate pace, shaking her head as she did so.

As soon as Rosabelle's carriage drew up at Shearing's imposing portico, the master of the house appeared and took her himself into the entrance hall. Here he gave her parasol to the footman and gave him some instructions. Then he walked with her to the drawing room. 'I'm so glad you came,' he said simply, and smiled at her, his eyes telling her how well she looked in her blue and white outfit. 'And I have an agreeable surprise for you. We have other neighbours—or almost neighbours—here. They called quite out of the blue.'

Rosabelle's heart missed a beat. The afternoon suddenly seemed full of pitfalls—other neighbours? Another session of walking a tightrope, keeping guard on one's tongue, fencing with words? At best, these neighbours, whoever they were, might be astonished at how little she remembered of them. At worst they might ask about 'Rosabelle', mention the word 'twin'—even comment on the likeness between them! It was truly said that the liar's path is fraught with danger!

Desperately rallying her forces—she must just keep the conversation in channels of her own choosing!—she entered the sitting room. An elegantly dressed gentleman was standing by the mantelpiece, one well-shod foot resting on the fender. The lady sat on a chair nearby, her green silk gros de Naples dress, her curled feather bonnet, her fine kid gloves and slippers proclaiming the lady of high fashion. As far as she knew she had never seen them before in her life. They were complete strangers.

Chapter Six

Feeling rather like Mary Queen of Scots mounting the scaffold, Rosabelle advanced into the room. Miss Winbolt came forward and greeted her kindly.

'Miss Kelland! I'm so glad you came! May I introduce you? Miss Kelland, Mr and Mrs Harpenden.'

Heavens—she had never even heard of them! But…her hostess had said 'introduce'. There was a chance, after all! Hardly knowing what she was doing she gave a vague smile in the Harpendens' general direction and curtsied.

'Mr and Mrs Harpenden are the proud new owners of Adwell Park, near Reading, Miss Kelland. So apart from yourself we are all newcomers to the area,' said Mr Winbolt.

'Oh!' Rosabelle's smile grew warmer, and she joined in the ensuing conversation with a pleasure unmarred by any fear of discovery. The afternoon passed quickly. The only difficulty Rosabelle encountered was in suppressing her own knowledge of London when the company talked of the amusements, the theatres, the parks, the customs of the capital. But since their manners were very good they only touched lightly on experiences that they did not expect her to share.

Questions about Temperley, Shearings, the countryside generally, she was able to deal with comparatively easily, and for the rest she found they had a style of conversation and behaviour which was totally to her taste. The company was in such good accord when the time came for the visit to end that the Harpendens pressed her to join Emily and Philip Winbolt when they next visited Adwell Park.

'Thank you. I…I…' Rosabelle hardly knew what to say. She did not expect to be in Berkshire for very much longer, but she could hardly say as much. In the end she fell back on the state of her father's health. 'I hope to be able to come. It is very kind of you.'

'Of course she will come, I shall see to it myself.' Mr Winbolt gave Rosabelle a smile, but spoke quite firmly. Rosabelle flushed as she saw Mrs Harpenden look surprised, then cast one discreetly raised eyebrow at Miss Winbolt. Philip's sister smiled blandly back, but a message had been received and understood, and, though the Harpendens were too well-mannered to say anything there and then, it was clear from their attitude as they took their leave that they were intrigued by the situation. Rosabelle was left to wonder what they said to Philip as he escorted them to the door. After they had left the room Emily Winbolt insisted that Rosabelle should stay a little longer.

'They have a journey to make, and you live practically next door. You can surely stay half an hour more—I have some fashion plates to show you. I cannot say that I like many of the new styles, but one has to keep up!'

'In London, perhaps, but surely not here in the country!'

'My dear Miss Kelland, when one is as lovely as you, one can wear anything at all and still look entirely delightful—though, if I may say so, that is a very pretty dress. But since the good Lord saw fit to give Philip all the looks in our family, I have to take more pains—wherever I am!'

'Are you talking nonsense as usual, Emily?' Philip Winbolt came into the drawing room, shaking his head and looking amused. 'It must be in the air. Mary Harpenden talked a lot of nonsense, too. Oh, surely you are not yet going, Miss Kelland? Can you not wait until it is a little cooler?'

'I really ought to be ready to go when John comes, and he should be here any minute.'

'I...I...er...I'm afraid I have a confession to make. When you arrived I took the liberty of telling John not to return for you. I shall take you back to Temperley myself.'

Miss Winbolt looked with interest to see how her guest would take this, but her brother paid her no attention. With a glance at the colour rising in Rosabelle's cheeks he went on, 'I have a great deal of respect for your independent spirit, Miss Kelland, but this is a very trivial matter. It was really not sensible to take up your servant's time when I have all the leisure in the world, and would take pleasure in performing this small service.'

Confusion, not anger, had been the cause of Rosabelle's colour. But since it seemed to be expected of her, she simulated annoyance. 'He is, however, my servant, Mr Winbolt,' she said coldly. ''I should have preferred to have been consulted.'

'I've done it again,' Mr Winbolt said ruefully. 'I've offended you. Will I never learn?' He looked so cast down that Rosabelle's tender heart was touched. She exerted herself to reassure him.

'It was a very kind thought, both for John Bostock and for me. I am sure you meant well, Mr Winbolt.'

Mr Winbolt's sister seemed to be having difficulty in suppressing a laugh, but when her brother gave her a look she turned it hastily into a cough. Philip turned back to Rosabelle and went on, 'No, you are annoyed with me—and with reason.'

'I...I assure you that I am not at all annoyed...any longer, that is. Allow me to thank you for your thoughtfulness, Mr Winbolt.' He still looked uncertain, so she added persuasively, 'Please, let us forget the matter.'

Miss Winbolt shook her head in amused disbelief, as Philip gave Rosabelle a sweet smile with no hint of satisfaction in it. 'You are very generous. Er...may I show you something? It's in the winter garden.'

'But, Philip,' exclaimed Miss Winbolt, 'Miss Kelland and I were talking fashions before you came in! I wanted to show her the journals you brought back from London.'

'Can that wait till the next time, Emily? I want to show Miss Kelland something which won't last even as long as the fashions in the fashion plates.'

He was regarded with exasperated affection. 'Very well. But I hope you realise what a good sister I am. You don't deserve me.'

He came back to her and kissed her. 'You are the dearest, most deserving, kindest sister that ever was, Emily. Now, Miss Kelland, prepare to be amazed.'

He led Rosabelle through the house to the south side. Here the somewhat neglected glasshouse of Joseph Winbolt's day had been transformed into an oasis of greenery. Tropical shrubs and plants of all sorts flourished in the warm and slightly humid air.

'It's…it's…I've never seen anything like it before,' said Rosabelle, gazing round in wonder.

'I am pleased you like it. I would have shown it to you when you last came, but we had so little time—and besides, it wasn't really ready for visitors. There was practically nothing here then.'

'Nothing here?' said Rosabelle, gazing round at the profusion of plants. Mr Winbolt smiled.

'Things grow very quickly in this atmosphere, and I have numbers of friends who know of my interest and send me plants, as well.'

He led her to a bench on which was a mass of delicate, starlike, white flowers. They were small, but filled the air with a sweet scent. Rosabelle was entranced. 'Oh, how beautiful! What are they?'

'Orchids. Epidendrums. A friend at Kew sent them to me. They're a distant cousin of the orchids at Harden. And over here there are some special ferns…' He took her over to another bench, then another, and another, pointing out the rarities, and waiting while she examined them, one by one. They came back to the beginning, and Rosabelle looked around her.

'If I had not already forgiven you for sending John back, I would surely do so now, Mr Winbolt. I would not have missed this for the world.'

She looked up at him, her delight still reflected in her eyes. What she saw in his made her tremble. Panic-stricken she stammered, 'Mr Winbolt, I… We must go back! Please.…'

Her voice died away as he took her hand and raised it to his lips. A mixture of enchantment and desire almost overcame her, and when he released it she could not stop herself from letting the hand rest against his cheek.

'Please,' she whispered. 'Please. You mustn't…'

He took her hand again and drew her closer, slowly, almost reluctantly, as if he knew he ought not, but could not help himself. Then, still holding her hand, he put his other arm round her. They stared into each other's eyes, like two people in a trance. Mr Winbolt tightened his arm and bent his head... Their lips met. After an initial hesitation Rosabelle found herself returning his kiss with fervour.

'My darling!' he murmured. There was an unusual unevenness in his voice, as if a struggle was taking place behind the calm exterior. 'Darling Annabelle!'

Annabelle? But she was not Annabelle! Rosabelle came to her senses with a shock, and wrenched herself free. 'No, no! You mustn't!' she cried. 'Oh, you've spoiled everything! How dare you, Mr Winbolt!' She could not continue. It was too much! She had betrayed not only herself but her sister, too! Taking refuge in anger, she said bitterly, 'I did not think you were the sort of man to take advantage of a guest in such a disgraceful manner! Pray let me pass—I wish to return to the drawing room! Immediately!'

Mr Winbolt looked surprised, then a dull red rose in his cheeks. 'Forgive me,' he said stiffly. 'I...I don't know what came over me. I thought you...' He stopped and pressed his lips firmly together. Then he said, 'I apologise for my behaviour, Miss Kelland. I assure you I had nothing of this sort in my mind when I invited you to see the winter garden. I thought only of giving you pleasure.' They both found his choice of words unfortunate. Rosabelle gasped and tried to look angrier than ever, Philip hastened to explain. 'I mean—'

'I know what you mean, sir. But I still wish to go back to your sister. Indeed, I should never have left her. It is

not at all suitable for me to be here alone with you. I
suppose I have only myself to blame for what happened.'

'You must not blame yourself, Miss Kelland! The fault
was all mine...the sweetness of your response went to
my head.'

The unpalatable truth contained in this remark resulted
in a complete and perfectly genuine loss of temper. 'That
is too much!' Rosabelle cried. 'I have heard enough! I
did not respond, sir! You misunderstood me. *I did not
respond!*' She stormed out of the winter garden, and ran
back along the corridor to the drawing room. Outside the
room she stopped short. What could she say to Mr
Winbolt's sister?

Fortunately that lady was immersed in a journal and
did not hear her. When Rosabelle finally entered the
room, she merely looked up with a smile and said, 'I
hope the winter garden had more to offer than these journals, Miss Kelland. I have seldom seen so many hideous
dresses.'

By the time Rosabelle had made some reply and examined the page Emily had open in front of her, Mr
Winbolt had arrived. He looked composed but unusually
stern. Rosabelle refused to meet his eyes.

'I think I must go,' she said, trying to sound natural.
'My father will wonder where I am.'

'I shall see you home, Miss Kelland,' Mr Winbolt said,
and added when Rosabelle looked doubtful, 'You will be
safe with me, I assure you.'

'Of course,' she said nervously. 'In any case, it isn't
far.'

Mr Winbolt looked grimmer than ever. 'Shall we go?'
he asked.

Rosabelle took her leave of Miss Winbolt, and was
escorted out to the carriage. It was a curricle—Mr

Winbolt intended to drive her himself. Reluctantly she allowed him to help her in, withdrawing her hand as soon as she could balance. Emily waved them goodbye and they set off.

They drove in silence for a mile or so, then Rosabelle decided that she must make an effort to speak. Something had to be done about the difficult situation in which they found themselves. Accordingly, she began rather shakily.

'Mr Winbolt, you must be wondering what…'

He interrupted her. 'Forgive me, but I do not really feel any need for further discussion of the events in the winter garden. Except to say that I am sorry. You were right—I did misunderstand you, but, in any case, the fault was mine. I assure you my actions will not be repeated.'

He sounded so decisive, so final, that Rosabelle was not sure how to continue. In any case, what could she say? Her false identity made it impossible for her to say what she really wanted to say. Left to herself, she would have found some way of telling him that she would welcome a closer friendship between them, a friendship which might in time grow into something warmer. But she could not plunge into a confession without thinking very carefully of the possible consequences. No, it was better to remain silent, to let him think she was still angry. She stole a glance at him. He looked calm enough, but she sensed he was not happy.

'You took me by surprise in the winter garden,' she said softly.

'Really? I have said I am sorry,' he said stiffly.

'I…I may have given you some reason to think I was encouraging you…'

'I now know you were not. Can we not put this tedious subject aside, Miss Kelland?'

In spite of his continued coolness she persisted. 'I...I would like to think we were still friends.'

'Friends!' This time his tone was so bitter that her tender heart smote her. She made an impulsive movement towards him, but hastily put her hand back in her lap. This was no time for weakness. But the gesture had caught his eye, and a small frown of mystification appeared on his face. There was a silence after which he seemed to come to a decision.

'I have to confess that you puzzle me, Miss Kelland,' he said thoughtfully, looking at the offending hand. 'You made your indifference to me clear enough at the start of our acquaintance, but I had come to believe...that there might be some hope for me in the future.'

'No, no!' Rosabelle cried, her own regret causing her to speak with great emphasis. 'You must not hope—I can offer you nothing but friendship. Anything else is quite out of the question.'

'Do I repel you, perhaps?' She shook her head, and he went on, 'In that case, need you be so...so very final?'

'I must! I cannot permit you to indulge in hopes which can only be disappointed. Believe me, I cannot regard you in...in any light other than that of a friend.'

'I see.'

Conscious of his intent gaze she managed to keep her face under careful control. Finally he said, 'I am disappointed, naturally. However, let that be forgotten. My sister would be sorry to lose your company.'

'And I hers,' said Rosabelle a touch sadly. It was hard—oh, how hard it was!—to insist on friendship, largely with his sister, when the thought of this man's love was so tempting.

There was silence in the carriage again for the rest of the journey. Then he said, 'We have reached Temperley.

I hope you will not let your mind dwell too much on
what happened today, Miss Kelland. I assure you that I
regret it. You will have my friendship, if that is what you
wish.'

His voice lacked its normal sympathetic flexibility, that
undercurrent of humour and understanding, which she
had learned to depend on. Their farewells were briefly
conventional. Rosabelle was anxious to escape to her
bedroom, where she could give way to her misery, and
Mr Winbolt seemed abstracted. She left him at the door
and went in, full of doubt, self-reproach, and a fierce,
bitter regret.

One of the girls had let her in, but when she was halfway up the stairs Becky came hurrying up towards her.

'Becky, I'm very tired. I think I shall just go to bed—
perhaps I'm coming down with a cold?'

But Becky paid no attention. 'There's a letter, Miss
Belle. From Miss Annabelle. It came this afternoon, by
special delivery.'

'What? Where is it?'

Rosabelle opened the missive with trembling fingers.
She scanned the pages eagerly, half relieved, half dread-
ing what she would find.

My dear Sister

What a surprise we have for you! Aunt Laura's
doctors have suggested that she should seek a cure
at a watering place, and Giles has given his consent.
I believe he intends to take us to Bath, and this
means that I shall be able to leave Aunt Laura in
his care while I pay you all a quick overnight visit.
Temperley is only a few miles out of our way. What
a pity it is that you are unable to accommodate us
all! But Aunt Laura insists that Temperley is no fit

place for a second invalid. She and Giles will stay
with friends of hers in Reading while I am at
Temperley, and I will rejoin them there. It will be
delightful to see you and Papa again.

Aunt Laura sends her love—and so do I. I shall
write again to give you the exact day as soon as the
details have been settled to Giles' satisfaction. It will
certainly be within the next week or not long after.
What a great deal we shall have to talk about!

Your loving Twin

'She's coming. Annabelle is coming back,' Rosabelle
said. She was stunned. Coming on top of the recent scene
with Mr Winbolt, this seemed to be both a deliverance
and a thunderbolt. She didn't know what she felt.

'When?'

'Very shortly. Colonel Stanton is taking my godmother
and Annabelle to Bath, and they will stay at Reading on
their way. Annabelle has arranged to come here alone on
a short visit. We shall be able to change over again then.'

'Thank goodness for that! Oh, don't look like that,
Miss Belle. I shall be sorrier to see you go than I can
well say, but it's time you went back where you belong.
Before any real damage is done.'

Rosabelle had recovered from the initial shock and
feeling was returning to her numbed senses. 'I rather
think,' said Rosabelle wearily as she turned away, the
letter fluttering to the ground, 'I rather think, Becky, that
the damage has already been done.' Slow tears started
trickling down her cheeks as she went on up the stairs,
and shut the door of her room behind her.

Philip Winbolt was hardly in a better frame of mind
as he drove back to Shearings. He was angry with himself

for his disastrous loss of control in the winter garden. It had not been his intention to reveal his feelings so early in their friendship. On several previous occasions he had noticed that Annabelle withdrew from him when he showed his admiration, and he had decided that his courtship of her must be patient and slow. So why had he acted so impulsively? It was quite out of character—he normally prided himself on his self-discipline.

The truth was that Annabelle's pleasure in those plants, the intimate atmosphere of the winter garden, her obvious delight in his company, had totally unnerved him. He had quite simply lost his head. Perhaps the heady perfume of those damned flowers had played a part? And he had ended up apparently having destroyed any chance of winning her. But…

But that was the puzzle! His instinct, which was usually sound, told him that Annabelle was not indifferent to him! His instinct had led him to believe that Annabelle Kelland's early feelings towards him had changed materially—so much so that she would at least listen to him with patience, if not yet with pleasure. The last thing he had expected was that she would dismiss his aspirations altogether!

His mind returned to the scene in the winter garden. Surely her anger had been somewhat overplayed? Whatever she said afterwards, she *had* encouraged him—her response to his kiss had been surprisingly ardent. And what was the significance of that gesture in the carriage? Though she had withdrawn it immediately, he would swear that her hand had stretched out of its own accord towards him. But, in that case, why had she then refused so adamantly to regard him as a possible suitor? It was all a mystery…

Had she some secret attachment unknown to the neighbourhood? An unwise early marriage, or something of that nature? But from what he had heard Annabelle Kelland had never left Temperley in her life. There were no hidden corners, nothing on which to base such a suspicion. So why, why, why? As he drove on he grew impatient with the lack of answers. His faith in the girl he had grown to love battled with doubts about her sincerity, her honesty. Was Annabelle Kelland the girl he thought he knew? Or was she a tease, a woman driven by caprice, or worse, a woman with some sort of shameful past, which made marriage impossible? He resolved to find out.

But Mr Winbolt was forced to leave his plans in abeyance, when his sister told him the next day that Annabelle was ill.

'What happened in the winter garden yesterday, Philip? Or is it tactless of me to ask?'

'I showed Miss Kelland the plants. Including the orchid Charles Dantry sent me.'

'And?'

'And what?'

'Did she like it?'

'Very much.'

'Did you talk of…anything else?'

'A little, but not much.'

Miss Winbolt looked at her brother with some sympathy. 'I can see that this is forbidden ground. Very well. But I think you ought to know that I've just had this note from Miss Kelland putting off our rendezvous on Thursday because she is ill.'

'Ill! Let me see!'

The note was polite but brief. Miss Kelland thanked Miss Winbolt for the very pleasant afternoon she had spent with them. She had much enjoyed meeting their friends, and the winter garden had given her a great deal of pleasure. Unfortunately she was now confined to her room with a particularly virulent cold. She sincerely hoped that she had not been infectious the day before. It would clearly not be advisable for Miss Winbolt to call as they had arranged on Thursday. The note concluded with suitable greetings, but there was no mention of a future meeting.

'I wonder…'

'What?'

'She might really be ill, I suppose…'

'What reason would she have for pretence? But ill or not, this note makes it perfectly clear that, for the moment, the lady does not wish to see either of us.'

He walked to the window and without turning said, 'I…I made a mistake yesterday, Emily.'

'In the winter garden?'

He turned and nodded. 'I told her of my feelings for her. It was far too early.'

'Is that all?'

'I kissed her.'

'You brute! Is…is that all?'

'Yes! Except that she became quite distressed. And very angry.'

'You kissed her and she became distressed? So distressed that she is ill today? Either you were very clumsy, Philip, which I refuse to believe, or there is something wrong with the woman! I swear I would be extremely flattered if a personable young man—who, by the way, would have every reason to think that I was attracted to him—kissed me and told me he loved me, whatever I actually felt about him. I certainly shouldn't take to my bed the next day, and refuse to meet even his sister!'

'So you too think there is something odd about it?'

'Very. I don't know what to make of Miss Kelland. She seems to change with the wind! I could not have imagined the girl I met in October being such a coward. Yet I was not half so attracted to her then, either. It's very strange… You…you don't think she's a tease, do you, Philip? There are such women—they enjoy being chased, but dislike the consequences.'

'I don't know. I wouldn't have thought Miss Kelland like that at all. And there were not even any significant "consequences", as you so charmingly call them. I am not an animal.'

'Of course not. I was being foolish. But I have to confess I am at a standstill. I simply don't understand our Miss Kelland. Would you like me to try calling at Temperley? I could take some fruit for her.'

'Would you? I would value your opinion on the situation. For all we know she might be really ill.'

'I shall call this afternoon.'

There was never a chance that either of the Winbolts would see Rosabelle, for she was determined not to be seen. The letter from Annabelle had brought home to her how vital it was that she should avoid all contact with them until she left Temperley. If the change back to the real Annabelle was to remain unremarked, the immediate impact of Rosabelle's personality must have a chance to fade. The present situation had come about by accident, but if it had been planned it could not be bettered—a cooling off between herself and Philip Winbolt, an excuse to see less of them in the future. Annabelle could quite naturally let the acquaintance gradually fade if she so wished, and in time Philip would forget his love for Annabelle Kelland. In the seclusion of her bedchamber

Rosabelle wept bitter tears over the loss of love and future happiness, but she rose the next day fully resolved—the Winbolts would not meet Rosabelle Ordway again.

Miss Winbolt duly arrived at Temperley with her gift of fruit, but was told that Miss Kelland was unable to receive visitors. Becky took her into the parlour, and offered to deliver a message or a note, if Miss Winbolt wished.

'I shall not disturb the invalid. Pray give her my best wishes for a speedy recovery, if you will, Mrs Bostock. Is there anything we can do? You must be very busy with two invalids on your hands.'

Becky looked slightly uncomfortable. 'Thank you, ma'am. You're very kind. But Miss Kelland's sister is due to arrive any day now. She will take charge, I'm sure.'

'Her sister from London? That's good news.'

'Yes. Being so close, they understand one another wonderfully well.'

'So close?'

'Miss Annabelle and Mrs Ordway are twins, ma'am.'

'Twins! How interesting! I don't believe I knew that. And how fortunate for Miss Kelland at this time. Will the neighbourhood see anything of Mrs Ordway while she is here?'

'I couldn't say, ma'am,' said Becky stolidly. 'But I do know that she can't stay long.'

'That's a pity. I should have liked to meet her. Well, Mrs Bostock, I'm sure Miss Kelland is in good hands. Have you already sent for Dr Jardine, or would you like me to call in on my way home?'

'Thank you, ma'am, but I'm not sure he's needed yet.'

'Then I'll take my leave. Perhaps you'd be good

enough to let me know when Miss Kelland is well
enough for visitors?'

'Certainly, ma'am,' said Becky.

'However, I am not sure she will,' said Emily when
she got home. 'There was something distinctly off-
putting in the good Mrs Bostock's manner. Whatever we
have done, we seem to have offended Miss Kelland beyond present forgiveness. You may set your mind at rest
on one score, at least, Pip. I do not believe her to be
seriously ill at all.'

'I don't understand it,' said Philip. 'Almost her last
words to me were that she valued her friendship with us.
What has happened in the meantime?'

'I agree it's odd… They've heard from her sister—but
that can hardly be it.'

'Mrs Ordway? There were some nasty rumours circulating about Stephen Ordway, the husband, at one time.
But that's a year or two back, and the man's been dead
for some time. I doubt that has anything to do with it.'

Emily was growing tired of the subject. She was fond
of her brother and would help him all she could, but she
was beginning to think that he ought to forget Annabelle
Kelland. The girl was proving to be disappointingly ca-
pricious.

'Well, she is coming next week on a short visit. If Miss
Kelland needs further care, I think we can leave it to Mrs
Ordway to provide it. Do look at these bonnets, Philip!
I think the milliners have gone mad!'

Chapter Seven

Though she had known happiness in her childhood, from the time of her marriage to Stephen Ordway, Rosabelle Ordway's life had been one of self-doubt, shame and misery. During the marriage her unhappiness had bordered on despair, and her anxieties had once or twice turned into pure terror. Stephen's death had brought a measure of relief, though worry over his debts had overshadowed her life. Then Giles Stanton had taken over with his threats and jeers, his implacable determination to see nothing good in her.

Her lack of self-esteem reinforced by his presence, her nervous system shattered by the events surrounding Stephen's death, her health affected by time spent nursing her godmother, she had been near to collapse. She had escaped at Easter just in time—or so it had seemed. Escape, freedom for a while from the atmosphere at Upper Brook Street, had been all she had wanted.

Then she had met Philip Winbolt, and the brief moments of delight she had recently experienced in his company had been an unexpected, a miraculous bonus.

But now she was filled with a pain she had not experienced before. For the first time in her life she had fallen in love, deeply in love, with a man who was everything a woman could desire—honorable, kind, amusing, energetic, and with sufficient standing in the world to offer his wife security along with all the rest... She had good reason to believe that he would have married her, if only... But it was impossible. She had embarked on a deception which ruled out any happy end—indeed, she would not see him ever again. And she had no one but herself to blame.

How could she possibly tell him that she was a liar and deceiver? A married woman, not the girl he thought her. And if he forgave her for that, what sort of wife would Stephen Ordway's widow make for a distinguished man such as Philip Winbolt? No, better by far not to let herself be tempted. At first she wept bitter tears, and, when her tears dried up, she lay awake into the small hours, staring hopelessly into the dark...

But she was no longer the poor, nervous creature she had been before Easter. She faced her pain with courage and determination, bolstering her rediscovered self-respect with the thought that a man like Philip Winbolt had nearly loved her... She refused to allow her mind to dwell on what might have been. Instead she began to make plans for the future, wondered what Annabelle had done about Giles Stanton's blind prejudice, and made a decision that, whatever had happened in London, she would cast off once and for all the black heritage of Stephen's malice and deceit. She would go to Bath, look after Aunt Laura, and, when they returned to London, she would run Giles Stanton's house for him so well that he would be forced to respect her.

As the week wore on Rosabelle grew increasingly impatient to be gone from Temperley, anxious to be free of the risk of meeting—or seeking—the Winbolts. She was prepared to face whatever might be waiting for her in London and her sole aim was to get away as quickly and as quietly as possible. So it was with relief that she saw John coming up the drive with a letter. It must be from Annabelle and would contain news of her release. She met him at the door, took the letter from him and opened it eagerly. It was indeed from Annabelle. She hurried through to the parlour and sat down, impatiently scanning the sheet of paper.

Dearest Sister

This will be as great a shock to you as it is to me. Colonel Stanton—for I cannot bring myself to call him anything else, unless it is The Monster— has decided in his wisdom that we should be better off going to Buxton! He is quite adamant. Apparently, he intends to visit his father in the vicinity, though he has not informed me of the fact. I had to learn even that much from Aunt Laura! I suspect that this is not his only reason, however, though I cannot imagine what any other could be. He can surely hardly be serious when he hints that my character may have something to do with his decision! I wonder whether Aunt Laura and I made the mistake of appearing too pleased with the notion of going to Bath? For such a killjoy as Colonel Stanton, the temptation to change his plans must have been quite irresistible. But let us forget the less pleasant aspects of life in Upper Brook Street!

The sad truth is that by the time you receive this letter we shall be on our way north to Buxton, and it will be impossible for me to see you for seven or eight weeks! Words cannot express how sorry I am.

I assure you, my darling sister, I would have hired a chaise and come alone if it had been possible, but the change of plan was sprung on us with hardly a day's notice, and I have been kept exceedingly busy. Colonel Stanton is all consideration! I expect he wanted to spare us the pain of learning too soon that we were not to enjoy the excessive dissipations of life in Bath! I understand that Buxton will provide me with 'fewer opportunities to parade' myself. I quote.

Since I shall not be seeing you in person for some time, I send you my love, and best assurances that I am happier than I may seem! Life with the Monster in the house is at least never dull. And you may have an easy mind about Aunt Laura. She continues to improve, and, however little I deserve it, she seems to be very happy with

Your loving Twin.

'What is it, Miss Belle? You're as white as a sheet! Has something happened to Miss Annabelle?' Becky came in to the parlour to find Rosabelle staring at the wall.

'She isn't coming, Becky.' Rosabelle's voice was devoid of life. 'She's on her way to Buxton. Giles Stanton has changed his mind about taking them to Bath,'

'Not coming? Why ever not? Where's Buxton?'

'It's a watering place in the North. There isn't the slightest possibility that Annabelle can come to Temperley before the end of August. Even then it is quite possible that Colonel Stanton will change his mind again, and take her to…to the Antipodes or the even to the moon! I shall never get away! Here, read the letter!' Rosabelle got up and walked agitatedly about the room, while Becky put her glasses on and read Annabelle's letter.

'It's too much, Becky! Much too much! I can't bear it! I've worked so hard to discipline myself to look forward, to forget… And now it will be two months or more before I can escape. What am I to do? Oh, what am I to do?' Rosabelle threw herself down on the sofa and burst into tears.

'There, there, my dear.' Becky took Rosabelle in her arms and stroked her hair as if she was a child. 'You'll manage. You've managed all this time without a foot wrong, and you'll do it again. Hush, Miss Belle! There's no need for this, my honey.'

After a while Rosabelle grew calmer, and Becky got up to go. But Rosabelle clutched the housekeeper's hand. 'No! Don't go. I need you, Becky. There's no one else I can talk to. I don't know what to do. Help me!'

'It's Mr Winbolt, isn't it, Miss Belle?'

Rosabelle looked at the kindly, rosy face, regarding her with such concern. Becky had been right, after all, in her gloomy prophecies. 'Yes. It's Mr Winbolt. You were right to warn me… I should have heeded you more.'

'As to that, I hardly expected you to, Miss Belle. Mr Winbolt is as fine a gentleman as I've seen.' Becky sat for a while in thought, then she said, 'Have you tried speaking to your papa about this, Miss Belle?'

'Papa? No, of course not!'

'I think you should. He's ever so much better than he was. And he is your own father.'

'But he would only be annoyed at being disturbed—you know what he's like, Becky.'

'I should try all the same. He's a clever man, your papa. And you need someone to talk to—you said so yourself. You never know. Why don't you try?'

At first Rosabelle rejected the suggestion out of hand—
it seemed absurd. Her father had not taken the slightest
interest in any of them for years, so why should he start
now? But as the day wore on the idea of consulting her
father grew more tempting. Becky was right—Papa was
clever. Moreover he would certainly take a dispassionate
view of her case—if he gave any opinion at all, it would
be realistic. Besides, who else was there to consult?

Becky was a darling—she gave comfort to her former
nurslings whenever they needed it, and had been the re-
cipient of many a childish confidence. But this was no
childish matter. It concerned the personal affairs of a
neighbour, a local landowner of some importance, and it
would be unfair to involve Becky in such a business.

By the evening, when her daily visit to her father was
due, Rosabelle had almost made up her mind. She would
see what sort of mood her father was in, and if he seemed
at all receptive she would consult him.

When she first entered her father's bedchamber she
thought he was asleep and her heart sank. But as she went
quietly over to his chair, she saw that his eyes were open
and he was staring into the fire. The candles had not been
lit, and his book was lying neglected on the table nearby.

'Are you feeling well, Papa?'

'Yes, yes.' Mr Kelland roused himself and looked at
his daughter. 'It's Rosa, isn't it?'

'Yes, Papa. I'm afraid Anna can't be here for some
time. Lady Ordway has taken her to Buxton.'

'Buxton, eh? Well I suppose it's time Anna saw a bit
of the world. I've been a bit selfish in keeping her here.
It's an odd place to go, though, Buxton.'

'Papa,' said Rosabelle, taking a deep breath. 'Papa, I
wish to talk to you—may I?'

'Why not? I've finished my book. I was just sitting here…thinking…'

'You looked sad when I came in—what were you thinking about?'

'The past. But it's a useless occupation. What did you want to say?'

'It's rather private, Papa. May I tell Walters not to interrupt?'

'He's in his room. You can tell him that I shan't need him for an hour or two.'

This accomplished, Rosa sat down by her father and said, 'Papa, I'm in something of a quandary. I don't know what to do.'

'Being in a quandary means you don't know what to do, Rosa. Don't waste words.'

'Forgive me.' Rosabelle took another breath and began again. 'I need your advice.'

Mr Kelland frowned, but said, 'Go on.'

'The fact that Anna's return has been delayed has caused me some difficulty…' She hesitated, trying to choose her words. But when she saw her father shift impatiently in his chair she hurried to tell him of her friendship with the Winbolts, and its latest development.

'It never does any good, mixing too much with neighbours. You should have followed Anna's example, and kept clear of them. Still, it's done now. So what do you want me to say? Did you tell Winbolt that you and Anna changed places? Is that the trouble? I notice he hasn't been round here this past week.'

'Papa! I didn't think you paid much attention to what went on!'

'It's difficult not to, when horses and carriages are forever crunching up the drive and the damned doorbell is ringing all the time! I should be in a room overlooking the back—that would be more peaceful.'

'Not with the stables close by, Papa,' said Rosa patiently. 'But I haven't told Mr Winbolt anything. I wanted to go back to London without him ever knowing.'

'His,' said Mr Kelland.

'His?'

'His ever knowing. Go on.'

'So I've been keeping out of the Winbolt's way to make it easier for Anna to take over…' Her lips trembled. 'And now she's not coming for weeks and weeks…'

'If you're going to cry, go somewhere else, Rosa! Crying won't help, and I can't stand it.'

Rosabelle got up, wiping her eyes. 'I'll go, Papa. I'm only disturbing you.' She started to walk to the door.

'You can stay if you promise to keep calm. You need to make some decisions. Is that why you want my help?'

'Yes, Papa.'

'Then sit down here and talk sensibly.'

'Yes, Papa.'

'Your problem is that you've got yourself into some sort of tangle with Winbolt, from which you thought you could extricate yourself by going back to London. Is that it?'

'Yes, Papa.'

'And how was Anna going to manage when she took your place again?'

'Oh, I didn't compromise her, Papa! I was always careful to…to keep my distance. Mostly.'

'What does that mean?'

'It wouldn't be difficult for Anna to resume her former relationship with the Winbolts when she returns. Though I did think originally that it would do her good to mix a little. She's getting to be as much of a recluse as…oh! I beg pardon, Papa.'

'As much of a recluse as I, eh?'

'Well, yes! And she's still too young to shut herself away! Before we changed places and she went to London she hadn't seen anything of life in Society.'

'It doesn't seem to have done you much good.'

Rosabelle bit her lip and looked down. 'That was different. I was…unlucky.'

'It was obvious that you didn't love Stephen Ordway. But Laura Ordway wanted the match, and you would have flown over the moon for her. I should never have consented to it.' Rosabelle was silent, and after a moment he asked abruptly, 'What about Winbolt? Do you love him?'

'Yes,' said Rosabelle. 'Yes, I do.'

'Enough to want to marry him?'

Painful colour rose in Rosabelle's cheeks. 'Yes. But that is impossible.'

'Because of your deception? He'll get over that.'

'I wish I had your confidence. But there's something else. Stephen was…was…'

'I can guess what Stephen was, Rosa. And you think that Winbolt would repudiate you because you were married to such a man?'

'Yes,' she whispered. 'Or feel he had to…to withdraw from Society himself if he married me.'

'I can reassure you on the first question: a young man in love—really in love—will forgive almost anything, including the small deception you and Anna have practised. Love makes idiots of us all. And on the second… Only you can know how closely you were associated with Stephen Ordway's activities. I would think not at all. I doubt you could be held to blame for them in anyone's

eyes—whether Winbolt's or those of Society. You're being over-scrupulous, Rosa.'

'What am I to do?'

'It's my opinion that you ought to take the chance fate
has given you, and use your extra months to fix Winbolt's
interest. It shouldn't be difficult. You're a beautiful
young woman, and he's a warm-blooded male.'

'Should I confess the truth?'

Mr Kelland had taken up another book. 'Whatever you
think best. I should give yourself a little while before
doing anything rash. Make sure he's besotted enough
first.'

'But how can I face them?'

'You can't play at being sick for months, and you can't
avoid the Winbolts if you're not—unless you wish to
become a recluse, like me. You're going to have to meet
them again, aren't you?' He opened his book, and started
leafing through it.

'I...I suppose so. Thank you, Papa.'

'Think it over by yourself. Make up your own mind.
Er...take Walters down with you and give him some
more candles, Rosa. I expect he's sulking. He hates to be
shut out of anything. The exercise will do him good. And
Rosa! Make sure you close the door carefully on your
way out—'

'I know, Papa! The draught is most unpleasant when
I don't.'

Rosabelle collected Walters and went thoughtfully
downstairs, and on into the kitchen to see that he was
given the candles. Here she found Becky who waited till
Walters had shuffled away again, then asked, 'Well? How
did you get on?'

'You were right. It did help to talk to Papa. But I'm

still not sure what I should do.' She told Becky what her father had recommended.

'Why don't you try? It's better than moping in the house for two months. And you couldn't be much unhappier than you are, Miss Belle. What have you got to lose?'

'Not much, it's true.'

'There's no need to rush it. Take your time, and it will come right, you'll see. I'm a great believer in Providence—you haven't been given this time without good reason.'

'I hope you're right. But whether I succeed or fail...'

'You won't fail, Miss Belle! But you must have it all in the open before Miss Annabelle comes back, mind.'

'Of course, I will! I wouldn't leave Anna with a problem like that!'

'From the bits I've seen of that letter, Miss Annabelle is solving a few problems of her own, and enjoying it!'

'What do you mean?'

'It seems to me that there's rather a lot of Colonel Stanton in it.'

'But that's because he's so awful!' Rosabelle was horrified. 'No, Becky, you're wrong! You must be! Anna and Giles Stanton? Impossible!'

The weather turned somewhat cooler that week, and Rosabelle was able to work in the garden, following Becky's advice and taking her time. And as she gradually put the flower beds in order, she tried to do the same with her thoughts. In the evenings she visited her father, and though he never referred to their conversation and was as taciturn as ever, she now felt his support was there if she should need it.

Slowly, in the calm after the storm of her outburst

earlier in the week, influenced by her father's talk of fate and Becky's of Providence, her spirits lifted by an idyllic spell of clear skies and temperate breezes, she adopted a more philosophical approach to her problems. She would carry on as before, trying where she could to show Philip Winbolt that she was not the adventuress he might otherwise believe her to be when he learned the truth. The rest was up to fate. Let the future take care of itself!

Miss Winbolt was invited to tea and shown round the garden. Though there was a degree of stiffness in her manner at first, she gradually unbent, and before the visit was halfway through the two young ladies were enjoying each other's company almost as much as ever.

'And…your brother? Is he well?' asked Rosabelle, somewhat self-consciously.

'Very well, thank you. He was pleased to hear you had recovered from your…indisposition.'

'I'm sorry I couldn't see you. I had no desire to offend you, believe me,' said Rosabelle. 'But I received some bad news, and felt much worse as a result.'

'Bad news? Not too serious, I hope.'

'Not really. My sister has been forced to postpone her visit. She has had to go to Buxton.'

There was a pause, then Miss Winbolt said, 'Buxton? I haven't ever been there. Philip and I intended to call there when we visited the Lake District some years ago, but it somehow didn't happen.'

Happy to turn the subject away from her sister, Rosabelle said, 'The Lake District? Oh, I should love to see the Lakes! Do tell me about it!'

The visit passed off as well as could have been hoped, and a return invitation for the following Thursday was given and accepted.

'My brother will be in London for the day, so I shall be glad of your company, Miss Kelland,' said Emily blandly.

'He won't be there?' Rosabelle was not sure whether to be sorry or glad that her first encounter with Philip Winbolt was postponed.

'I confess I chose the day deliberately.' Miss Winbolt studied her hostess. 'It was my impression,' she said carefully, 'that when you were last in his company you were…not at ease. I thought you might prefer to see less of him in future. Or am I wrong?'

The sensitive colour flooded into Rosabelle's cheeks, but she spoke with dignity.

'Your brother was everything that was kind, Miss Winbolt. I will not hide from you—nor from him—that there are…circumstances which caused me some difficulty, and continue to do so. But I hope to overcome them in time. I believe I would enjoy his company as much as I do yours. On the other hand I would perfectly understand if he wishes to regard me as more your friend than his.'

'We shall see! I'm glad to have settled that slight awkwardness. Shall we keep to Thursday for this time, however?'

'Miss Winbolt—'

'Could you see your way to calling me Emily? I am not one for great ceremony.'

'I should be very pleased to, Emily! My name is—'

'Annabelle. Yes, I know. May I call you Anna?'

'Er…yes. Of course.'

If Miss Winbolt was surprised at the reluctance in Rosabelle's tone, she did not allow it to put her off. Instead she merely said, 'Till Thursday, then. I shall ask your advice on our ornamental pool. Philip wants to fill it with carp. Goodbye—Anna.'

* * *

However, Rosabelle was to see Philip Winbolt sooner rather than later. Only a couple of days later she was working in the garden as usual, when she became aware of a tall figure standing behind her.

'Mr Winbolt! Oh, you startled me.'

'It seems to be a habit of mine. I'm sorry.' Rosabelle had scrambled to her feet, and he held out his hand. 'Emily tells me you are better.'

'No, don't shake hands with me. Mine are covered in earth. Look.' She held out a grubby hand. He took it, and released it quite normally.

'A little dirt never hurt anyone. Do you think me such an exquisite?'

'No! But…'

'Emily also told me that you might enjoy my company, after all. As a friend, of course.' He seemed to be waiting. There was still a coolness in his manner which was very different from his former warmth.

'I…I should like that,' said Rosabelle somewhat nervously.

'It's all I am asking of you, Miss Kelland! Friendship. Nothing more. You needn't look so frightened,' he said, somewhat impatiently. 'I've taken note of your wishes.'

'It…it wasn't that at all,' she stammered. 'But I didn't expect to see you today.'

'I had some business down the road, which I wanted to complete before going to London. Emily said you were working in the garden, and she asked me to bring you some plants—John Bostock has them.'

'Thank you!' They fell into step up the path to the house. 'Do you often have business in London?'

'I like to keep in regular touch with my grandfather. And he insists that I take a full part in any discussions with our agents and trustees. The Winbolt estate owns

some property in London near St Giles, and I'm trying
to persuade my grandfather to get rid of it. It's in a terrible state, and I will take no rents from the poor devils
who have to live there.'

'So you will sell it to someone else who will?'

'Wrong! It's being pulled down. But it all takes discussion and time.' He looked around him. 'And it seems
such a waste of this glorious weather to spend it in a
city!' He hesitated, then said abruptly, 'Are you fit
enough for a walk, Miss Kelland? I feel like stretching
my legs a little. But perhaps you would rather not?'

Rosabelle looked down so that he should not see the
delight in her eyes. 'I shall wash this dirt off my hands
and fetch my hat,' she said demurely. 'May I suggest you
could use a little water yourself?'

He looked down at his hands and smiled. 'It might be
as well.'

They took the lane down to the river. The river pop-
ulation was out in force. Ducks, moorhens, coots were
parading their families, a kingfisher was busy in the
reeds, and as they walked along the bank sudden plops
and splashes ahead of them gave evidence of escaping
water rats. They even caught sight of an otter, twisting
and turning in the river.

'It's so beautiful here,' sighed Rosabelle. 'I never want
to leave it.'

'You love the country so much?' Rosabelle nodded,
and he continued, 'My sister and I both prefer life in the
country, but she occasionally feels the need to see what
is happening in the city. I'm not sure what she will do if
she ever marries.'

'*If* she marries? How unbrotherly you are! Miss
Winbolt is bound to marry one day.'

'My sister said that you were going to call her by her given name.'

'Emily, then.'

'Emily was engaged once, but she broke it off. There were good reasons. It was several years ago, but though I think she is very nearly over it, it has made her wary. She hasn't shown much interest in anyone else since. The path of true love doesn't seem to run very smoothly in our family, Miss Kelland—' He stopped. 'I'm sorry,' he said. 'Have you seen the swans?'

He said no more about Emily's personal affairs, or his own, for the rest of the afternoon. Instead their conversation ranged widely, from reforms on the Shearings estate—about which Rosabelle knew nothing, but believed she managed to conceal her ignorance rather well—to a lively argument on the rival merits of *Waverley* and *Emma*, about which she knew a great deal.

In the heat of the discussion he regained some of his natural warmth, and she found herself once again drawn to him—his humour, his sympathy, his love of life. He never once gave the slightest indication that he regarded her as anything but a friend, however, and afterwards, when she turned the walk over in her mind, she could not remember that he had ever touched her unnecessarily. When they reached the house again she held out her hand.

'I enjoyed our walk, Mr Winbolt,' she said.

'So did I. Though I still think that Miss Austen's technique and restraint in *Emma* far outweigh the big guns in *Waverley*.'

'Oh, pray do not open that subject again! I am exhausted!' Rosabelle laughingly protested.

'You defended your position manfully. And what is conversation for, if not to debate our likes and dislikes?'

'Say our preferences, rather. I, too, rate Miss Austen's works very highly. Good night, Mr Winbolt. And have a safe journey to London.'

'I shall be back quite soon—and then we can debate more preferences, perhaps. Good night, Miss Kelland.'

After that Rosabelle saw one or both of the Winbolts nearly every day. Walks, rides, drives, and visits to each other's houses occupied many happy hours. Perhaps Rosabelle would have been less carefree if she had known that Philip Winbolt kept a more careful eye on her than she realised. In spite of his open manner and gentle ways, Mr Winbolt was far from being a fool. He may have appeared to seek nothing but friendship from Miss Kelland. He certainly treated her much as he treated his own sister.

But he soon found that, in spite of his suspicions and doubts, he was still as much in love with her as ever, and, since that was the case, he was determined to unravel the mystery which surrounded her. He gathered tiny facts and inconsistencies, and hoarded them as a squirrel hoards nuts. For instance, why did Annabelle, who had successfully run Temperley for so long, know nothing of the new systems in farming—even though one or two were in place on her own land?

Why was her behaviour in the second episode with Carter so inconsistent with her behaviour in the first? Why, since then, had she appeared to be ill at ease when-ever she met any of the villagers in his company? She visited them regularly alone, and was popular with them, he knew that from hearsay. So why be uneasy when she met them in his or Emily's company?

Why was she so reluctant to be involved with their other neighbours? She usually found an excuse not to be

present at larger gatherings. Was she company-shy? He
hadn't forgotten how tense she had become when he told
her that the Harpendens were at Shearings. But she had
relaxed afterwards, and the Harpendens had been
charmed by her.

He did not share his thoughts with his sister, though
he made a careful note of what she said about Annabelle.

'Why do you suppose Annabelle Kelland objects to
being called "Anna", Philip?'

'Does she?'

'She seemed rather hesitant. I wondered whether she
thought me too forward. Yet…she was very friendly otherwise…I tell you, Pip, I feel like a weathercock when I
think about her. At the moment I like her as much as
anyone I have ever known. But there have been times…
She puzzles me. She appears to have humour and courage
and spirit. But why was she so cast down when Rosabelle
Ordway couldn't come after all? She said it had made
her ill, and I have to say she looked it when I first saw
her afterwards! I can't believe the mere absence of a sister would do that to any normal person. I'm prepared to
wager that you wouldn't take to your bed if I didn't visit
you when I ought! And fond as I am of you, I certainly
wouldn't refuse to see other callers if you went away.'

Philip laughed, 'I should hope not, indeed!'

'Perhaps it's different if one is a twin.'

'A twin?'

'They're twins—didn't you know?'

'No, I didn't,' said Mr Winbolt thoughtfully. 'Who
said so?'

'Mrs Bostock. She was their nurse at one time.'

Philip was silent for some time, then he said slowly,
'That might just be it!' He thought again. 'No—surely

not! I can't believe it! But...but it would account for a
lot...if there was a twin sister.' He saw his sister looking
at him, and smiled at her cheerfully. 'I mean, it would
account for her being ill, perhaps.'

Chapter Eight

The thought was fantastic, but Mr Winbolt could not dismiss it. The apparent inconsistencies in Annabelle Kelland's behaviour could be explained by the existence of a twin who had changed places with her. If such an exchange had taken place, it was an outrageous piece of trickery—though it would not have been for mere amusement, he was sure. He tried to tell himself that it was all the product of an over-fertile imagination, a result of his anxiety to get to the bottom of the mystery surrounding the girl, but it was no use. He knew the notion would continue to plague him until he gave it closer examination. He would treat it as a pastime, an exercise in logic, such as he had enjoyed at Cambridge. 'First assemble your data, Winbolt,' his tutor had exhorted him, 'examine it carefully, and then produce a hypothesis.'

What were the facts? Annabelle Kelland, an intelligent girl who had spent years running the Temperley estate, had tried and failed to hide her complete ignorance of even the basic notions of modern farming. Annabelle Kelland, who had met him at least ten times before, had seemed not to recognise him after Easter, when they had met for the eleventh time. Annabelle Kelland, who had

previously been indifferent to him to the point of rude-
ness, had changed her attitude to him between one meeting and the next—a change which had taken place so
arbitrarily that he could not possibly attribute it to his
powers of charm and persuasion, much as he would have
liked to.

Annabelle Kelland, who had never before wasted a
moment in his company, had agreed—no! *suggested* that
they should ride back to Temperley together, and when
they arrived she had offered him wine and biscuits and
the like, welcoming him with a grace and charm which
he had never before observed in her. There were the two
episodes with Carter. Before Easter, Annabelle Kelland
had resented his assistance with the man, but after Easter,
she had accepted it more than gratefully!

Emily's suggestion, that the sister from London had
exercised a civilising influence during her visit, might
explain some of it, but not all. He went over in his mind
other small incidents which had disconcerted him at the
time, and came to the conclusion that they could all be
explained if the girl at present at Temperley was not
Annabelle Kelland at all.

Over and above all these details there was evidence of
a different kind—not suitable for a court of law, but convincing, nonetheless. He had admired Annabelle Kelland
before Easter, had thought that with time she could turn
into the bride he was seeking. But he had fallen in love
with her, quite suddenly, quite arbitrarily, but with no
doubt or reservation, when he had helped her over the
stile by the river in early June. She had seemed a different
woman altogether—and perhaps she was!

So what else? It was a fact that Annabelle Kelland had
a sister, and it was beyond reasonable doubt that they
were twins. Though the girl at present at Temperley had

implied that this was not the case, she had not actually said so. Her 'not very much older' could have meant a matter of minutes. But *why* had she prevaricated, if not to lead him off the track?

Were the Kelland twins identical? If the girl at present at Temperley was *not* Annabelle, then they must be for the imposture to succeed as it had. That was something which shouldn't be difficult to find out.

Furthermore, if the girl he had first met was the real Annabelle, and the one now at Temperley was not, then they must have changed places some time after Easter. He knew both girls had been at Temperley then, and the wrong girl could have gone back to London. The difference in 'Annabelle', which Emily and he ascribed to illness, would thus be easily explained!

Though Mr Winbolt had begun this exercise with scepticism, the more he thought about it, the more convinced he became that it was the case. If he could confirm that the twins were, in fact, identical, that would clinch it. He pondered over this for some time, for the last thing he wanted was to let the girl at Temperley, or Emily, or anyone else, become aware of his interest.

An unexpected opportunity came during a visit to one of his tenants. It had been his uncle's practice to make regular calls on the farms on the estate, and Mr Winbolt had followed his example. On this occasion the lady of the house had invited him in for a glass of ale. The day was hot, so he sat down gratefully at the kitchen table, and chatted comfortably with the family. The conversation turned to his Uncle Joseph.

'He was a fine man, Mr Winbolt. Not soft, but you knew where you were with him.'

'I'm sorry to say that I hardly knew him, Mrs Pegg.

Just towards the end he invited me down to see the place.
But he didn't seem to want me to stay more than a night.'

'Ay, that's Mr Winbolt for you,' said the farmer's
wife. 'The kindest man you could ask for if you were in
trouble, but he never wanted company. He and Mr
Kelland up at Temperley made a right good pair, though
your uncle at least cared for the land, and you can't really
say that about Mr Kelland. It's young Miss Kelland who
runs the estate at Temperley. And that's what I meant
about your uncle, Mr Winbolt. He was kind to Miss
Kelland and spent a lot of time with her, teaching her
what she needed to know. They had some rare arguments—about fencing and draining mostly—but they understood each other, they did. She was really upset when
he died.'

'It's a novel idea to me—a young lady looking after
the estate. It can't happen often.'

'Well, she had to, more or less, Mr Kelland not being
interested, like. And from the time she was a child Miss
Annabelle was always eager to learn about the land. Mr
Winbolt taught her a good bit, and John Bostock the rest.
She was a bit of a tomboy, mind, but…well, she had to
be, didn't she? Not like her sister.'

'Was she not like her sister? I thought they were
twins.'

'They're like two peas out of the same pod! But Miss
Rosabelle was taken away when she was nobbut a little
child to live in a grand house in London with her godmother. A Lady Ordway. She only spent the summers
here. She was…gentler. Quieter. Both lovely girls—but
then the late Mrs Kelland was a lovely lady.'

'I expect they played tricks, did they? There were some
fellows at school—twins—and they used to have the
masters at sixes and sevens.'

'I won't say as they didn't, Mr Winbolt. Monkeys they were, sometimes—Miss Annabelle pretending to be Miss Rosabelle, and the other way round. Even Becky Bostock who reared them couldn't always tell which was which! Not always. But they were good-hearted children, all the same. I often wonder how Miss Rosabelle is getting on. She married Lady Ordway's son, but he died and she was left a widow, poor thing. She was here for a while at Easter, and folk said as how she looked very frail. But still the image of her sister. Did you never meet her?'

'We were away at the time, Mrs Pegg.'

'Ah, yes. She went back just about the middle of May.'

So the Kelland twins were identical—his case was just about complete! Now what? For the first time Philip Winbolt started to think of the consequences of his investigation. Having proved the theory to his own satisfaction, what was he going to do about it?

Somewhat to his surprise he found that he had no desire to expose Rosabelle Ordway for the fraud she undoubtedly was. He had admired Annabelle Kelland during his short acquaintance with her, and, because the inheritance of his uncle's estate had brought thoughts of marriage and of founding a family, he had even thought of her as a possible wife. But the girl he loved, more deeply with every day that passed, was the girl at Temperley now—gentle, vulnerable, and in need of help. His discovery had not changed his feelings for her, not by a hair. Indeed, he felt a greater need to protect her, to shield her from disgrace and exposure.

But though he had proved his theory correct, his work was not yet finished. The reason behind this reckless attempt to deceive him and the rest of the neighbourhood was still a mystery. Not for one instant did he believe

that it had been undertaken lightly. It was no trick for the
sisters' amusement, nor, he thought, for any frivolous
cause, such as giving Annabelle an opportunity to see
London and town life. No, he suspected that it had been
born of desperation, and his instinct told him that the
desperation had been Rosabelle's. Nothing could have
appealed more to Philip Winbolt's chivalrous nature.
Rosabelle Ordway, not Annabelle Kelland, needed a
champion. And one was to hand.

Having sorted out his feelings in the matter, Mr
Winbolt considered what he would do next. Should he
confide in anyone else? Rosabelle herself? Emily? The
household at Temperley certainly knew of the substitu-
tion—now that he knew the truth he could see that there
had been several indications of that. But, on balance, he
thought it best to keep his discovery strictly to himself
until he knew more about this masquerade. If, as he suspected, it had something to do with Stephen Ordway's
misdeeds, it was possible that Rosabelle might take fright
if he confronted her—he might well lose her completely.
And it was tempting to think that, given time, she might
learn to trust him, even confide in him of her own accord.

So Philip Winbolt embarked on a deception of his
own. And, though he was as anxious as ever to help
Rosabelle, there was no denying that the situation intrigued him, even appealed to his sense of humour.

'Tell me, Rosa, has Philip Winbolt succumbed to your
charms yet?'

'Not yet, Papa,' said Rosabelle. As usual she and her
father were sitting one evening in his room, though now
that it was hotter they were by the window, catching a
faint breath of air. There had been a change in Mr
Kelland in recent weeks. Instead of remaining in his chair

all day he had started to walk about the room, and the pile of books on his table had diminished.

'Why not?'

'I…I don't know. He seems to have taken what I said to heart. That I wanted a friend, not a lover.'

'Rubbish! Either he's cooling off, or he's biding his time, and I'm inclined to believe the latter. You're still interested in him, are you?'

'Oh, yes, Papa! That will not change. I love Mr Winbolt.'

'Then you'd better do something about it!'

'I…I don't know what that could be.'

'Good God, girl! Didn't your godmother teach you anything?'

'Not really, Papa. She said it wasn't necessary. She arranged for Stephen to marry me before I was brought out. So you might say that I never learned the arts of attraction.'

He looked at the face in front of him, dark blue eyes with a hint of sadness in their depths, sensitive mouth which could curve into a totally enchanting smile, dark gold hair framing the delicate lines of cheek and throat. He frowned.

'She was right. You don't need any arts. But what was the woman thinking of, marrying you off to that misbegotten son of hers, before you were out of the schoolroom? I should have realised…'

'Oh, no, Papa! You mustn't blame yourself. I was very ready to oblige Aunt Laura.'

'And afterwards?'

She turned her head away. 'We realised we had made a dreadful mistake, Aunt Laura and I. A dreadful mistake.' Then she looked back at her father. 'You know,

Papa, whatever happens between Mr Winbolt and me, this stay at Temperley has done me a lot of good.'

'I'm glad to hear it—the imposture has had its merits, after all. In what way has it done you good, precisely?'

'Being here, and talking to you and Becky, and the people round about—especially the Winbolts and their friends—has taught me so much. I had never realised before how extraordinary my life in London was. I was always so close to Aunt Laura, that I didn't meet many other people. Then marriage to Stephen followed as soon as I was old enough. And though I can see now that the marriage was doomed from the start, I was convinced at the time that the fault was all mine.

'He was always telling me I was a failure... The atmosphere in that house just before he died was...the stuff of nightmares. And after his death Giles Stanton came, and made me feel even worse. Here at Temperley I've had time to reflect, and I can now see that I was far too young, and far too inexperienced, to help Stephen. I think it was an impossible task anyway—certainly towards the end no one could have saved him...' She fell silent.

'And that thought makes you feel better?'

'Of course not! But I've learned to stop blaming myself!'

'I hadn't realised how bad it was for you, Rosa. But then, I've haven't taken much notice of anything in recent years. Perhaps I, too, have learned something from your stay here.' Mr Kelland moved restlessly in his chair. 'Well, what about the Winbolts? What are we to do about them? I think you should ask the young man to come and see me. It's high time.'

'Papa! You won't...'

'I'm not about to ask his intentions, if that is what you're afraid of!' he said testily. 'I'm not a complete fool.

But I do want to see the fellow for myself. I don't intend to fail you a second time, Rosabelle. Ask him if he plays chess.'

The upshot of this conversation was that Mr Kelland had an evening's chess with Mr Winbolt which he enjoyed so much that it was repeated. It became a regular engagement, and each player soon learned to respect his opponent—and not only in a game of chess. Philip Winbolt discovered to his surprise that Rosabelle's father had the same quirky sense of humour as the Winbolt family, though he was somewhat out of practice in using it. Mr Kelland found Philip Winbolt to be what he called sensible, a man who seldom spoke or moved without thinking, but when he did, it was to the purpose. Just the man he would have chosen for either of his daughters— but especially Rosabelle.

Time was moving on, and news of Annabelle's return from Buxton was already overdue. Communication between the sisters had continued despite the distance between them, and in her letters Rosabelle had been open— more open than she perhaps realised—about her feelings for Philip Winbolt. Not that she was indiscreet. When writing to one another, the sisters still kept up the fiction that Annabelle was in Berkshire and Rosabelle with the Ordways, and anyone reading them would only learn that Annabelle Kelland of Temperley was finding companionship, and perhaps more, with her neighbour, Philip Winbolt. The difficulties this attraction brought in its train were not mentioned, but they would be obvious to both sisters.

In fact, Rosabelle felt that her friendship with the Winbolts, and Philip Winbolt in particular, was becoming

more securely founded with every day that passed. But
when she asked herself if it was secure enough to stand
the test of a confession, she hesitated. Philip Winbolt, to
use her father's word, did not yet appear 'besotted'
enough. Indeed he had every appearance of having forgotten his passion, replacing it instead with a rather
placid friendship. And try as she might, she could not
bring herself to employ any arts to change it—not while
the secret of her true identity lay between them. She was
caught in a circular trap of her own making. She could
not confess without feeling absolutely secure of his regard; she could not work to secure his regard without
having told him the truth! And time was running out.
Any day now she expected to hear news of Annabelle's
departure from Buxton.

But when the expected letter arrived it told her that
her sister had been delayed yet again. Much later, when
she learned the true reason for Annabelle's continued absence, Rosabelle realised that she ought to have been
worried beyond measure, but at the time she only felt she
had had a reprieve.

My dearest sister,
I am writing this note in great haste before we are
whisked away yet again. You will begin to think that
I have little desire to see you and Temperley again!
But I assure you that I have no intention of letting
another four years elapse before my next visit,
though I have found myself unable to keep my word
to come in August! Giles is taking us both away
from Buxton, though not back to London. He remains as high-handed as ever, and has not yet
deigned to inform us where we are going. I daresay
he would not even let me send this letter if he knew

I had written one!

But however mysterious our destination, you may be certain that we shall all be comfortably lodged. One of Giles's redeeming features—perhaps the only one!—is his care and attention for Aunt Laura. Sadly, this courtesy does not always extend to me. I sometimes think he would be quite happy to see me lodged in a cow byre. However, you may be easy in your mind—Aunt Laura would not permit it.

Aunt Laura and I have found Buxton society more interesting than we had expected, and we have on occasion enjoyed ourselves immensely. Once or twice I have even found myself basking in Giles's approval. He can be surprisingly agreeable when it pleases him!

I am afraid I can give you no firm date for our reunion—I cannot even slip away for a day or two to see you and Papa, as I would wish. But take comfort in the thought that entertaining me would limit the time you could spend in Mr Winbolt's company! I regret I cannot talk to you face to face about such an important matter, but I do not need to tell you that your happiness is very important to me. Aunt Laura and I both feel it may well lie with a man like Philip Winbolt, and we shall look forward to meeting him when the time is ripe. Meanwhile I shall do my best to earn Giles's approval more often. The trouble is we fall out so very frequently!

Aunt Laura sends her love, and I mine. We are both in perfect accord on your situation, so do your best to acquire me a brother-in-law as soon as possible, my darling twin.

Your loving Belle

PS Does Papa know? Please give him my love—I
am pleased he is so much better.

Rosabelle was still examining this letter when Becky
came to tell her that Miss Winbolt had called.

'Emily, what a pleasant surprise! I thought you were
going to be in Reading all day.'

'Philip had to come back earlier than expected—he has
to see someone at Shearings. So I asked him to drop me
here while he went on. He'll call for me in an hour. I
hope it's all right?'

'Of course it is! Can Becky get you anything?'

'Thank you, no. We ate so well at the Harpendens that
I may well not feel hungry till the day after tomorrow!
Anna, are you free on the last Saturday in September?
It's my birthday, and I've decided I'd like to have a party.
The Harpendens are coming, and one or two other friends
of ours. Do say you'll come!'

Rosabelle hesitated. She had always avoided going to
parties and large assemblies where she might meet numbers of local people—especially if the Winbolts were to
be present, too. But this sounded as if it would be harmless enough—an affair with their own friends... She
could hardly refuse an invitation to Emily's birthday
party.

'I'd love to,' she said, trying to sound as if she meant
it.

'Good! I'll send a proper invitation as soon as I have
them. We've ordered them from a place we know in
London. And I'm ordering a new dress, too.'

'Another one?'

'Of course! Anna, you have no idea how lucky you
are. You look enchanting whatever you wear, whereas
I...'

'What nonsense you talk, Emily! I shall look forward to seeing the new dress—what colour is it?'

'I haven't quite decided—we're going to London tomorrow for about three weeks, so I shall have time to consult with the dressmakers and have one made up.'

'Three weeks?'

'Yes. Grandpapa has sent for Philip—that's why we left Reading early. He wants him to see to some business. I don't know what it is. The lawyers are involved again— a tiresome affair. So Philip has decided to take some time and finish whatever it is off properly. As it is, some time in London suits me very well, though we've had such short notice. Anna! I've had a splendid idea! Why don't you come with us? We could have such fun, and you could get your dress for my party at the same time!'

'Oh, no!' There was panic in Rosabelle's voice, and Emily stared. Rosabelle forced a smile and softened her reply.

'I should love to come to London with you, but it will have to be on another occasion. You know very well that I'm not as free as you are, you....butterfly!'

'A very mundane one—a cabbage white, perhaps?'

'No, no! In your new dress you will be a peacock and dazzle everyone! Now tell me your ideas.'

They became involved in a discussion of sleeves and flounces, trimmings and waists, and when Philip Winbolt arrived they were deeply immersed in sarsnet and zephyrine, satin and Urling lace.

'I'll go away again, and come back in a couple of hours, shall I?'

'No, no! I've finished, Pip. Anna and I were just discussing our dresses for my party. She thinks I should go to Fanchon.' A thought struck her and she turned to Rosabelle. 'How on earth did you know about Fanchon,

Anna? I thought you had never left Temperley and she is purely a London phenomenon—I doubt she has ever heard of Berkshire!'

There was a fractional silence, then Rosabelle said hastily, 'I…I must have heard the name somewhere…'

'I expect Mrs Ordway has patronised her,' Mr Winbolt said, easily. 'And mentioned it in conversation. Are you coming to London with Emily? To order a dress?'

This time Rosabelle was prepared. She smiled and shook her head. 'I shall make do with our local dress-maker and what I can find in Reading.'

'But you shall have my pattern book from which to choose your style!' said Emily. 'I shall get one of the servants to bring it over tonight! We must go, Pip. I have a thousand things to do, and we set off early tomorrow morning, remember.'

'I promise to remember if you do, sister dear,' said Philip, smiling.

Emily shook her head at him, and took an affectionate farewell of Rosabelle. 'I shall see you as soon as I get back,' she said, 'and you shall be the first to see The Dress.'

Rosabelle shook hands with Philip and wished him a pleasant journey. He hardly replied. He seemed to be more concerned with helping Emily into the carriage.

Rosabelle went upstairs for her usual half-hour with her father, but she was feeling a little low. The Winbolts were going to be away three whole weeks! If it were not for her wretched situation she could have accepted Emily's invitation, gone with her to shop, be fitted for new dresses, visit the theatre—and spend time with Philip. Though she would not lack occupation at

Temperley, the prospect of three weeks without the Winbolts was dreary.

'Wasn't there to be a birthday party when they come back?' asked her father. 'I thought girls liked parties.'

'I do!'

'Well, think of a present for your friend and stop moping. Or is there some other reason?'

There was, though Rosabelle didn't feel like mentioning it. Judging by this evening's performance, Philip Winbolt was still far from losing his head over her. His farewell had been noticeably cool.

Mr Kelland suddenly sat up in his chair and stared out of the window. 'Good Lord! I haven't forgotten the day, have I? Did Winbolt say he was coming for a game of chess today?'

'No, Papa. Why?'

'He's coming back again up the drive. You'll have to tell him I haven't the time. No, I'll see him myself.'

But, as Mr Winbolt explained, he had merely brought the promised pattern book for Miss Kelland.

'Good!' said Rosabelle's father. 'I don't feel like chess this evening. It's too hot.'

'It is indeed, sir. I confess I'm not looking forward to spending time in London.'

'Madness! See Mr Winbolt out, my dear. You might take a turn with him to the gate—you haven't been out today.'

Rosabelle felt the colour rising in her cheeks. 'Mr Winbolt rode here, Papa. He doesn't want to have to lead his horse the length of the drive.'

'If you would keep me company, Miss Kelland, I will do so with pleasure. If you haven't been out today as your father says, then you need the air. Shall we go before it is dark?'

When they reached the door Mr Winbolt said, 'I have a better idea. I'll leave Thunderer where he is—he's happy in your stables. We can take a turn round the gardens, even go into the park, then I shall see you to your door and collect my horse. How does that strike you?'

'I'd…I think it an excellent idea,' Rosabelle said, trying to sound calm. 'I'll fetch my shawl.'

They went out into the garden. Though it had been hot during the day, summer was now looking slowly towards autumn, and the days were beginning to draw in. Swifts were wheeling and twisting through the air, a gaggle of rooks were noisily seeking out their favoured roosting spots, and the song of a blackbird or thrush could be heard from the other side of the garden. It was that time of day when the sun has disappeared but the sky is still light, and the merest whisper of a breeze freshens the air.

'You are not cold?'

'No, I have my shawl. Thank you for coming with the pattern book. It was kind, when I know you must be busy. You should have let one of the servants bring it.'

'And miss an opportunity for a few minutes' chat with you? We don't seem to have been alone together for weeks. I love Emily dearly, and I enjoy your father's company immensely—but I sometimes wish them a hundred miles away.'

'Mr Winbolt!'

'It's true! You probably don't realise it, but when more than one person is present you seem to disappear into the background, and I lose you.'

'I…I didn't think you noticed such things—not now.'

'Oh, I notice.' Rosabelle glanced at him. He was smiling at her, quite in his old, half-teasing, half-serious manner.

She felt the colour rising in her cheeks, and said, 'I'm not used to company, you see. But I...I am always glad to talk to you, Mr Winbolt.'

They had reached the edge of the garden. 'Are you tired? Or shall we go a little further?'

'I'm not tired,' was all she said, but Philip Winbolt smiled, raised an eyebrow and took her hand in his. She left it there.

They went out of the wicket gate and turned down the lane. The light was now fading and, with the exception of the solitary blackbird, the birds had fallen silent.

'Listen!' They stood while the exquisite trills and flourishes were borne to them on the breeze. When the song came to an end they waited for a moment still held by its magic.

'London has nothing to compare with all this!' said Rosabelle softly.

'Nor with you.'

She looked round, not sure she had heard him correctly, but his face was in shadow. 'Mr Winbolt—' she began nervously.

'No, don't say it!' He put a finger on her lips. 'You remember the second time we went out for a ride together? You wanted us to pretend we had never met before.' She nodded and he went on softly, 'Now it's my turn. Can we not pretend tonight that there are no secrets between us, no barriers? Can you pretend—just for a few moments—that we are two young lovers out for a walk in the twilight, listening to the sounds of the night... If I were to take you into my arms, like this...would you be shocked and angry?' He waited, but when she said nothing, he drew her closer and gazed into her eyes.

'My love,' he said. 'My very dearest love.' He kissed her carefully at first, almost as if he was afraid she would fly away, but then his arms tightened and he kissed her again.

'Philip, no—' Rosabelle's protest, which had come too late for any conviction, was silenced by his third kiss. 'Philip…' she breathed, and suddenly found herself responding to him, lost in such a tumult of feeling that she hardly knew what she was doing. When he lifted his head she gave a little cry and pulled it down again so that his mouth covered hers once more…

When the kiss finally ended, Rosabelle still held on to Philip's arms, not trusting her legs to support her. They were both breathing rapidly.

He said, 'I swear you have the strangest effect on me, you…you enchantress! I start with every intention of treating you as the rare and wonderful being you are, I tell myself I mustn't hurt you, mustn't frighten you. But when I have you in my arms, when you respond as you do, I forget everything except your witchery!'

Rosabelle shook her head. Reaction was setting in. She had behaved disgracefully. Nothing in her upbringing had ever sanctioned behaviour like this. She tried to pull away, but he wouldn't let her.

'Don't! Don't tell me that you didn't want me to kiss you. Don't spoil that moment! You can't tell me that you don't love me this time. I really wouldn't believe you. Not this time.'

'I couldn't do that! I do love you. But I'm…I'm ashamed of myself. I don't know what happened to me. What must you think of me?'

'Everything that is good, believe me.'

She hardly heard him. 'I…I have never behaved like that before—never even felt like that before,' she said miserably.

He hesitated, then said in a curious voice, 'Never?'

'No.' The memory of her farce of a marriage to Stephen Ordway flashed into her mind, destroying her calm. 'Useless, devoid of natural feeling, shameless, wanton…' Her voice rose in panic. 'What sort of woman am I?'

'Stop this, Ro—role playing! You can't seriously believe what you're saying! Listen to me!' He took her by the shoulders. 'You are like no woman I have ever known. Lovely, gentle, amusing, kind…and totally desirable—do you want me to go on?'

She looked at him dully. 'But you don't know…'

'Then tell me! Trust me!'

Chapter Nine

Rosabelle looked at Philip Winbolt in confusion and distress. Was this the long-awaited moment? Had the time come to tell him the truth? She was still off-balance, unable to think clearly, governed by strong emotions never before experienced—or even suspected. In spite of his reassuring words she still had a sense of shame at her passionate response to his kisses, her loss of all control; the memory of her husband's cruel taunts and lewd suggestions had been vividly resurrected in her mind.

How could anyone love her so much that he could forgive her deception? If he asked to know more about her marriage, what could she tell him? Would he turn away in disgust if she revealed the sordid details, the degradation that marriage to Stephen Ordway had brought? Was she brave enough to risk it? She stole a glance at Philip Winbolt. It was now nearly dark, and the newly risen moon slanted across his face, giving it an unfamiliar sternness.

'I…I *can't*!' she said and hid her face in her hands. A shuddering sob escaped her.

The air was heavy with Philip's disappointment. He seemed about to protest, even to force the truth out of her. But then his face softened and he took her into his arms again, this time cradling her gently in them. 'Don't! Please! I didn't mean to upset you. It's just that I want so badly to help you, to have you trust me. And I'm sorry that you don't seem able to.'

'I will, Philip, I will! But not yet!'

'I suppose I understand—after all, you have not known me for all that long, though it seems like a lifetime to me. But, *whatever* your secret is, my love and friendship for you will not change. Believe me.'

Rosabelle turned away and shook her head. Philip refused to let her hide from him. He took her face in his hands and said firmly, 'Listen to me! I could persuade you to tell me if I really tried. You love me, I know, and I've told you what I feel for you. But I'm foolish enough to want you to confide in me of your own free will, without any persuasion or pressure. Am I being mad?'

'No! But I can't tell you tonight! It's…it's late—and I need time!'

He looked at her for a moment, then nodded. 'I can understand that. I didn't mean to bring matters to a head tonight, I wanted to take things slowly, carefully, but now I've rushed you, after all! It's all because of my call to London, of course, and the fact that I found I couldn't go away for three weeks without seeing you once more. If I could ignore my grandfather's summons, I would, I assure you, but I can't! Something which has been brewing for a long time has reached a crisis, and he needs my help in sorting it out. And this time we must put an end to it once and for all. But three weeks seems a very long time before I can see you again!'

Rosabelle nodded. 'It is a long time,' she said softly.

He smiled and bent his head to kiss her again, very gently. After a moment he cleared his throat, and said firmly, 'Perhaps it's as well that we have to postpone our discussion, otherwise I really might not be able to concentrate on Winbolt business as I should! But, listen to me—while I'm away, I want you to remember that I have sworn to you that I love you. Hold on to that and let it give you courage to tell me everything. It will make no difference to my feelings for you, I promise you. Will you do that?'

He continued to hold her, waiting until she looked into his eyes.

'It's hard...I wish you weren't going, Philip...'

He kissed her gently on the lips and silenced her. 'So do I.'

She took a deep breath. 'I will tell you—when you come back,' she said gravely. 'I promise.'

He saw her safely back inside the house, raised her hand to his lips and kissed it, and it was as if the fervour of the kiss passed through the hand, into the rest of her body, bringing new hope and new life.

'Miss me a little,' he whispered. 'And smile for me now.'

Putting aside her doubts and fears, Rosabelle smiled at Philip Winbolt. If the smile was a little uncertain at first, it grew in answer to the old familiar quizzical gleam in his eye, until her face sparkled with love and laughter.

That smile haunted Philip throughout his weeks in London. He was fond of his grandfather and normally enjoyed time spent with him on business connected with the Winbolt estates. But on this occasion the sessions with lawyers and agents seemed unusually long and tedious. Lord Winbolt was in his eighties but, though physically frail, he was still in full possession of his considerable faculties, and he was at first surprised and then annoyed at his grandson's lack of concentration.

'What the devil is wrong with you, Philip? You're usually bang up to the mark, but Harrison has twice made an error which passed you by, and it is quite obvious that you can hardly wait to be finished! What's going on?' He grew sarcastic. 'Or does all the business involved in your inheritance of half a million pounds or more bore you? Not to mention the title.'

'I hope the title won't be vacant for some time yet, sir. But no, I'm not bored.'

'You must be in love, then.' He gave Philip a hard look. 'Is that it? Who is she?'

'I…I'm not absolutely sure.'

'What? What on earth does that mean? You'd better explain yourself, sir! I'm not having my heir marrying a nobody!'

'Grandfather, I promise you I have no intention of disgracing the family name! But I would rather not discuss the lady with you until…certain matters have been cleared up.'

He remained adamant in this refusal though Lord Winbolt tried to move him with promises, pleas and, finally, threats.

'Trust me, Grandfather. When the time comes I will tell you everything—I'll bring her to see you. You will approve, I am sure.'

'Oh, very well, very well. You were always a headstrong, obstinate young puppy. But I never found you lacking in sense. What about your sister? Any beaux in that direction?'

'No, but there's time yet.'

'She's five-and-twenty, sir! High time she was married. She'd make a good wife, though it's a pity she didn't take after her mother—she was a real little beauty! Emily isn't still pining for young Colesworth, is she?'

'I think she's over him now, though it took some time. His defection was a shock.'

'A sad business. Very sad. But it must be five or six years ago now. Has it made her difficult to please?'

'No, but it *has* made her cautious. She's a very rich young woman since my mother's fortune became hers, and past experience has made her a touch suspicious of young men who pretend to admire her.'

'I said no good would come of that money, and look what happened! What did your mother mean by leaving it to Emily, not you?'

'She knew very well that I already had more than enough, sir! But rest your mind about Emily. She'll find someone when the time comes.'

'I hope she may not leave it too late! Where is she now, by the way?'

'At her dressmaker's. She's having a new dress.'

'Another one? She ordered three the last time she was here.'

'This one is for a party we're giving at Shearings—to celebrate Emily's birthday.'

'No cause for celebration there! Twenty-five and not married yet. Better to keep quiet about it. Remind me to see about a small gift for her.'

Philip's time was not totally taken up with business matters. When Emily was otherwise occupied, he enjoyed several convivial sessions at various London clubs. Here, during the course of conversation with his friends and acquaintances he managed, quite casually, to introduce the name of Ordway. But though he heard numerous rumours, and a certain amount of speculation, there was nothing definite. Whatever Ordway and his circle had been up to, they had kept it very quiet. However, the picture he began to form was bad enough to explain why Rosabelle Ordway would be reluctant to talk about her husband.

'You seem to be interested in Ordway and his cronies—I can't imagine why. They were never your sort, Winbolt,' said one acquaintance. 'But I'll tell you one thing. Ordway wasn't the ringleader. That was a man called Selder, but no one outside ever saw him—we only ever heard the name. He came out of nowhere and stayed well in the background. I don't know what became of him—the group seemed to split up after Ordway died and I haven't heard a whisper of Selder since then. But if you ever do come across him, I'd advise you to treat him with caution. From what I've been told, he's the nastiest customer you're ever likely to meet.'

One thing Philip made time for early in his stay was to visit the Ordway house in Upper Brook Street. But the knocker was off the door, and the house was closed. The family were clearly away, along with many other London families at this time of year. He turned away, and came face to face with a well-dressed gentleman, who was standing at the foot of the steps.

'Excuse me, sir. Were you hoping to see Lady Ordway? I'm afraid they're out of town.'

This agreed with what Rosabelle had told him—that her sister was going to Buxton. The stranger seemed to be well-informed, and Philip decided that he might learn more from him. He joined the gentleman and they started to walk towards Grosvenor Square.

'That is a pity. I had hoped to deliver a message from Mrs Ordway's sister,' Philip said, 'You know the

Ordways, perhaps? Can you give me their direction, sir? My name is Winbolt.'

'I am delighted to make your acquaintance, Mr Winbolt. Julian Falkirk at your service.'

Mr Falkirk appeared to be about the same age as Philip, a dark-haired man of average height, but powerful build. He had an air of distinction about him, and his voice was curiously agreeable—husky and deep. Philip would have described him as an ugly man, but when he smiled, as he did now, his face was transformed into something magnetically attractive. He went on, 'But I regret I am unable to oblige you with the Ordways' address. I believe they intended to go to Bath, but they appear to have changed their minds. Is Mrs Ordway's sister with you in London?'

'No. Only my own sister.'

The two walked across the square and down towards Piccadilly. Mr Falkirk proved to be an intelligent, interesting companion, and very knowledgeable about London life. When they reached the corner of St James's Street Philip paused and held out his hand. 'Goodbye, Falkirk. I turn off here. I might well follow your recommendation and take my sister to *'The Taming of the Shrew'* tonight. I don't believe she has seen it staged before. Thank you.'

Mr Falkirk smiled. 'I've half a mind to see it again myself. You might well find me there. Goodbye, Winbolt. I hope you manage to trace the Ordways. Would you care to tell me where you're staying—in case I hear anything?'

'In Arlington Street with my grandfather. But the matter is not urgent. It can wait.'

Mr Falkirk strolled away down Piccadilly. But once out of sight he abandoned his casual air, and walked quickly and purposefully towards the maze of small streets beyond Leicester Square. Here he searched through several disreputable-looking taverns until he found the man he wanted.

'Burrows, find out all you can about a certain Philip Winbolt. He's asking a lot of questions about Ordway, and today I found him at the house in Upper Brook Street.'

'Where does he live?' Burrows asked laconically.

'Not in London. That's something I'd like you to find out. But he and his sister are staying in Arlington Street at the moment. With a grandfather.'

'Winbolt…let me think… That'd be Lord Winbolt. He lives in Arlington Street. When d'you want it?'

'Before tonight.'

'Have a heart, Selder—' There was a sudden silence during which the air fairly crackled with menace. Burrows grew pale.

'I'm sorry. It slipped out.'

'Did it? How dangerous. For you, I mean.'

'It won't happen again…Falkirk.'

'Good. I wouldn't like to lose you—you're quite useful. I want to know about the Winbolts before tonight, Burrows.'

The result of Burrows's researches was so interesting that Mr Falkirk dressed with particular care that evening, and set off to see *The Taming of the Shrew* for the second time.

Somehow Philip was not surprised to see Mr Falkirk at the theatre. He had appeared to be a man who liked company, and, as he had explained, most of his friends were out of London at the moment. The play proved to be everything he had claimed, and at supper afterwards, he and Emily speculated with much imagination, and a great deal of amusement, on the possibility of future happiness for the hero and heroine. Emily was more animated than Philip had seen her for a long time.

'But, sir, Katharine was merely pretending to be submissive! I'm sure she is still a clever, strong-minded woman. She had not changed essentially at all, and I fear Petruchio is due for an unpleasant surprise.'

'Not at all, not at all! Petruchio knows very well what sort of wife he has acquired. It's a game they are both playing.'

'You mean he *wants* a termagant for a wife?'

'No, no. But he wants a wife who knows her own mind. I think most intelligent men do.'

Philip had been content to watch the sparring match, but now he intervened. 'I think some men do. But if someone has to have the last word, then it should surely be the husband.'

In the argument that followed Philip watched Julian Falkirk closely. The Winbolt brother and sister had been orphaned at an early age, and Philip was accustomed to guarding his sister's interests. When Colesworth had nearly broken her heart, Philip had supported his sister in her distress, had taken her away on a long tour of the Lake District to help her recover, and had, since then, discreetly vetted any would-be successors. As it turned out, his efforts had till now proved unnecessary—Emily had never taken an interest in any one of them.

Julian Falkirk seemed on the surface to be eminently suitable—presentable, amusing, and, from what he said, of the same sort of background as their own. Since the Winbolts were not great mixers in fashionable circles, and since Falkirk had met Philip only by chance that morning, he was unlikely to be a professional fortune-hunter. There hadn't been time for him to hear gossip about Emily's inheritance. Still, it wouldn't do any harm to set some enquiries in motion.

The time came for them to part company. 'Goodnight, Miss Winbolt,' said Falkirk. 'Today, when I found that the Ordways had still not returned to London I was somewhat cast down. But see! It has resulted in a very pleasant evening.'

'You know the Ordways, sir?'

'Slightly. But more by way of business. Mrs Ordway might be able to help me with some papers I need.'

'Her sister has told me that they are in Buxton at the moment. But they should be back before long, I think. Goodnight, Mr Falkirk.' Emily smiled and offered him her hand. He took it and touched it fleetingly with his lips.

'Goodnight, Miss Winbolt. And thank you for a most…interesting evening.'

Philip met with only moderate success in his enquiries. Julian Falkirk was very popular at the clubs, being someone who had a fund of excellent stories, held his wine well, and, though willing to play deep, never played beyond his ability to pay. He had been a captain in the Army, and had fought with distinction at Waterloo. After the war he had remained abroad and had been a frequent, though elusive, visitor to London. Until recently.

But then a radical change had taken place in Julian Falkirk's fortunes. He was a distant cousin of the present Lord Banagher, a very distant cousin, but a series of misfortunes in the Banagher family had resulted in a disastrous lack of heirs. As a result, when the present Lord Banagher died, which report said could be at any moment, Julian Falkirk would inherit the title.

The matrons of society now regarded him with benev-

olence, and were looking forward to cultivating his acquaintance when Society returned to the capital. Heir to
a barony, moderately wealthy, charming in company, not
even the worst of the tabbies could claim that there had
ever been any scandal associated with him. His only fault
seemed to be that he was still somewhat elusive, and
though he danced and conversed amiably enough during
the last season, he had never seemed particularly interested in any of the young ladies who were paraded before
him.

It had to be said that Mr Falkirk did not parade his
interest in Miss Winbolt, either. He was apparently in no
hurry to pursue the acquaintance, for neither Philip nor
Emily saw anything of him for over a week after the
theatre visit. He might almost have been out of town. But
on his return he was so charming that Emily grew more
interested in him with every day that passed. Though
their conversations may not have been exceptionally
long, she found them more stimulating than any others.
He teased her about her love of shopping, he shared her
intense interest in drama and the theatre, and he listened
sympathetically to her enthusiastic descriptions of the
beauties of Berkshire.

A more handsome man would have made her cautious,
but Mr Falkirk's lack of looks disarmed her. The fact that
he obviously prized intelligence and initiative in a
woman was most reassuring to someone who thought of
herself as plain. Philip watched and did his best to hide
his anxiety. With all his heart he wanted Emily to find
someone with whom she could be happy. He was not yet
certain that Julian Falkirk was that man.

Then, to Philip's dismay, on the eve of their return to
Berkshire, he heard his sister issue an invitation to

Falkirk for her birthday party. This development was as unexpected as it was unwelcome, but he found it impossible to think of anything to say against it. It was highly out of character, for Emily was usually a cautious creature. She was clearly more interested in Julian Falkirk than he had realised. To do Falkirk justice, the fellow demurred, hesitated, said everything that was proper…but the end result was that Julian Falkirk's name had been added to the list of those invited to the party at Shearings on the following weekend. He had friends nearby, he said, with whom he could stay.

'You don't approve, Pip?'

The Winbolts were in the carriage on their way back to Berkshire. It had become clear to Philip that Emily was having second thoughts about her invitation to Mr Falkirk, and was looking for reassurance.

'I don't exactly disapprove, Emmie,' said Philip, deliberately using an affectionate name from childhood. 'I was a little surprised. We don't know much about him.'

'That's because he has lived abroad a great deal of the time,' said Emily eagerly. 'He was at Waterloo, and before that he fought alongside the Prussians.'

'Ah. That might account for it. Er…where has he been since 1815? Did he say?'

'I gathered that he's been with the Army of Occupation.'

'Has he said anything about his family? The Banaghers haven't the best of reputations.'

'Philip! I don't like you in this mood! There isn't the slightest need to be so suspicious. Mr Falkirk is only a distant connection of the present Lord Banagher. You mustn't tar him with the same brush. His family own a castle on a lake in the south, which he is due to inherit any day. It's very beautiful there. He has always been something of a rover, but now he is beginning to feel that he ought to settle down.'

'He appears to have plenty to live on,' said Philip, trying to find something positive to say. 'Just…just don't rush into anything, Emmie. It isn't like you.'

'I know, Pip dear. You're afraid I'll make another mistake. Don't worry—I'm not going to lose my head over Mr Falkirk. But I have to confess that he's the most interesting man I have met in a long time! And he is not coming to stay for a month—only a few hours on my birthday.'

The warm weather held throughout the weeks the Winbolts were in London. Rosabelle ordered her dress, made her usual visits to the sick round the Temperley estate, sat in the garden in the shade of the trees, went for walks along the river, and quite failed in all of this activity to put Philip Winbolt out of her mind. Sometimes she could picture herself living forever more in idyllic happiness at Shearings, but at other times she was despondent, unable to see a future with him anywhere. Then she would remind herself of his words and take heart again. Her father was getting more active. He even came down one afternoon to sit with her in the garden, and said several times how pleasant it was.

'I had quite forgotten how agreeable it can be in the open air. My room is very hot in the afternoons. I should do this more often. When is young Winbolt coming back?'

'On Friday, I believe, Papa. Emily's party is the day after.'

'Hmm. Leaving it a bit late, aren't they?'

'They have a very competent housekeeper, she will see that the servants do everything necessary. Emily says in her note that Mr Winbolt has too much to do to leave London earlier.'

'I take it that you haven't yet spoken to him?'

'He did ask me a little about it—the night before he left. But…I wasn't ready. Don't say anything, Papa! I know it was foolish, but when it came to the point I just couldn't do it! It was he who suggested waiting till he came back, not I! He…he is very kind.'

'Kind? Bah! I told you. He's in love with you! Don't waste any more of his time, Rosabelle. Tell him! I'll warrant he'll take you in his arms and swear it makes not an atom of difference. Tell him soon.'

Rosabelle's smile, her enchantingly sweet, sparkling, vulnerable smile, lit her face. 'I will, Papa. I will.'

Her father's face softened. He stretched out his hand to hers. 'I want to see you made happy, my dear. And Philip Winbolt is the man to do it.'

Philip and Emily arrived home in a carriage laden down with packages and parcels of every size. Rosabelle had been warned of their arrival and was at Shearings to greet them.

'Emily! How many dresses did you intend to buy? There's more than one here, I'll swear!'

'Well, it would have seemed such a wasted opportunity, Anna dear. Three weeks with nothing to do but look at the shops and choose materials!'

'During the day,' said Philip. 'She had better things to do in the evenings. How are you?' He came over and took Rosabelle's hand. 'Have you missed me?' he said softly, taking her hand to his lips.

The look in his eyes caused delicate colour to rise in Rosabelle's cheeks. 'I…yes, I have,' she said.

Emily had been busy with her boxes and parcels, but now she looked sharply at her brother. She seemed about to say something, but he gave a faint shake of his head, and she changed her mind. Then she turned to Rosabelle.

'Anna, I have to show you my dress—it is a dream! You were quite right about Fanchon. Come! We'll go to my bedchamber right away.'

Laughing, Philip said, 'I can see that my sister has her own priorities. Who am I to interfere? I'll go and see what's been going on at Shearings while we've been away. I'll be back in less than an hour, however, so don't linger over your rhapsodies!' With that he left the room and the two young ladies ascended the stairs to a handsome room on the first floor.

The new dress was produced and greeted with awe. In truth, its rich, wine-red silk top and thin cream gossamer skirt were extremely flattering to Emily's colouring, and her figure was shown to full advantage by the slightly longer, closely-fitting bodice.

'You don't think the waist is too low?' Emily asked anxiously. 'Madame Fanchon said it was going to be all the fashion, but I'm really not sure.'

'I shouldn't argue with her. That bodice is absolutely right for you. I hadn't realised what a tiny waist you have, Emily. I like the little point in front—that's very elegant.'

'I was very taken with the sleeves—see?' Emily lifted up the short oversleeves of wine red, to display the short, delicate, gossamer silk undersleeves ending in a pointed fall of lace and silk. Every detail was pored over and admired by Rosabelle, delighted that her friend had been so successful in her search for a dress worthy of the occasion.

'And what have you found, my friend?' asked Emily when the dress had been given, along with all the rest, to be put away.

Rosabelle smiled and said. 'Guess the colour!'

'Blue,' said Emily promptly.

'Wrong—it's azure! Blue is far too commonplace a name for the colour of my dress—according to the silk merchant in Reading. And I've taken some lace from one of my mother's old dresses to trim it. You'll like it. But you're the important one on Saturday, and that dress makes you into a star. It is truly beautiful!'

'Anna, I've invited someone I met in town. He's Lord Banagher's heir. His name is Falkirk. Mr Julian Falkirk.'

'Oh?'

'Don't say "Oh?" in that significant way! You mustn't read more into a simple invitation than there is! I simply like him, and I think you will, too. He isn't particularly handsome, but he's a sensible man and very easy to talk to. I shall look forward to hearing your opinion of him.'

'What about your brother? Does he like him?'

'Philip's protective instincts are always aroused when I show interest in anyone. He's reserving judgement. But I'm sure he'll like Mr Falkirk more when he sees him here at Shearings. I might call on you to support me. Philip will listen to you.'

Rosabelle grew pink and said, 'What makes you think that?'

'Oh, Anna! I have eyes! And I've known Philip a long time. He's besotted with you! And there is no one I would rather have as a sister—you must know that. But I won't say any more until one of you tells me that it is all settled. I have a feeling that I won't have long to wait.'

The maid came back at that moment to say that Mr
Winbolt was asking for them. Emily gave Rosabelle an
unladylike wink, and hugged her. They both collapsed
into laughter, then calmed down and descended the stairs
in a dignified manner.

'It's a great nuisance,' said Philip as they entered the
drawing room. 'I have to ride over to Johnson's farm
tonight—apparently Johnson injured himself pretty badly
yesterday, and I need to see him and settle what we'll do
while he's out of action.'

'But Johnson's farm is miles away!' exclaimed Emily.
'And it's already late!'

'I know,' said Philip, looking at Rosabelle. 'It's…
inconvenient. There are other, more important, things I
wished to do.' He turned to Emily. 'But I can't put it off
till after the weekend—and tomorrow is your birthday.
I'll go tonight and stay at the Falcon in Theal. That way
I can see Johnson early tomorrow, assess what to do and
be back in time for the party.'

'I'll tell Mrs Hopkins to pack a bag for you,' said
Emily and hurried out.

Philip went over to Rosabelle and took her into his
arms. 'I've missed you. Oh, how I've missed you!' was
all he said, but Rosabelle felt his love enveloping her
once again. She gave him her enchanting smile.

'I've missed you, too, Philip. And I'm ready now to
tell you everything. But it will take some time—it's a
long story.'

'We'll have all the time we need tomorrow, my love—
no, confound it! It's Emily's party! I'm sorry, but all this
time I have looked forward to seeing you; I arrive home
to find that you are ready to trust me as I had hoped—
and I cannot stay to hear you!'

'Johnson is bad?'

'Very. He's likely to lose a leg. I have to see him and do what I can to reassure him.'

'Of course. We can wait. After all, we have the rest of our lives.'

'But now that I know you love me, I want the rest of our lives to begin as soon as possible!'

'So do I, Philip—oh, so do I! But it seems we must wait till after the party—and, after all, it is Emily's day tomorrow.'

'So I must wait till Sunday then?'

'On Sunday I shall tell you the whole sad story. And then—'

'And then…' He drew her to him.

There was a sound of loud coughing from outside the door and Emily entered the room. 'It's all ready. When do you expect to be back, Philip?'

'I shan't know till I see Johnson. However, I shall certainly be here in time for your party, Emily. I wouldn't dare miss that! But perhaps you should get that cough of yours seen to?'

Rosabelle had many dresses equal to Emily's in style and modishness in the house in Upper Brook Street, but she had seldom dressed there with as much pleasurable anticipation as she did at Temperley on the evening of Emily's party. The dress she wore was not ambitious in style, for she had thought it better not to test the skills of the local dressmaker too far. The bodice was plain, and the skirt full and simply cut. But she had been very fortunate to find the length of 'azure' silk at the silk merchant's in Reading. The beautiful material shimmered in candlelight, and the intense blue kept its colour where paler shades would have faded. Her mother's lace was valuable and the dressmaker had draped it over the bodice and round the hem with considerable success.

The whole of Temperley's small household shared Rosabelle's pleasure—they had all watched her increasing confidence and happiness in the past weeks, and thought they knew how to account for it. Even Mr Kelland insisted on seeing his daughter before she set out for Shearings.

'My dear girl!' he said. He was not accustomed to emotion, and found difficulty in expressing it. But the sight of his gentle, anxious daughter's transformation into a laughing, radiant beauty overcame his inhibitions. 'My dear girl—you look…wonderful! Irresistible! Enchanting! I am so proud of you.'

'Papa! Thank you! And thank you for looking out Mama's jewellery for me.'

'You look just like her, Rosabelle. Just like my Rosanna. That diamond collar was my wedding present to her.' Mr Kelland coughed and cleared his throat. 'I should have come with you. But I daresay John will see you safely there and back. And I have no doubt whatever that young Winbolt will keep an eye on you at the party. Enjoy yourself.'

Rosabelle went over and hugged him, without thought for her finery. 'Thank you, Papa. Not just for the jewellery, but for everything else.'

'Well, well. That's enough. Off you go. Don't keep the horses standing about.'

Chapter Ten

Shearings was *en fête*. All the huge double doors which linked the rooms on the ground floor were open. Hundreds of candles burned in the chandeliers and wall lights, and the house was full of great bowls of autumn leaves and flowers. The Winbolts had brought Mrs Hopkins, the housekeeper, with them from London when they had first come to Shearings, and she had proved more than worthy of their trust in leaving her to it. Extra help had been engaged locally, and Maynard, Lord Winbolt's butler, had condescended to join the household for the week leading up to the party. He and Mrs Hopkins were old friends and together they had worked to produce superb food and wines in fitting surroundings. Emily might well be pleased with the preparations for her birthday celebration.

Rosabelle had not realised, when she had accepted the invitation, that it was to be such a huge affair. She would have been far more reluctant to come, had she known that practically the whole neighbourhood had been invited. But she comforted herself with the knowledge that Philip, who was the most important person in her life after all, would soon know the truth anyway. So she came into the hall, after leaving her cloak with the footman, prepared to enjoy the evening.

'Annabelle! Where've you been all these months? We've hardly seen you! Y're looking deucedly well, girl!'

Rosabelle turned round to find a large lady beaming at her. She had a weatherbeaten face, was dressed in purple satin, and had two lavishly curling feathers waving in her hair. The face was dimly familiar, but the name eluded her. Lady Harbury?…Harbottle? Har… Heavens! What was the woman's name?

'Ah, Lady Harwarden! There you are!' Philip Winbolt appeared at Lady Harwarden's side. 'And I see that our neighbour from Temperley has arrived, too. You are both very welcome.'

'How are ye, Winbolt? This is a splendid affair, indeed it is! I never saw anything like it when y'r Uncle Joseph was alive! Not that he was mean, mind—he just couldn't stand a lot of noise and fuss. Where's your sister?'

'She's in the drawing room, ma'am.'

'I'll seek her out straight away. Oh, by the by, Annabelle—what about the horse?'

'Horse?' said Rosabelle blankly.

'Y'can't have forgotten! How much d'ye think she's worth?'

'I…I haven't—'

'Come on, girl! You've had long enough to think about it!'

'Now, ma'am,' said Philip smoothly, taking Lady Harwarden's arm. 'I won't let you bully my guests in this shameless manner. It's not the right occasion for business matters. And if you don't find Emily soon, you won't see her at all—she'll be dancing. Talk to Miss Kelland some other time. Come, I'll find you a glass of wine and then take you to my sister.'

'Y're quite right, of course, Winbolt. I'll see you later, Annabelle!'

Philip bore Lady Harwarden off and Rosabelle breathed again. She mingled with the other guests, finding with relief that she remembered most of them quite well—especially when she could take her time about it. In due course, when she thought that Lady Harwarden would be safely out of the way, she went in search of Emily.

Emily was surrounded by a group of young people, most of whom Rosabelle could remember from the summers spent at Temperley during her childhood. She joined them with fair confidence. The young woman holding the stage at present was Georgiana Smythe— Georgie, they had called her.

'Anna! You're late! And you live practically next door—shame on you!' said Emily, smiling and kissing her cheek. 'I sent Philip to find you, but he came back with Lady Harwarden.' She saw Rosabelle's eyes go over the group, and said softly, 'No, my guest from London has not yet arrived. He said he would be late.'

One of the young men asked Emily if she would dance and with a smile at Rosabelle she went off in the direction of the music.

'Will you dance, too, Anna? Or will you accuse me again of treading on your toes? I've been taking lessons—this is an easy one.' Rosabelle looked into the anxious eyes of a gangling youth and smiled her enchanting smile.

'And I've been learning manners. I'd be delighted to dance with you, Freddy!'

After the set was finished Rosabelle and her partner

rejoined the group. Rosabelle was panting slightly, for
Freddy Norland's energetic style had rather taken it out
of her. She met Philip's quizzical smile with fortitude,
however, and thanked her partner prettily. She turned to
Philip.

'Stop looking at me like that!' she whispered. 'I shall
burst out laughing, and that would never do. Poor lad!'

'If I looked at you the way I really want,' said Philip,
equally softly, 'the poor lad and all the rest of them
would be shocked.'

Rosabelle took refuge behind her fan and turned away.
But after a moment or two she turned back. 'How is
Johnson?'

'In a bad way. But I think he'll pull through. I've
brought a man in to keep the farm running.'

A burst of laughter drew their attention back to the
group.

'Anna,' said Emily. 'Georgie has been telling me such
tales. Did you and your sister really get up to such
tricks?'

'I'm not sure,' Rosabelle said carefully. 'Which ones
do you mean, Georgie?'

'Well, Rosa wasn't there at all for the best one,' said
Georgie. 'You remember, Anna? When we fell into the
mill pond? That was a lark!'

'Oh, yes,' said Rosabelle. 'Yes, that was very amusing.'

Then Georgie said, catastrophically, 'I'm hopeless at
telling stories—you tell it, Anna!'

'Er…'

'I'm sure Anna would tell it brilliantly,' said Philip.
'But if you get your story, I shall miss the dance I've
been promised! The set is just being made up. I propose
to take your Scheherezade away! Or—' he turned to

Rosabelle with well simulated anxiety '—am I being presumptuous? Would you prefer me to forgo dancing with you?'

'No, no!' said Rosabelle. 'I'm sure Georgie can tell the story just as well as I could—or even better.'

'I would put money on that,' murmured Philip.

'I beg your pardon?'

'Nothing, nothing. Come, we shall miss it unless you hurry.'

'I didn't promise any dance to you,' hissed Rosabelle as he led her away.

'No, but you were glad I intervened, weren't you?'

'Wha-what do you mean?'

'My dearest girl—tell me honestly. Would you rather tell a stale old story to a bunch of people, most of whom know it better than you do—or would you rather dance with me? You look enchanting, by the way.'

'There's no competition, if you put it like that,' said Rosabelle and gave herself up to the enjoyment of dancing with Philip.

The party continued without any further crises. Though Philip was careful not to make too much of it, Rosabelle was conscious of his care and attention all the time. For the first time in years—perhaps the first time in her life—she felt she could look forward to the future with a light heart.

This happy situation changed dramatically halfway through the evening.

'My dear Miss Winbolt, what a splendid occasion! How fortunate for me that we met in London!'

Rosabelle heard the words from the flower-bedecked alcove in which she was sitting, somewhat hidden from view. There was a sound of breaking glass, and looking down she saw that she had dropped her wine glass. The wine had spilled out on the floor, and splashes of it were staining the hem of her dress. Red. The colour of blood.

'What is it? What's wrong?' Philip's voice broke through the waves of faintness which were threatening to overwhelm her.

'I...I don't feel well...'

'Come, I'll help you upstairs. One of the maids will take care of you. Put your arm through mine.'

'No! Not that way!' she whispered. He had begun to lead her past the owner of that hateful voice. 'I'd...I'd like some air. Take me into the garden, Philip.'

'But you'll be cold—'

'Take me outside!' Her voice was still low, but the intense feeling in it impressed him. He led her to the side door which opened into the garden room. Here he snatched up a wrap which was lying on one of the benches and helped her put it on. They went outside.

He took her to a small gazebo, set with ornamental stone seats. 'Sit here. Now tell me what caused all this.'

Rosabelle wasn't ready. Confused and frightened, she had to have time to think! 'I'd like a glass of water, Philip,' she whispered. 'Do you think you could fetch one? I'll be all right here.'

'Of course.' He strode away.

What was she to do? Oh, what could she do? She was well nigh certain that the voice belonged to Selder. He was here in the house. He had said he would be back, but he had disappeared after Stephen had died—more than a year ago, now—and she had come to think he had given up. She had apparently been mistaken. By what catastrophic coincidence had he come here to Shearings? Or was it a coincidence? Had Selder tracked her down as he said he would?

The thought terrified her, and she half rose, ready for flight. But second thoughts prevailed. She could not avoid him—even if she fled, questions would be asked and Selder would easily find out where to look next. She tried to subdue her rising panic—she must stay calm and think sensibly, if not for her own sake, then for Philip's. He must be protected at all costs from Selder's anger... She must think...

Selder had obviously met Emily in London. It was a Mr Falkirk who had made such an impression on Emily, but there had been no mention of a second stranger... Oh God, what was she to do? Falkirk *must* be the man she had known as Selder... She shut her eyes as the dreadful memories returned, the appalling state of Stephen's poor, battered body, his groans... Whatever happened, Philip must not be put in a position where he would do anything to arouse the man's enmity. She had seen what Selder did to those he regarded as a threat.

And yet if Philip learned what sort of man Emily had invited to Shearings there would surely be some sort of confrontation. But how could she prevent it...? Pretend not to know him! Continue to be Annabelle! That was it! She must...she *must* persuade Selder that he had found the wrong sister. It was the only way she could think of to protect herself and her friends.

'I'm sorry it took so long. I had to make a latecomer welcome—someone I would have sooner not welcomed at all to tell the truth.' Philip sat down at her side and put his arm around her. 'Here—I brought a little brandy, as well. Drink it.'

Rosabelle sipped the brandy. Its warmth spread through her veins, but it could not dismiss her feeling of dread. 'Who was it?' she asked.

'A man called Falkirk. We met him in London, and

Emily was rather taken with him. She invited him for tonight, and he has just arrived. What's this? You're shivering again. What is it, my darling?'

'Philip, hold me! Hold me tight.'

'Hush, Rosa, hush! You're safe with me. Nothing can harm you.'

Rosabelle clung to him for a minute, drinking in his warmth and the feeling of security in his arms. Then she drew back and stared at him. 'You called me Rosa,' she whispered.

'A…a slip of the tongue.'

'I don't believe you,' she said. 'Why would you make such a mistake? That's not it at all! You know! You know I'm not Anna.' He nodded, never taking his eyes from her face. 'How long have you known?' she demanded.

'I haven't been absolutely certain till this moment. But I've suspected as much for several weeks.'

'Who told you?'

'No one. You did.'

'Me?'

'Let's say I worked it out. I fell in love with you after Easter, Rosa. It was you, not Annabelle, that I found myself in love with.'

'Does Emily know, too?'

'I haven't told anyone else. Why did you do it?'

'I…I was ill. I needed a rest. There were reasons why I couldn't simply abandon my godmother in London. So—Anna took my place.' She paused, then asked, not looking at him, 'Do you know about Stephen, too?'

'Know what?' he said carefully. 'I know you're his widow, if that is what you mean. Do you…do you still mourn him, Rosa?'

'No,' she said sadly. 'I never did.' She looked at him

sombrely. 'I was glad when he died—and so was he. He...he wasn't the sort of person someone...someone like you would want to...to associate with.'

'Yes, I know,' he said gravely.

Rosabelle let out her breath in a long shuddering sigh. 'I was so frightened of telling you. Are you sure that it doesn't make a difference to the way you feel?'

'Not the slightest in the world—didn't I tell you so?'

'Yes, but I didn't know then what you meant.' The relief was too much for Rosabelle's overstretched nerves. She burst into tears. 'Philip,' she sobbed, 'Philip, I love you so much!'

There followed an interval during which Mr Winbolt did his best to demonstrate that he returned these sentiments in full. After a while she grew calm again, and he said quietly, 'Tell me why you were so upset.'

'Before I do, will you promise me something first?'

'What is it?'

'I want to—I *must* carry on pretending to be Anna. For the moment. Will you help me?'

'Of course. But why?'

'I can't change back without telling Anna first.'

'That's understandable. But it doesn't begin to explain why you were in such distress. Tell me the real reason, Rosa. Don't put me off.'

'No. I...' Rosabelle took a deep breath and forced herself to speak calmly. 'I think I might know Mr Falkirk, though I didn't...didn't remember his name. And if he is the man I know, then he will recognise me. It would be better for everyone if I can persuade him that I am not Rosabelle Ordway.'

'Are you saying that it was Falkirk who caused that shock?'

'I heard his voice—and thought I recognised it. I can't be sure until I've seen him.'

'Tell me why you don't want him to know you.'

'I...I can't.'

Philip regarded her in silence. 'Did he make advances to you when you were married to Stephen Ordway? Is that it? Are you afraid he'll repeat them?'

Rosabelle stared at him. This might be as good a reason as she was likely to find, though it fell a long way short of the truth. It might keep Philip safe. She hung her head. 'Yes,' she said. 'Please, Philip. Help me to convince him I am Anna.'

Philip was silent, then he sighed. 'I'm sure there's more to it than this. Can't you tell me?'

'Not...not yet. I'll tell you later.'

'I have a double reason for it, you know—Emily, and now you.' He looked at the set face before him. 'But I think that's all I'm going to get out of you for the moment.'

'Promise you'll leave it,' said Rosabelle clutching his arm. 'If we can make him believe I'm Anna, he'll go away to London and we shan't see him again. We can convince Emily that he isn't for her, I'm sure. Promise, please promise! When he's safely away I'll tell you the whole story.'

He frowned at the note of desperation in her voice, then his face softened. 'Very well. For the moment. Now tidy yourself up, and we'll go in. Otherwise it'll be all over the county that I've seduced Annabelle Kelland—and then how should we manage?'

When Philip and Rosabelle returned to the house they found Emily in the supper room, being plied with food by Julian Falkirk.

'Anna!' she cried. 'And Philip, too! Come here at

once. I've been waiting all evening to introduce my acquaintance from London to my friend. Mr Falkirk, Miss Kelland.'

Julian Falkirk had been standing with his back to the room. Now he turned round. He stared for a long moment, then smiled. 'Rosabelle Ordway!' he exclaimed. 'What a very pleasant surprise! I quite thought I had lost track of you!' He turned to Emily. 'Mrs Ordway is an old friend,' he said. 'Her husband and I were very close.' He turned back to Rosabelle. 'Isn't that so?' he asked impudently, challenging her, threatening her, reminding her of the past and what he could do.

The man before her was indeed Selder. Drawing on all her strength, Rosabelle kept her eyes clear of any previous knowledge of the man and smiled apologetically. Philip came to the rescue. He shook his head ruefully. 'Falkirk, you have just lost me an argument. When I was told that this lady here and her sister were identical twins—"as like as two peas in a pod" was the phrase used, I believe—I refused to entertain the notion that two people could possibly be so alike. But you say you know Mrs Ordway?'

'I do,' said Falkirk.

'And you think to see her here?'

'I'm certain of it.'

'What if I were to tell you that this lady is her sister, Annabelle Kelland?'

'Of course she's Annabelle!' said Emily. 'She lives with her father at Temperley, quite near here. Mrs Ordway lives in London. Did you say you knew her, Mr Falkirk?'

'Er…yes.' Falkirk frowned. 'I thought so,' he said. He turned to Rosabelle, and eyed her speculatively. His eyes were hard, obsidian, like a snake's. She gave him a cool look in return and raised her chin. He suddenly smiled and said, 'Forgive me, Miss Kelland. I'm sorry I mistook you. The likeness is amazing, truly amazing.'

'You are excused, sir. I am well used to being taken for my twin, though it can sometimes be embarrassing.'

'Well, now that's settled, may we have some food? It's always the same—one never gets anything to eat at one's own parties,' said Philip. 'Come, my little case of mistaken identity! If I know Maynard, he has a few delicacies put away for the deserving. We'll see you later, Falkirk.' Philip offered Rosabelle his arm and led her away.

'You were very good,' he said as they made their escape. 'All the same, my love, we'll have to spend some time talking to him later. I don't want to give the impression that we're avoiding him.'

But all of Rosabelle's courage was required when later that night Falkirk asked her to dance with him. Philip was already dancing with someone else, and so was Emily. To refuse would be somewhat pointed, and he had a suspiciously watchful air about him. Mr Falkirk was far from convinced.

'Tell me, Miss Kelland,' he began as they started towards the room set aside for dancing, 'do you know your sister's present address? Or when she intends to return to London? She has something of mine in her care, and I should like to collect it.'

'I'm afraid I can't help you with either, Mr Falkirk. I haven't heard from my sister for several weeks. Indeed, I shall take her to task when I do see her. I believe her to be with her godmother still.'

'Ah, yes, Lady Ordway. Are the two ladies alone? It sounds a dangerous enterprise to me.'

'Dangerous? Surely not! I understand that Colonel Stanton, Lady Ordway's nephew, is with them.'

'I see...Giles Stanton, eh? Of course, the Stantons have an estate in Derbyshire, have they not?'

Rosabelle looked enquiringly at Mr Falkirk. 'I really don't know. You seem concerned?'

'Well, I shouldn't have said that Stanton was the best escort for two ladies in the wilds of the North.'

Rosabelle was just about to agree, when she remembered that Annabelle was not supposed to have met Giles Stanton. 'Really? You know Colonel Stanton?'

'No, but I've heard of him. He has the reputation of being a ruthless sort of chap.'

If Rosabelle had not been so afraid of arousing any sort of curiosity in this man she would have questioned him further. It was true that Annabelle's recent silence had worried her. But she would not give 'Julian Falkirk' an opening.

'He's Stephen Ordway's heir, after all,' she said airily. 'My sister seems to fall out with him quite regularly, but I can hardly believe he would do anything to give rise to scandal.'

'Of course not,' said Mr Falkirk. The irony in his voice was not lost on Rosabelle, though she gave no sign that she noticed. Instead she turned the conversation to talk of the rooms, the music, all the various topics in which comparative strangers can take refuge.

By the end of the evening Rosabelle was exhausted. The effort of keeping up a front in the face of Mr Falkirk's unremitting interest had taken its toll. Emily had noticed the manner in which her London guest's eyes had constantly followed Miss Kelland, and she was distinctly put out. Rosabelle saw it, but could do nothing to help her friend. Indeed, one small consolation in the affair was the hope that Julian Falkirk's behaviour would give Emily a distaste for him. When the Temperley carriage was announced Rosabelle was horrified to hear Mr Falkirk offer to escort it.

'I feel I owe it to Miss Kelland's sister,' he said smoothly. 'The roads are dangerous at night.'

'Not here, sir,' said Philip curtly. 'And, in any case, the lady has already accepted the offer of an escort from me. I promised her father.'

'Ah, then I shall wish you goodnight.' He turned to Emily, 'Thank you for a very pleasant evening, Miss Winbolt. If you would let me know the next time you are coming to London, I shall procure some theatre tickets for you. I can usually be sure of the best seats.'

Rosabelle was delighted to observe that there was nothing in Emily's manner to encourage him. 'Thank you, but I do not think I shall be in London for some time. Goodnight, Mr Falkirk.'

Mr Falkirk was unabashed. He smiled, that slow, magnetic, charismatic smile. Rosabelle could hardly restrain another shudder.

'Goodnight, Miss Winbolt.' A bow, another look at Rosabelle, and he was gone! Rosabelle could have cried with relief.

'Emily—'

'I see there's a stain on the hem of your dress, Anna. What a pity. I hope it will come out.'

Rosabelle looked down. She had forgotten about the wine. The marks had faded to a dull brown. 'Becky will know what to do. Emily, I hope you enjoyed your party. It was a wonderful occasion.'

'Of course I did! But I think my dress was a mistake.

The colour doesn't really suit me. Goodnight. Philip will see you home.'

'Shall I see you tomorrow?'

'I expect so. I'm a little tired. Goodnight, Philip.' Emily turned away and went slowly up the stairs.

Philip looked at her retreating back with a frown in his eyes. Then he turned and took Rosabelle's arm. 'She's unhappy, but I don't think anything I could say at the moment would help her. I wish I'd never met Falkirk!'

'She's unhappy now, Philip, but she will be saved a lot of unhappiness in the future if she forgets him, believe me. He is not the sort of man she ought to know.'

'I believe you. Shall we go to Temperley?'

'There's no need for you to come! How will you get back?'

'My darling, dearest Rosa! I regard this evening as our unofficial engagement! If you think I would let you drive home alone, you are clearly deranged! I shall fly back on wings of love! Or, John Bostock will lend me a horse, if you prefer.'

Laughing, they ran out to the waiting carriage. From an upstairs window, Emily watched them, heartache in her eyes.

A whole week went by without any sign of Julian Falkirk, and Rosabelle started to breathe freely again. It had been a week of mixed fortunes. Emily was clearly depressed. The thought of being twenty-five had not seemed to trouble her before her party, but now she often referred to her age, and lack of prospects. However, she appeared to have forgotten her pique at Julian Falkirk's interest in Rosabelle, and was as friendly as ever. She brought up the subject of her future.

'One has to look facts in the eye, Anna. It is clear that

you and Pip are made for each other. Indeed, I cannot
imagine why you have not announced your engagement
already. And when you marry, you will hardly want a
third living with you.'

'Emily! Without wishing to discuss household arrangements which are still hypothetical, I swear that Shearings
would be big enough for a host of sisters—and especially
ones as nice as you! And I'm sure you will agree that
we can make nothing official until I have managed to be
in touch with my own sister! I have written to her three
times at least, but I think the letters must have gone
astray.'

Emily put her hand on Rosabelle's arm. 'Don't look
so anxious. When Pip and I were in the Lakes no one
heard from us for weeks! It is quite remote in some parts,
you know. I expect your sister will write as soon as she
returns to civilisation.'

'You make it sound like the moon! But it is October
now. It's rather late in the season to be jaunting round in
the wilds of the North! I am sure it cannot suit Lady
Ordway.'

'You'll hear soon, I'll warrant you. Now, tell me. Are
you coming with Pip and me to Lady Harwarden's?'

Rosabelle smiled. She had no intention of going near
the good lady till she could find out more about that
horse! 'I'm afraid I have a previous engagement,' she
said, trying to sound regretful.

Rosabelle had much the same discussion with Philip.
'I want to tell the world that we belong,' he said. 'Is
that so unreasonable?'

'My darling Philip, we do belong—isn't that what matters? And you must admit that you can hardly announce
your betrothal to Annabelle Kelland, and then marry

Rosabelle Ordway! It simply wouldn't do! What would the neighbourhood say?'

'Damn the neighbourhood!' Then he smiled. 'Yes, yes! You're right, I suppose. We can't have two Rosabelle Ordways roaming the country. Where is that sister of yours?'

Rosabelle's face clouded over. 'I don't know, Philip. I'm worried.'

'Darling Rosa, don't look like that. From what I saw of Anna when she was at Temperley I would say that she is very well able to take care of herself—and Lady Ordway, too.'

'But Giles Stanton went with them, and I am not at all sure she is safe with him!'

'Stanton? Giles Stanton? You say he is with them? Why?'

'He is Aunt Laura's nephew and Stephen's heir. His mother was Sir John Ordway's elder sister.'

'I thought Giles was in France, or Vienna. Somewhere in Europe, anyway.'

'He came back last year, when the Duke of Wellington returned to England, though he still spends time abroad.'

'Then Anna is in the best possible hands. I knew Giles Stanton in the Peninsula. A great fellow.'

'Really?' said Rosabelle doubtfully.

''I can imagine the ladies finding him somewhat harsh. He doesn't waste time on civilities.'

'No!' said Rosabelle with feeling.

'But he's absolutely straight. Anna couldn't ask for a better escort—and, after all, my love, they're not in the wilds of Estramadura, only Derbyshire!'

'So why doesn't she write?' demanded his love.

On the day that the Winbolts visited Lady Harwarden, Rosabelle, whose previous engagement was entirely fictitious, stayed at home. She felt restless. She was no happier than Philip about the delay in announcing their engagement, but until she could see Annabelle, or at least communicate with her, she was determined not to make their exchange of identity public. Her father agreed with her.

'Anna did this as a favour to you, Rosa. You can't end the deception without consulting her. You don't know how it might affect her.'

'No, Papa. But Philip and I—'

'Want to be engaged, get married all in five minutes! Heaven defend me from the impatience of lovers! You're not children—you can wait. Go out for a walk and leave me in peace.'

Now that the weather was less agreeable Mr Kelland had once more taken up his position by the fire, complete with his books. Though he was no longer quite so absorbed in them—Philip came several evenings a week to play chess and converse, and Rosabelle often stayed a while to talk with him—today he was impatient to finish a new criticism of the art of the Greeks and had little time for his daughter.

Rosa waited until she was certain that the Winbolts would be well on their way to Harwarden Place, then wandered out into the park. The day was overcast, with dark clouds scudding across the sky. The wind was tossing the branches of the trees, bringing down showers of leaves. It would soon be winter.

She had been at Temperley now for nearly six months. Half a year. What changes there had been in her life! She wondered how Annabelle was getting on with Giles Stanton. Had he changed his opinion of 'Rosabelle Ordway'? Becky was convinced that Annabelle was attracted to Giles, but how could she be? And yet…Philip liked him.

It was strange that the two men should know each other. Not so strange, perhaps—they were of an age, and it was fashionable for young men of their generation to go into the army. Philip appeared to know him well, so perhaps she had been mistaken in his character…

'What would you say if I told you that I had found your sister, Rosabelle?'

She whirled round. Selder was leaning against one of the oak trees, looking at her mockingly. In spite of the shock Rosabelle kept her head—and remembered to call him by the right name.

'Mr Falkirk! What are you doing here?'

'I thought you might like to know where Annabelle is.'

Rosabelle kept her head. 'Annabelle? What do you mean? I'm Anna.'

'Are you? Well, that remains to be seen.'

'You are talking nonsense, sir. Did you say that you had Mrs Ordway's direction?'

'No, not exactly. The lovely widow Ordway is keeping well out of my way. She's not in Buxton. But if she's with Giles Stanton then I might know where to look next. Or am I wasting my time? Is Rosabelle Ordway in front of me here and now?'

'I can't stand here trading rubbish with you, Mr Falkirk. Either you know Rosa's address, or you don't. If you do, then I should be obliged if you would give it to me. If, in spite of what you say, you don't, then I will waste no more of your time—or my own.'

'I'm damned if I can decide… Let us say, for the sake of argument, that you are Miss Annabelle Kelland, Rosabelle. I'd like you to give her a message if you will.'

'I've already told you, sir. I have no idea where my sister is!'

'Tell her that she has something her husband gave her—something I want back. She'll know what it is. Tell her that I'll take it by force if I need to—she knows what that means, too. You're looking pale, Rosabelle. Have I brought back memories?'

'No, but I don't like the menace in your voice, sir. You are making me very anxious for my sister. And I wish you would stop calling me Rosabelle!'

'She's in no danger as long as she does what I say. You see she gets the message.' He turned to go.

'Mr Falkirk!'

'Yes?'

'I...I really haven't an idea where Rosa is. How can I tell her anything?'

'In that case, let's hope you find her before I do, eh? The message would come more...agreeably from you. I'll call again.'

'No!' But Rosabelle's cry was lost in the wind. Selder had gone.

Chapter Eleven

Rosabelle sat down on a fallen tree trunk, her head in a whirl. What had Selder meant? What was it that he wanted? As far as she knew, she had nothing of his—Stephen had not given her anything. She and Aunt Laura had nursed Stephen constantly until he had died, his frail constitution unable to withstand the terrible beating he had suffered at Selder's hands. He had muttered in delirium, obviously desperate about money, but he hadn't been in a state to say or do anything coherent, and, even if he had, he couldn't have communicated with anyone outside.

No one else had been allowed near him—she and Aunt Laura had been desperate to protect the family name from the shame and scandal which would surely follow if his activities became public. Aunt Laura's doctor had treated him, but even he had never been alone with his patient. The story they gave the world was that Stephen had fallen down a flight of steps, and such was his reputation that no one had questioned it. Whatever the doctor thought privately, he had supported the tale—largely, Rosabelle was sure, for Aunt Laura's sake.

What was she to do now? It didn't take long for

Rosabelle to decide that there was little enough she *could*
do. She couldn't communicate with Annabelle, and it was
too late to call Falkirk back. Her hands were tied. The
temptation to confide in Philip, to lay her burden on his
shoulders, was very strong... But the sight of Stephen's
body rose in her mind's eye, and she buried her face in
her hands. She could not! She could not expose her beloved Philip to the risk of suffering a similar fate. And
to tell her father would be tantamount to telling Philip.
She must work it out on her own.

Her thoughts ran this way and that, like a squirrel
caught in a cage. What if Falkirk found Anna before she
had been warned that he was searching for her, believing
her to be Rosabelle Ordway, and in possession of something he wanted? The thought of what he might do to
Anna, innocent of the background to all this, chilled her
blood. But how could she prevent it? What could she tell
him when he came? After a while she came to the conclusion that there was really no decision to be made. She
had no choice.

She would write to Anna again that night, begging her
to get in touch immediately. But if there was still no
response before Falkirk returned, then she would have to
tell him the truth—that she was indeed Rosabelle
Ordway. If Anna was at risk, there was nothing else she
could do. She realised she was chilled to the bone, and
made her way slowly indoors.

Another week followed, a week of anxiety and tension
for Rosabelle. It was difficult to meet Philip every day
without letting him see how tormented she was—she had
no idea what she would reply if he were to ask her what
was wrong. But just as she was sure he was on the point
of confronting her, news came from London that Lord

Winbolt was ill. Philip set off for Arlington Street straight away and Rosabelle's immediate problem was solved. She grieved for Philip's grandfather for she knew how close the family was, but for herself, she didn't know whether to be relieved or sorry.

Though some of the tension disappeared with Philip's departure, she missed his quiet strength, the reassurance of his presence. A few days later Emily came to see her with the news that Lord Winbolt was no longer in danger, but that Philip was remaining in London for the moment to arrange his grandfather's affairs, and incidentally to make sure Lord Winbolt did not exert himself too soon.

'He had asked me to join him there in a day or two, when Grandpapa might need more distraction. He's a bad invalid and a worse convalescent! Meanwhile I am to look after you, Anna. Philip is worried about you—he says you are too pale. Is there something wrong? Something you can tell me?'

'Darling Emily—you mustn't let Philip's excess of concern infect you too! You have enough to worry about, without adding my problems to your list. I shall come about. Tell me, will Lord Winbolt make a full recovery?'

'We think so—though at his age nothing can be certain. I don't know how Philip will take it if Grandpapa dies. He is very fond of him.'

'When…when did you say you were to leave for London?'

'I'm not sure—as soon as Philip gives me the word. It won't be long.'

Towards the end of that week, however, Rosabelle had a most unwelcome return visitor. Falkirk appeared when

she was out for a walk, almost as suddenly as he had the
previous time.

'Well, well, if it isn't the beautiful Miss Kelland—or
the lovely Mrs Ordway!'

Rosabelle braced herself. 'Mr Falkirk! You gave me a
fright. You've found my sister?'

'Not yet, though I have people searching for her.
Stanton has spirited her well out of the way. But perhaps
you know where they are…Miss Kelland? Perhaps you
managed to get a message to her. Did you?'

Rosabelle's heart was racing. The moment of decision
had arrived. There had been no word from Anna, so she
must tell Falkirk the truth. She wished fleetingly, passionately that Philip was beside her, but there was no
point in delaying any further.

'There was no need to send any message, Selder. I will
no longer prevaricate. You were right in the first place.
I am Rosabelle Ordway.'

In one stride Falkirk covered the space between them
and was holding her arm in cruel fingers. *'Don't call me
Selder!'* he hissed. 'The name is Falkirk—get it?' He
gave her a shake.

'Yes,' Rosabelle said. 'Let…let me go. You're hurting
me.'

He released her, patting her arm in a travesty of concern. 'My apologies. I tend to lose my temper when
someone reminds me of other, less fortunate, times. So
you *are* Rosabelle Ordway, eh?'

Rosabelle nodded.

'Then tell me where the packet of papers is.'

'So it's papers you want?'

'Don't waste my time. You know very well what they
are.'

'You're wrong. I know nothing of any papers. Stephen

never mentioned them. He certainly didn't pass them to me. Nor to Lady Ordway.'

'No? I find that hard to believe!'

'You have to! I swear I have nothing, nothing at all, of yours! Ah!'

Falkirk had taken her wrist and had twisted it up behind her back. He said softly into her ear, 'I'll remember you're a lady and treat you more gently than others who lie to me. For the moment. But I shan't give up. I've a mind to become respectable, my dear, and those papers represent a threat to my plans. Tell me where the packet is.' He gave another vicious jerk.

Rosabelle cried out with the pain. 'You could break every bone in my body,' she cried, 'just as you did with Stephen. But I can't tell you what I don't know! Stephen didn't tell me anything of papers of yours. I swear that is the truth!' The desperation in her voice seemed to convince him. He released her again and took a step back.

'I think I'm beginning to believe you—you don't know,' he said slowly. 'You have no idea what I'm talking about. And shall I tell you why? Because you're lying to me now, not earlier. I don't believe you're Stephen Ordway's widow at all. You're out to save your sister, aren't you…*Annabelle Kelland*!'

Rosabelle stared at him in amazement. She had not expected this! 'You're wrong! I'm Rosabelle Ordway, I swear!'

'Swear away, darling!' He put his hand at the back of her neck and pulled her towards him again. His other arm pinned her to him. 'You're beautiful enough, I give you that. But as you said yourself, the two of you are often confused. Identical twins, they all said that. Enticing little morsels, both of you. And if I had the time I'd find out if you had more go than your sister. At least you aren't saddled with a pathetic rat of a husband.'

Rosabelle stared into the black, snake's eyes so close to her own. 'Let me go!' she said, refusing to show any sign of fear. 'I have nothing to tell you, and nor has my sister.'

'I wonder…' He smiled, then bent his head and kissed her slowly. His arm held her to him so that she couldn't move, couldn't breathe, and the hand at the back of her neck was cruelly tight. Rosabelle felt as if she was suffocating…

'Mr Falkirk! Anna!'

Falkirk whirled round, holding Rosabelle like a shield in front of him. But when her tormentor saw who had interrupted them he let her go. She stumbled over to a tree and held on to it, drawing air, grateful, cool, fresh air, into her lungs in deep gulps. Falkirk bowed gracefully, smiling all the time.

'Why, it's Miss Winbolt. I thought you were in London with your brother.'

'Evidently.' Emily's voice was full of shocked distaste.

Rosabelle wanted to speak, to protest at the contempt she could see in Emily's face, but her throat was dry. She could only croak her friend's name.

'Emily—'

'Pray forgive me for interrupting this…this idyll. I had no idea you knew each other so well.' This time Emily's voice was icy.

Falkirk started to laugh. 'We don't! I was merely testing Miss Kelland. To see if she was as easy a conquest as her sister—any man's for the asking.'

'That's not true!' Rosabelle cried hoarsely, finding her voice in her outrage. 'I fought you off then as I tried to just now, Selder—' He turned back towards her, and the clearing was suddenly crackling with menace. She drew in her breath and went on, 'I mean…I mean Falkirk— I've…I've *seldom* met anyone who fills me with more repulsion and horror!'

'It's clear that your sister has confided a good deal in you, Annabelle, though not enough, it seems. Seldom such repulsion and horror, eh? Brave words. But does she mean them, Miss Winbolt?'

Emily looked from one to the other, at Rosabelle's pallor and the tension in Falkirk's stance. 'I am not sure, sir,' she said slowly. 'But I can see that Miss Kelland is not well.'

'Please, Emily, please help me back to Temperley.'

'Are you sure you wouldn't prefer Mr Falkirk to take you?' Emily's voice was still cool. It was clear that she was not altogether convinced.

Falkirk smiled and shook his head. 'Forgive me for my lack of gallantry, ma'am! But it's time I was away. There's work to be done elsewhere—in the North. If you should learn the whereabouts of your sister, or of any papers, Annabelle—then you can reach me in London through the landlord of the Swan with Two Necks. In Lad Lane.'

'No!' cried Rosabelle despairingly. 'Don't go! You must leave my sister alone! I tell you—I swear to you, I am Rosabelle Ordway!'

'Tell that to her poor fool of a brother,' laughed Falkirk, nodding at Emily. 'But take care! He might believe you—and how do think he would feel about having a shop-soiled widow for a wife, instead of the innocent, untouched bride of his dreams?' He untied his horse, mounted and rode away, still laughing.

Rosabelle collapsed against the tree and put her head in her hands. There was silence in the clearing. When

she looked up again Emily was still standing there, looking at her expressionlessly.

'Did you believe him, Emily?'

'When I met Mr Falkirk in London he was…different.
I thought that I might at long last have found someone I
could trust—the way I trusted you. But he's not the man
I thought at all.'

'Emily—'

'And apparently you are not the woman I thought, either.'

'Believe me, Emily. I am.'

'You swore to him that your name was Rosabelle.'

'It is. I was actually telling him the truth, but he didn't
believe me,' Rosabelle said in despair.

'I find that strange. You have always called yourself
Annabelle. Either you lied to him, or you've been acting
a lie all this while to me, and to Philip. To everyone here,
in fact.'

'I…I'm sorry. I had to. But Philip knows who I really
am. And my father.'

'Does Philip know about Mr Falkirk?'

Rosabelle was weary, wearier than she had been for a
long time. Once again the past was smearing her with its
lies and guilt and deceit, and at the moment she was too
heartsick to defend herself. 'Know what exactly?' she
said. 'What do you think there is to know about Mr
Falkirk?'

'That you had a liaison with him in the past.'

'That's not true, Emily. He was lying. But I'm not
going to argue with you. You've known Falkirk for a
month at the most. You've been my friend since Easter,
and you must know how I feel about Philip. You will
have to make up your own mind about Mr Falkirk and
me.' She straightened herself up and took a step forward.

She was shivering in the cool, autumn air. 'Now I'm afraid that I must get back to Temperley. Will you help me, or shall I go on my own?'

'I'll help you. I'm not a monster. I can see that you are exhausted. Besides, my horse is at the house. Mrs Bostock told me you were in the spinney, and I left him there and walked down. I came to tell you that Philip has arranged for me to go to London tomorrow.'

'I see.'

'Why did you do it, Anna…Rosabelle? Oh I don't know what to call you, what to think! It's impossible!'

They had been walking slowly back in direction of the house, but now Rosabelle stopped and faced Emily. 'You have had sadness in your life, Emily, it hasn't always been easy for you, I know. But believe me, your life has been a bed of roses compared with parts of mine. Try not to judge me harshly. At Easter when Anna offered me a respite from a situation which was very nearly intolerable I took it. We didn't think it would do anyone any harm—it was to be for a month or six weeks at the most.'

'So why haven't you changed back again?' Emily's voice had not softened.

'I don't know where Anna is! Somewhere in the North with my godmother and Giles Stanton, but I have no idea where. She hasn't been in touch for weeks.'

They resumed their path. 'So you changed over at Easter. That would account for quite a lot. Has Philip known for all that time?'

'No, only since the night of your party, though I think he had guessed before that. I love him, Emily. I wouldn't do anything to hurt him.'

Emily said nothing until the house was in sight. Then she said, 'It has been a shock. I don't know what to say.

It's a long time since I trusted anyone as much as I thought I could trust you. When I first met you I felt you were direct, open, frank. But was that you or was it your sister? You see, I don't know.'

It was Rosabelle's turn to be silent. There was something she wanted to say, though it was not easy in the face of Emily's hostility. She waited until Emily was about to take her leave and it could wait no longer.

'Emily, I'd like to ask you, for all our sakes, not to broadcast my real identity. I don't wish to deceive anyone for one moment longer than necessary, but Anna must be consulted first.' She paused but Emily did not respond. Rosabelle went on, 'Philip is in agreement with me on this.'

'Very well…Anna,' said Emily coldly. 'I'll try not to let anyone know.'

'And…and…'

Emily interrupted her, saying angrily, 'If you wish me to promise not to tell my brother about this morning, then I cannot.'

'But—'

'I'm no tale-bearer. I won't volunteer anything. But if he asks me then I shall tell him the truth. You are wasting your time if you're asking me to deceive him. Goodbye…Anna.'

Still with a face of stone Emily mounted and rode off, without even pausing for her groom. He had to gallop to catch up with her.

When Emily arrived in London she found her grandfather very nearly back to normal. Philip was happy to leave him in her care while he attended to business in the town. But in the evening when they lingered over dinner she was not able to avoid all mention of matters in Berkshire, and she found it very hard to hide her hurt at the deception which had been practised on her, to pretend that all was well. She had never had secrets from her brother before. After several occasions on which she had evaded a direct answer Philip finally said, 'Emily, you are not usually so reluctant to tell me all the gossip. How is everyone at Temperley?'

'I...I didn't manage to see a great deal of them,' said his sister, taking a large sip of her wine.

'Why not? Why didn't you? I asked you particularly to keep an eye on...my lady love.'

This reproach from her adored brother was too much. Emily burst out, 'Oh, this is unbearable! Tell me, Pip, why do you never call your "lady love" by her given name?'

There was a pause. Then Philip said slowly, 'I...see... So that's it. Rosa has told you the truth. Or did you guess it for yourself?'

'Let's say I found it out,' said his sister bitterly.

'But how? No one else outside Temperley knows.'

Emily couldn't help herself. 'No one?' she asked with a curl of her lip.

'Who then? Who could you possibly have seen? Falkirk?' Emily took another sip of her wine, avoiding his eyes. 'Are you saying that Falkirk told you? That's impossible—we've convinced him that she's Anna. Why are you laughing?'

'It's all so terribly, ironically funny!' said Emily, laughing a little hysterically. 'I thought she was Anna, you know she's Rosa, she told Falkirk she was Rosa, and he said...' She could hardly get the words out for laughing. 'He said he didn't believe her. He thinks she's Anna! And afterwards she swore to me she was Rosa! Oh, Pip,

how difficult it is to see the truth for the web of lies and
deceit she has woven!'

Philip came round the table and took her glass of wine
away from her. 'You're not making sense, Emily. When
did this conversation take place? And where?'

She sat back and looked at him, half-wanting to tell,
half-reluctant. 'The day before I came away. In the spinney.' When he seemed to be waiting for more, she said
defiantly, 'Ask some more questions. I said I would answer questions, though I wouldn't volunteer anything.
Ask me another question, Pip!'

'God damn it! This isn't a game! You tell me!' He saw
her shocked face. She had never in her life heard such a
tone from him. He took her hand and said more gently,
'It's not a game, Emily! It's deadly serious. I must know
what happened. Try to tell me it all! Falkirk was in the
spinney, you say.'

'He...he was kissing her. He said he wanted to compare her with her sister, to see if she...if she was as ready
to receive his advances. He meant Rosabelle Ordway
had...had kissed him, Philip. In the past.'

'Go on. What did Rosa reply?'

'She denied it, of course. She was angry. She said she
had fought him off this time and before.' Emily thought
a moment. 'It was strange. I didn't really understand what
she said next. And just for a moment I thought he
would...would kill her. But that's not likely, is it?'

'What did she say?'

'I thought for a minute that she had said something
like ''selder''—but then she corrected herself and began
again. She...she was really frightened. She said she had
seldom met anyone who filled her with such...such repulsion and horror. I think those were her words. He
repeated them afterwards.'

'Selder!'

'You know the word?'

'It's a name. My God! So that's it.' Philip had been crouching at her side, but now he got up and walked away. 'Selder!' He came back and crouched down beside her again, his face close to hers. 'What happened next?'

'Anna looked ill. She asked me to help her back to the house. I…I was angry and said something about Falkirk helping her, but Falkirk said he couldn't stop. That he had things to do in the North. He said something about her sister and papers…he asked her to get in touch with him.'

'Where?'

'At an inn in Lad Lane. The Swan with Two Necks.'

'I know it! It's a coaching inn. Anything else?'

'Falkirk started to go and Rosa screamed at him. She swore she was Rosabelle Ordway, that he should leave her sister alone.'

'My poor girl! What did Falkirk say?'

'He started to laugh. He…he didn't say much more.'

'I want everything, Emily. What did Falkirk say?'

'Pip, I don't want to tell you!'

'Come on, Emily. You've done wonders, my dear girl. Finish it!'

'He said that you would be disappointed. That you wouldn't want to marry a…a shop-soiled widow instead of the bride of your dreams.'

Philip got up, slamming one fist into the other. 'I'd like to kill him! I may well, unless the hangman gets him first.' He looked at Emily, who was gazing at him with tears rolling down her cheeks. 'Don't worry, Emmie. You were right to tell me. You've saved me a great deal of heartache. As for you—you've had a luckier escape than you could possibly imagine.'

* * *

Philip's first impulse was to go with all speed to the
inn, and throttle Falkirk until he got the truth out of him.
But second, wiser thoughts prevailed. 'Don't go at it like
a bull at a fence, Mr Winbolt!' his army instructor used
to say. 'A good officer uses strategy—that's what wins
the day. Don't let the fellow know what you're up to till
he's got it in the neck!'

So he sent one of the more cunning stable lads to The
Swan with Two Necks, and contented himself with mak-
ing enquiries of his grandfather's physician about
Stephen Ordway's death.

'A shocking business,' said Sir James. 'Cottrell is the
Ordway man. He said the injuries were quite dreadful.
Hardly an unbroken bone in the whole body. Those two
poor women—Lady Ordway and her daughter-in-law. He
was full of admiration for them. They nursed him themselves to the end.'

'He is supposed to have fallen, isn't he? Down the
cellar steps.'

'Yes. That was the story.' Sir James thereupon closed
his mouth very firmly and refused to discuss the matter
any more, however cunningly Philip tried. It was obvious
that Stephen Ordway's death had not been all that it
seemed, but that the medical profession had closed ranks
on it.

The stable lad came back with the news that Falkirk
was still lodged in Lad Lane and had paid his shot for
another week. So far so good. Then Philip started to visit
the clubs and taverns he knew Falkirk frequented, never
mentioning the man's name, but always looking to come
across him as if by accident. But when he finally ran his
quarry to ground it was truly by chance. He was on his
way to leave a note at Giles's lodgings, asking him to
get in touch as soon as possible. At the corner of Charles

Street he met the very man he had been seeking. He should have thought of it! Falkirk had clearly been calling at the Ordway house again.

'Why, Falkirk!' he called genially. 'What a surprise! Have you been trying the Ordways again? Are they home?'

'No!' Falkirk was apparently in none too good a mood. 'It's time they were back.'

'I don't think Miss Kelland has heard from them, either, though it's some time since I spoke to her, of course.'

'You haven't seen her recently?'

'No—my grandfather has been ill. I came to London soon after Emily's party, and I haven't been able to go back since. I've hardly spoken to a soul.'

'What about Miss Winbolt?'

Philip allowed himself a puzzled smile. 'My sister? Well, yes, I suppose I've spoken to her—she came to London a day or two ago. But we've not had time for chatter. She's well, if that's what you're asking. A bit quiet, perhaps. But that's only to be expected.'

'Expected?' Mr Falkirk asked sharply. Philip allowed himself to look slightly surprised. He said earnestly, 'Of course! She's very fond of my grandfather. She spends all her time with him. Are you going my way, Falkirk? As far as Arlington Street?'

They fell into step. 'I've just been calling at Stanton's place to see if they know anything there. Miss Kelland asked me to, and I felt I couldn't return to Berkshire without having tried. I'm afraid the housekeeper there is as ignorant as we are. But tell me—why are you so eager to see them? You're not a friend of Stanton's, are you? It was Mrs Ordway you wished to see, if I remember rightly.'

Falkirk gave Philip another sharp look, but Mr
Winbolt's face was innocent. 'Yes,' he said slowly. 'She
has some papers…of mine.'

'Papers?'

Falkirk seemed to make up his mind. 'To be honest
with you, Winbolt, it's a matter of some delicacy. Mrs
Ordway and I…well, you know how it is. Stephen
Ordway was a poor fish, and Rosabelle is a beautiful
woman—and a passionate one. The affair is over now,
of course, but at the time I wrote her some letters…'

'And you'd like them back?'

'That's it! I don't like to think of them falling into the
wrong hands.'

'Has Mrs Ordway refused to let you have them?'

'No. She'd be very happy to return them, I think. But
she's away.'

'But what is the urgency? Or are you contemplating
matrimony?'

Falkirk gave his flashing, magnetic smile. 'There's
nothing I would like more! Especially as I now have the
Banagher name to think of! But I don't think Miss
Winbolt would have me.'

Philip experienced some difficulty in keeping his feelings—and his hands—to himself. The insolence! The in-
fernal nerve of the villain! But he said with a laugh, 'I
can quite understand why you'd like to clear the record
before attempting anything of that nature. Women can be
peculiar about such things. Well, if I hear of any letters
I'll let you know.'

They had now reached the corner of Arlington Street.
'By the way, Falkirk.' His voice dropped to a confidential
level. 'If you should see Miss Kelland, you won't mention any letters to her, will you? I shouldn't like her to
learn that her sister had had an affair—she's such a coun-

try girl *au fond*. And we don't want her to get any ideas, do we?' He winked.

It was clear that Falkirk thought he was a fool. 'No, of course not, Winbolt,' he said, quite failing to hide the mockery in his tone. 'Pray give her my regards when you see her. And remember me to your sister, of course. *Au revoir!*'

When Mr Winbolt told his sister that he was paying a fleeting visit to Berkshire, she clutched his sleeve and said, 'No, Pip! I shouldn't have told you about Rosabelle. I've thought a lot about it, and I now believe I was wrong. She's innocent.'

'What do you think I'm going to do, Emmie?'

'I thought you were going down to break off your engagement.'

'You're a fool, dear girl. I never thought for one instant that the girl in Berkshire, whatever her name, whatever her history, was anything but innocent! Pig-headed, perhaps. Ridiculously protective, certainly—'

'Protective!'

'Of me. Odd, isn't it?'

'Protective of you?'

'I think so. And that reminds me. I don't want you to go out while I'm away. It will only be for a day or two. Send Betty or one of the footmen for anything you want. And if Falkirk calls, pretend you're not at home. I don't want you to see him.'

Emily shuddered. 'I don't, either. I didn't like the Falkirk I saw in that spinney.'

'You'll promise me, then?'

'Yes.'

'Good! Keep Grandfather amused while I'm gone. I'll be back as soon as I can.'

*   *   *

Philip set off very early the next morning, taking the Winbolt carriage with him, for he intended to persuade Rosabelle to come back with him to London. It was high time that all the mysteries which had bedevilled their relationship were cleared up. The problem of Annabelle would have to wait until they could trace her, but for the rest, he was not going to be satisfied with anything less than the whole truth.

He arrived at Shearings, changed and rode over to Temperley straight away. Becky let him in.

'Why, Mr Winbolt! What a surprise! Miss Belle is with her father—'

'Thank you!' said Philip grimly, and went upstairs to Mr Kelland's room. Here he found father and daughter engaged in a chess tutorial.

'Sir,' began Philip.

'It's good to see you, young man! But, from the look of you, you have something serious to say. It's not bad news about Lord Winbolt I hope?'

'No, sir.'

'Good! Pray get it over with, and then you can set about cheering up this daughter of mine. I haven't seen a smile for days.'

'I'd like to speak to her in private, if you don't mind, sir.'

'Of course! Take her downstairs.'

Rosabelle had not been able to say a word. Philip's unexpected appearance so soon after Emily had arrived in London could only mean one thing—Emily had found it impossible, after all, to keep the events in the spinney to herself. Perhaps she hadn't even wanted to. Philip's manner was not encouraging. Was he about to repudiate her? Or worse, was he about to demand to know all about Falkirk's involvement with the Ordway family? That she would never tell him—it was too dangerous. It would be dangerous for him even to know Falkirk's real name.

'Now,' said Philip as he shut the parlour door behind him. 'Now, Rosabelle Ordway, I am not prepared to wait any longer. I want the truth! All of it!'

Chapter Twelve

Emily must still have been angry when she told her brother about the scene in the spinney, thought Rosabelle. And now he was angry, too. He looked forbidding.

'You know that Mr Falkirk was here, Philip?' she asked tentatively.

'I certainly do—Emily gave me a graphic description of your meeting. What she saw of it, that is. I gather she came on the scene halfway through. What does Falkirk want of you, Rosa?'

She turned her head away. 'You know what he wants. He would like me to…to be kind to him.'

'You mean to kiss him? I thought you had.'

'*He* kissed *me*, Philip. Against my will. Whatever Emily said—'

'We'll leave Emily out of it, Rosa. She may have told me what she saw and heard, but she doesn't know what lies behind it, does she?'

'She knows I'm really Rosa. She was…angry with me. I expect that's why she told you.'

'She'll come round. In fact, she was pleading your case before I left. And you mustn't blame her for telling me—

I made her tell. What are these papers Falkirk was talking about?'

Rosabelle's head came up with a start. 'Papers? I don't know, Philip! I don't know what he meant.'

'You haven't written him letters…or anything of that kind, have you?'

'No! Did Emily think they were letters?'

'I've told you. Leave Emily out of this.'

'I have never done anything or written anything to give…Falkirk the slightest encouragement. I find him repulsive,'

'Ah, yes! Repulsive. He fills you with repulsion and horror. Was that it?'

'I said that, yes. Emily has a good memory.'

'Is there nothing more you can tell me about Falkirk?'

'What could there be?' Rosabelle avoided Philip's eye. 'He was one of Stephen's friends. He's not…he's not a nice man. I am sorry if what your sister saw upset her, but if it means she has given up the thought of cultivating his acquaintance then it was worth it.'

'Emily is not at the moment my main concern, though I agree with you. Why are you fencing with me, Rosa? I thought you had promised to tell me the truth?'

Still avoiding his eye, Rosabelle said quietly, 'There are some things it is better for you not to know, Philip.'

'Falkirk's real name, for instance? Selder?'

'*What?*'

'Emily's hearing is better than you think. She heard you say "Selder". It didn't mean anything to her, but it does to me. And to you, I see.'

Rosabelle took him by the arms and gripped him hard, her knuckles white with the strain. 'Philip, please forget I said it! Please! And Emily must forget it, too. It's nothing, just a…a name. It has nothing to do with us.' She was deathly pale and shivering. Philip swore under his breath and broke her hold, wrapping his own arms round her. He held her close, trying to give her some of his own warmth. After a while the shivering stopped and she looked up.

'Rosa! Don't, don't be afraid. There's no need, there really isn't! Not while I'm here to protect you. Surely you know I love you?'

'Oh, Philip!' she said on a long shuddering sigh. 'I thought you had come to say that you wanted to have nothing more to do with me. What Emily saw and heard was so…so damning. I've been so unhappy.'

Philip sighed in exasperation. 'This has to stop!' He led her over to the sofa and made her sit down. Then he stood over her, tall, upright and challenging. 'Look at me, Rosabelle Ordway! What do you see? A fool? A rake? A braggart?'

She was surprised and indignant. 'Of course not! You're none of those! Why do you ask?'

'Then why do you keep thinking I shall behave like one?'

'I don't!'

'Oh, yes, you do!' He knelt down beside her. 'I have told you so many times that I have faith in you, that I honour you, that I want you to be my wife more than anything else in the world. I have said, more than once, I believe, that I love you and will continue to love you as long as I have breath in my body.'

'Oh, Philip—'

'No, I have to finish. I'm well past the age of being a young hothead, swearing to what he doesn't understand. I've lived long and fully in the world, Rosa. I've fallen in love and out of it again, I've made mistakes and got over them, I've fought hard in wars and worked hard afterwards for the things I believe in. I know what I want! Why won't you allow me to know my own mind?'

'I hadn't realised… Oh, Philip, forgive me!'

'No more doubts?' Her face was hidden in his shoulder, but she shook her head. 'Do you love me?'

'Oh, yes!'

'Then show me.'

She got up, pulled him to his feet and flung her arms about his neck, casting caution and propriety to the winds in her relief and happiness. She kissed him eagerly, passionate little kisses on his cheeks, his brow, his eyes…his lips. Here she lingered, and then Philip took over. The kiss lengthened, deepened until they were lost in each other, sinking down on to the sofa, all the while murmuring words of love and delight in each other.

Eventually Philip lifted his head. 'I…I think you've shown me,' he said, somewhat unsteadily.

'Was it enough?'

'It would never be enough, my darling, my love, my sweet life,' he said, lovingly putting her hair back from her face. 'But it'll do for now.' He laughed at her exclamation of dismay when she put her hand to her hair and found it falling down her back, at her confusion when she looked down at her dress, which was in considerable disarray.

'Instead of laughing, my own, why don't you help me find my hair pins?' said Rosabelle severely. 'Becky will be waiting to serve some tea. When did you last eat?'

'I had something before I left.'

'That must be six hours at least! Come, help me with this last hook, and I'll find Becky. No, Philip! Just hook it up!'

'Pity! In that case, while you see Becky I'll go to have a word with your father. I'll join you here in half an hour.' It was clear that his talk with her father was not to include her. Rosabelle was content. This was no more than normal procedure. Philip was about to ask her father for her hand in marriage. She went into the kitchen.

'Come in, Winbolt—don't keep the door open. Walters, disappear, man!'

Philip entered Mr Kelland's bedchamber, shut the door and advanced into the room. 'Are you busy, sir? I'd like to speak to you. It's about Rosa.'

'Oh?' said Mr Kelland with exaggerated surprise.

Philip laughed. 'As I'm sure you know, I want to marry her, sir. As soon as it can be arranged.'

'You have my blessing, if that's what you're asking. I like you, Winbolt, and I think you're the right man for her. But…'

'I know we have to wait till your daughters can take up their own identities again. And that can't happen till Anna's return.'

'Quite so. But after that I shall be delighted to welcome you as a son-in-law. You could hardly fail to be an improvement on the last.'

'Thank you, sir,' said Philip meekly.

Mr Kelland smiled thinly. 'I could have put that better, couldn't I? I ought to have said that you couldn't be improved on as a husband for Rosa.'

'Thank you. I shall be able to support her quite adequately. If you wish I can get my man of business to see you. Rosa will have settlements and all the rest.'

'Yes, yes. We'll go into that later, if you wish.'

'But…'

'But what?'

'There's the matter of her late husband.'

'I assure you that he's dead, if that's what you're worried about.'

'No, no! That's something I don't doubt. But how did he die? And why?'

Mr Kelland looked at him sharply. 'You feel there's a mystery, eh? Well, I can't help you. I don't know. I certainly don't believe the story the two women put about— that was an attempt to save the Ordway name. But Rosa has never confided in me.'

'I see…'

'But I agree with you. I've had my suspicions, too.'

'Do you feel you could share them with me?'

'Ordway was in with a very queer bunch of people. At one time I had enquiries made. He was a drug addict, of course—opium, laudanum, anything he could get hold of. And he was…' Mr Kelland grimaced. 'I read a lot, Winbolt. I am not easily shocked by what modern, rich, idle, young men get up to—it's mostly been done before. But when it concerns your own family… Ordway had…unnatural appetites.'

'You knew this? And you let your daughter marry him?' Philip didn't quite manage to conceal his disgust.

'Of course I didn't! Not until after they were married. And in any case, whatever suspicions I might have had beforehand, there was very little I could have done about it at the time. Lady Ordway practically forced Rosa to marry her son, and Rosa would have done anything to please her godmother.'

'All the same…'

'Yes, yes, you're right, of course. I failed in my duty towards my daughter. I should have refused to give my consent. But I just wasn't sufficiently interested enough to take a firmer stand. It would have caused a great deal of fuss. Oh, you needn't look so shocked! Lady Ordway had practically adopted Rosa. Except for the summer months, I hadn't seen anything of the child from the time she was six or seven. I've regretted it since, of course, especially in the last few months.'

Philip exerted himself to speak calmly. 'So you can't help me about Ordway?'

'Rosa is the one who knows the truth—or some of it. Get her to tell you, if you really want to know. But if you take my advice you'll leave well alone.'

'I'll…er…I'll think about it, sir,' said Philip briefly. He got up.

'Shut the door on your way out. Winbolt. It's damnably draughty in this room,' Rosabelle's father said as he picked up his book.

Philip went out, shutting the door very carefully behind him. Gentlemen did not slam doors.

After the substantial repast that Becky thought necessary, Rosabelle and Philip went outside. It was late in the afternoon on a clear day in the middle of October and the autumnal foliage was a blaze of red and gold in the light of the dying sun. Philip turned in the direction of the spinney.

'No, Philip. Let's go the other way.'

'Why? I want to see the spinney. I want to work out what direction Selder could have come from.'

'Please, Philip, please don't say that name—not even here! I tell you it's dangerous to know it. Why must you talk about him, anyway?' she said desperately.

'Because, dearest, loveliest Rosa,' said Philip, stopping and turning to face her, 'I intend to scotch this snake.'

'No!' Rosa's voice rose in desperation. 'No, I won't hear of it. You must leave him alone!'

'I can't. What about Anna? The man is determined to

get hold of those papers, whatever they are. He won't give up till he either finds them, or is stopped.'

'I know, I know! But you mustn't get involved. I'll manage somehow.'

Philip Winbolt seldom lost his temper, but at these words of Rosabelle's he exploded.

'What the hell do you think I am, Rosa?' he demanded fiercely. 'Your sister once called me a doormat, and, by Heaven, I think you regard me as one!'

'It's not that, Philip, it's not that at all!' she pleaded. 'But Selder is totally ruthless. I can't risk having you beaten unconscious, to die the way Stephen died. I couldn't bear it.'

'Good God, it's even worse than I thought! You don't think of me as a doormat. You think I'm like your rat of a husband. Ready to stand aside while you do battle with a villain like Falkirk! Abject enough to lie down, waiting to be kicked like a dog.'

Stunned by the strength of feeling in Philip's voice, Rosabelle couldn't say a word for a moment. But Philip didn't wait. He swept on, 'Well, I'm not about to crow like a cock on a dunghill about prowess in the art of defending myself. But I'm damned sure I'm not going to let you push me out of this fight. I've met worse men than Falkirk in my time, believe you me. And beaten them.'

Rosabelle found her voice. 'But you didn't see Stephen after Falkirk had finished with him,' she cried. 'I did! I tried to stem his bleeding, I bathed his head, I gave him more laudanum to ease the pain…' She couldn't go on. Tears were blinding her, her throat was constricted with feeling.

Philip took her into his arms. 'Hush. I know, I know. But Stephen wasn't a fighting man, my darling. He was

no match for the likes of Falkirk. You say you trust
me—'

'But not about this!'

'Yes, you must! This trust is just as important as any
other—you can't separate them. Face the truth. Your
troubles are now my troubles. I'm going to fight your
battles whether you let me or not, and I know I can win.
But I'll fight them a lot more easily if you are with me,
if you help me to learn exactly who or what my enemy
is. Have confidence in me. Tell me about Falkirk and the
rest. Or I shall know that, for all your brave words, you
don't really trust me at all.'

He held her eyes as she struggled to come to terms
with this new Philip. This wasn't the charming, humor-
ous, quizzical stranger who had captured her heart. Nor
the passionate lover whose kisses could inflame her with
strange and overwhelming sensations. Nor was this the
sympathetic, undemanding friend on whom she had
learned to depend. This was a man, ready to be her champion. It would be useless to deny him, for he would defend her whether she would or no.

She looked at him with new eyes, seeing the steel
which was disguised by Philip's exquisite manners, the
determination which lay beneath his air of charming dif-
fidence, the authority which he had till now not found it
necessary to parade. Philip was right. She had to let him
make his own decisions about risk and danger. Security
lay in working together. She took a step back and smiled.

'Where shall we start?' she asked.

They went to the spinney, where Philip took Rosabelle
carefully through her second meeting with Falkirk.

'It's clear that he's desperate for those papers.
Whatever they are, they must represent either a fortune,

or a threat which can't be ignored. I wonder which it is…' said Philip, as they walked round the little clearing.

'It's a threat. He said so. They must incriminate him in some way.'

'He was here by this tree, you say, when you first saw him?'

'Yes. Both times he came, he seemed to appear out of the blue. He was…just there!'

'Horse?'

'He had one the second time. I didn't notice the first time he came.'

'Where did you meet him the first time?'

'In the park.'

'The park is on the other side of the house from here, further away from the bridle path… If you didn't see a horse then he must have walked across the fields. Right! Now think back again to his second visit. This horse— did it look as if it had been ridden far?'

'I wasn't looking…but I don't think so.'

'I'll get one of the men to start asking questions. The bridle path leads to Harden Lane and on to the Reading road. The road on the other side of the fields comes into the Reading road about ten miles further on. He can start along those ten miles.'

'Why are you doing this, Philip?'

'So far, my love, Mr Julian Falkirk has been a bit of a mystery. He seems to come and go as he pleases. I want to track him down—whether he stays at an inn, or whether he knows anyone in the neighbourhood apart from ourselves. But that's only the beginning. Tomorrow, or the day after, I should like you to come to London with me. It's time you met my grandfather, and there's work we can do there.'

'London! But I can't!' said Rosabelle blankly. 'I'm not ready! I haven't any clothes…I can't leave Papa…'

Philip burst out laughing. 'You are a delight, Rosa! Mrs Bostock will help you to get ready, your father can do without your company, and as for clothes… You surely have some, and acquiring more can work to our advantage.'

'How?'

'You will have to gain admittance to the house in Upper Brook Street to look for the ones you left there! I assume there's a caretaker with keys?'

'The lawyers usually keep them. What…what do you want from Upper Brook Street?'

'Apart from your clothes? I want to look for some papers. Falkirk's precious papers.'

'They're not there!'

'How do you know? You didn't even know they existed when you were last in Upper Brook Street.'

'But what if Falkirk sees me?'

'Let me take care of that. Rosa! I'm serious when I say that I want you to meet Grandfather. Will you come?'

Rosabelle took a deep breath. It was a beginning, and she had promised to help him. 'Well, yes! I'd like to,' she said bravely.

However, she needed all her courage later that evening when Philip started to ask her about her life with Stephen Ordway. He was very patient, but the memories still had power to hurt. He led her gradually to the point where she had first started to suspect that her husband was engaged in unacceptable—or even illegal—activities.

'It was obvious to me very early that our marriage wasn't going to be a success,' she said.

Philip put a hand over hers. 'There's no need to go

further into that, Rosa. Your father told me what Ordway was like.'

'Thank you,' she said. 'But it had an effect on what happened later. He…he did try, you know. He was devoted to his mother, and wanted above anything to please her. And he and I had practically grown up together. But…he didn't trust me. And…it didn't work.' She shut her eyes, and when she opened them they were full of misery.

'He blamed me. He used to get very angry with me. And for a long time I accepted what he said and blamed myself. I…I tried to make myself acceptable to him, however much it went against my…my nature. But then he…he found what he really wanted. He told me he was in love with someone called Selder. At the time, that was all he said.'

She got up and walked about the room, refusing to look at him. The words came out jerkily, tension and shame in every syllable. 'I was humiliated and hurt, of course, when I thought Stephen had taken a mistress, but at the same time I was relieved. It meant that I was left in peace! And at least he seemed to be happier.'

Philip hardly dared breathe. Rosa's painful story was filling him with pity and anger, but he dared not interrupt her—not because of anything she might tell him about Falkirk, it was far more important than that. Rosa was at last ridding herself of a canker which had blighted her life for years, which might well be the source of that permanent look of sadness which he had seen at the back of her eyes. She must be allowed to continue.

'Then one day,' she went on, 'Aunt Laura and Stephen had a terrible quarrel. About me. And, as always, he blamed me for it. He still loved his mother deeply and he was badly upset at falling out with her. He…he

wanted to punish me. So that night after Aunt Laura had
gone to bed he brought Falkirk to the house. I didn't
understand at first. I had expected ''Selder'' to be a
woman. I was, in spite of everything, still so…innocent!'
This was said in bitter self-contempt.

'How old were you, Rosa?'

'I don't remember exactly. Nineteen? Twenty?'

'My God!'

'And when I did understand I was shocked beyond
measure. Stephen introduced us. He paraded his infatu-
ation with the man in front of me. But Falkirk…he
wasn't like that at all. Falkirk treated Stephen at first
rather as you might treat an importunate puppy. He even
seemed kind. Can you imagine it—in spite of the shock,
I quite liked him!'

'When did you change your mind?'

'Stephen used to boast to me about his friends, and it
gradu-ally became clear to me that Falkirk would do anything for money. It was a matter of business for him. He
and one or two others were making themselves very rich,
providing…desperate people with what they needed—
drugs, and…the other. And worse things than those,
even.'

'Worse?'

Rosa's reply came out of the darkness. She was walking round the edges of the room, out of range of the light
of the candles, as if she could not bear to be seen. 'Terrible…terrible things. Childre— I can't tell you. I won't!'

She stopped for a moment as her voice rose and her
breathing became more uneven. Philip longed to go over
to her, to fetch her forward into the light, to reassure her,
but forced himself to sit still. Better to let the whole ugly
story emerge as she wished to tell it. Then would be the
time for the cure.

She went on, 'But that was when I changed my mind about Falkirk. I was desperate, but there was nothing I could find to do about it. I was on my own. Stephen was besotted, of course. I couldn't confide in Aunt Laura, and I had no one else.'

'What about Anna and your father?'

'How could I go near them? I felt…unclean. I didn't want to taint their lives with what I knew. So I thanked God that Temperley was so many miles away and kept clear of it.' She stopped suddenly and in spite of himself Philip went over to hold her. But she pushed him away. 'I'd like to finish,' she said.

'Are you sure? We could leave the rest to tomorrow.'

'I want to finish! Then matters came to a head when Falkirk became bored with Stephen's slavish admiration. He found my aversion to him more intriguing. So he decided to…to switch his attention to me.'

Rosabelle had been almost invisible, a disembodied voice, telling its nightmare out of the dark. But now she came back and sat down as if her legs would no longer support her. Philip took one look at her chalk-white face and shadowed eyes and decided that enough was enough. Rosa needed a rest, whatever she said.

'I think we'll stop there tonight, my dearest love. You've had enough.'

'Have I? Perhaps I have. I wanted to finish it, Philip, but I don't think I can. I hadn't realised what this would do to me—living it all over again.'

'Would you like to leave it there altogether, Rosa darling? We can manage without the rest, I am sure.'

'No, no! I want to tell you everything now that we've started. A clean sheet.' She sighed. 'A clean sheet. Perhaps there'll be one after this. But perhaps it would wait till tomorrow.'

* * *

Rosabelle had expected to be haunted during the night with bad dreams and memories. But in fact she slept sweetly, undisturbed by nightmares of any kind, and woke the next morning feeling refreshed, and ready again to tell Philip anything he wanted to know.

He came over from Shearings at an hour which was only marginally acceptable in polite society. Becky was impressed.

'Well, bless me! I never expected to see Mr Winbolt at this hour. He used to be a very well-behaved young man before he knew you, Miss Belle!'

'Perhaps he doesn't feel he has to stand on ceremony with us any more, Becky. He…he's asked me to marry him. And I'm going to!'

'Oh, Miss Belle! I'm so pleased! Not that I didn't expect it, mind. But I did wonder, just occasionally, whether you'd manage to sort things out. Does he…does he know which of you he's marrying, Miss Rosa?'

'Yes, he does! And he loves me just the same. Becky, he wants to take me to London as soon as possible—to meet his grandfather. I'd like to go tomorrow. Can you and Martha start getting my things ready? I'll help you later, but I have business with Mr Winbolt first.'

'Business, is it?' Becky said to herself, as she watched Rosa run out to be greeted by Mr Winbolt. 'That's a very friendly form of business, if you ask me! Kissing in full view of anyone who cares to watch, indeed! Come along, Martha! There's work for us to do.'

Rosabelle put on a warm pelisse and she and Philip took to the park. It was still early and the sun was not yet warm, but they both wanted to be outside. There was less risk of being overheard in the fields, and the freshness of the country air helped to cleanse the effect of Rosabelle's story.

'You're sure you still want to do this, Rosa?' Philip asked.

'Quite sure. Besides, the most important part is still to come.'

'Very well. But you must stop the minute you've had enough.'

'It's doing me good, Philip. And I want now to rid myself of it all. I've kept quiet for so long.'

'Then tell me what happened when Falkirk turned his attention to you.'

'Stephen went wild. He wept, he raged, he swore vengeance—I think that's when he must have written those letters to his cousin.'

'Letters? What letters?'

'Oh, not what Falkirk wants. Just letters Stephen wrote to Giles Stanton, talking of broken hearts, accusing me of all sorts of misdemeanours. Giles believed what was in them, of course. And the fantasies Stephen had written in his diary.'

'Wait! That's not fair—Giles is a hard man, but he was never unjust.'

'I forgot. He's your friend. Though how a man like you could... Never mind! You've probably seen him under different circumstances. And I suppose he had no reason to suspect that it was all lies. He and Stephen had always been friends in the past. But I assure you, Philip, Giles could not have been more unsympathetic to me when we met.'

'I can see I'll have to have a word with him. But what happened between Stephen and Falkirk?'

'I kept well out of Falkirk's way, and he eventually forgot about me. But by this time Stephen had transferred his affections to another member of the group. At least, Kingsley used to frequent the house more often than Falkirk, so I assume that's what happened.'

'Kingsley.'

'John Kingsley. But you won't find him. He's dead. I don't know how, and I have no idea why, but I am practically certain that Falkirk either killed him or had him killed. That's what Stephen shouted that last evening. He was beside himself, shouting that he would ruin Falkirk, that he would see him hanged.'

'Is that why he had to die in turn?'

'I think so. Philip, that's why I'm so afraid. Those two, Falkirk and his henchman, Burrows, have nothing to lose!'

'Being afraid is useful, Rosa. It makes you careful. But it doesn't mean you have to give up and simply scuttle for cover.'

'I realise that. And Anna doesn't even know she has to!'

'Look, I'm not too worried about Anna. If Giles is with her she'll be safe. You may believe me on that. There's no one I'd rather have with Anna at this moment!'

'Very well, I'll try not to worry. When do we start for London?'

'Can you be ready tomorrow morning? All the dresses pressed and so on?'

'*All* the dresses! If I have a quarrel with Anna, it is on the subject of her wardrobe! She is obviously not interested in clothes.'

'My love, you have been entrancing me for six months in Anna's clothes! Don't criticise your sister too badly.'

They arrived in London the next afternoon. In spite of Rosabelle's strictures, the carriage was well laden with boxes and valises, much to Philip's amusement.

'It's as well we decided to engage a maid for you in London, rather than taking one of the girls from Temperley,' he said. 'She would have had to travel on the roof!'

'They're dear girls, all of them,' said Rosabelle. 'But I'm sufficiently well acquainted with London servants to know that an untrained girl from the country would be very unhappy among them. You're sure your sister will help me find one?'

'If I know Emily, she will be eager to make amends. Try to keep her feeling a little guilty about you—she'll do much more for you if she feels she owes you something.'

'You're an unnatural brother! I shall do no such thing!'

Rosabelle gazed eagerly about her as they came along the Bath Road towards London. She had travelled this road with her godmother, twice a year, once at the beginning of June and once back to London halfway through September. As a child she had eagerly counted the mile posts, the toll gates, the sights along the route which had indicated how much further they had to go— the bridge over the Kennet at Reading, Hounslow Heath and the junction where the main road to Lands End joined them, the Grand Junction Canal, the Star and Garter Inn at Kew Bridge, and then as they drew nearer to London, Holland House and the mansions along the road opposite Hyde Park. Soon they were bowling along Piccadilly and at last they turned into Arlington Street.

Chapter Thirteen

For a few minutes all was bustle and noise as grooms, footmen and other servants went about their business, and Philip led Rosabelle into the imposing, rather gloomy house which stood before them.

Lord Winbolt's butler met them at the door, and was good enough to acknowledge Miss Kelland by a slight softening of his stately demeanour.

'How is my grandfather, Maynard?' asked Philip, as the butler relieved him of his outer garments.

'Very well, Mr Philip,' the butler said. 'Er…he is in the upper drawing room.'

Philip stopped and gave the butler a hard stare.

'Miss Emily did her best, sir,' Maynard said, almost apologetically. 'But his lordship did not wish to receive Miss Kelland in his bedchamber.' This was a fairly free paraphrase of his lordship's blistering statement to the effect that he would be damned if his grandson's future bride would see him in his bedgown and nightcap, supping cat lap and generally behaving like a confounded dotard. 'Mrs Jackman is ready to take Miss Kelland to her room, Mr Philip.'

'If you will come this way, ma'am.' The housekeeper

curtsied and then led Rosabelle towards the very handsome staircase.

'Anna! You've arrived!' Emily came hurrying down the stairs, but at the bottom she paused and looked uncertain.

'Emily?' said Rosabelle. Then the two young ladies laughed and embraced each other. Emily put her arm round Rosabelle's waist and they followed Mrs Jackman up two flights of stairs.

'I've put you in one of the rooms at the back, Anna. It's quieter, and you have a view of the park. See?' Emily ushered into a delightful room overlooking Green Park.

'Thank you. But, er…Emily, I would like to straighten things out between us—'

'There's no need. Philip explained a little—enough to make me wish I had been more sympathetic that last time. I'm sorry, Anna.'

'Don't say that! And let's forget that episode. It has served its turn. But…my name really is Rosa, Emily.' Rosabelle looked apprehensively at her friend.

Emily kissed her. 'I shall remember. Now tell me, have you brought a maid? I've asked one of the girls here to help you in case you haven't. Then, if you wish, we can hire a proper ladies' maid tomorrow. I'll send for her and then you can refresh yourself after your journey. Do you wish for anything? Something to eat or drink, for example?'

'Thank you, but we stopped at Hammersmith.'

When the maid arrived Emily went downstairs and Rosabelle set about making herself presentable. A short while later she descended to the first floor and was shown into a beautifully proportioned room with a bow window overlooking the park. Philip and Emily were both there, and in a large armchair by the fire sat a gentleman, who was eyeing her with a great deal of interest. Though he was extremely old, his eye was keen and his air distinguished.

'Rosa, I'd like you to meet my grandfather, Lord Winbolt.'

'Hmph, so you've decided who you are, have you, young lady? My grandson has been telling me he's not absolutely sure.'

'That was a long time ago, sir!' said Philip. 'I'm absolutely certain now. Of that and other things. I intend to marry Mrs Ordway.'

'Yes, well, that's not a name I'm particularly fond of, I'm not surprised you wanted to change it. I think I shall call you Rosa. If you don't mind?' He gave her a fierce look from under bushy silver eyebrows.

'I should be pleased, sir.'

'Yes, well, sit down here and tell me about Shearings and your place in Berkshire, what's it called... Temperley? You were a Kelland, so I hear?'

Rosabelle bore up pretty well as Lord Winbolt put her through a catechism, which told him more than she perhaps realised. At the end of it he said, 'You're pretty enough—a very good-looking girl, in fact. You say your sister is exactly like you?'

'Yes, sir.'

'You must be a striking sight when you're together. I gather there's no fortune?'

'No, Lord Winbolt.' Rosa bit her lip.

'There's no need to look so cast down. Philip has more than enough for the two of you. And he'll have more when I'm gone.' Rosa blinked at this plain speaking, but Lord Winbolt smiled at her and called Philip over to him. 'She's pretty, she's modest—look at her blushes now!—

and she's sweet-natured. And I think she's probably no fool.'

'She's also demonstrably patient, Grandfather! Do you have to subject my beloved to such a trial?'

His grandfather chuckled. 'It's the only pleasure left to me, my boy! You'd have had more to complain about thirty years ago—I'd have given you a run for your money then! I have to say that I don't like the Ordway connection, but that can't be helped, I can't believe she was to blame for that. In any case, there was nothing wrong with the rest of Stephen Ordway's family. And the Kellands are good stock. You have my blessing, my boy.'

Philip smiled and drew Rosabelle to him. 'Thank you, Grandfather. I was sure you would give it.'

'But you'd still have married her if I hadn't, is that it?'

'I'm afraid so, sir.'

'Very well, very well. When is the wedding? Not too long ahead, I hope? I haven't all that much time.'

'As I told you, Grandfather, we have to wait until we can find Rosa's sister. But it will be as soon as we can arrange it after that, I promise you. Er…meanwhile…Rosa will be known under her sister's name in public.'

'What? Oh, yes! Of course. Well, I don't go out much, Philip. In fact, not at all. So there's no difficulty there.'

Rosabelle found that London was now a different place. The busy streets, the new buildings, the old quarters—all took on an additional brightness when Philip was there to laugh with her, escort her, admire the sights with her. And shopping with Emily was an excitingly new experience, too. Never before had she had a person of her own age in London ready to advise her on a length of material or the shape and colour of a new hat.

Emily was quite shockingly extravagant, and it was sometimes hard to refuse her generosity when Rosabelle decided that she couldn't afford a particularly suitable pair of gloves, or a desirable scarf. And her efforts were frequently in vain, for the same gloves or the identical scarf would later appear in the form of presents from Philip.

'You are teaching me bad habits, sir!' she laughed. 'You're training me to be a very unthrifty wife!'

'We have many problems, Rosa, my sweet, but having to be thrifty is not one of them. And while we are on the subject...I should like to take you to the Ordway lawyers this afternoon. We still have a lot to do.'

'Yes,' said Rosabelle, her smile dying. 'Of course. I had almost forgotten.'

'Good! It was what I intended. You've enchanted my grandfather, helped Emily spend even more than usual, and, I hope, enjoyed your respite from Falkirk and his friends. But now we shall take up the chase with renewed strength. I haven't yet mentioned what my man found out on the Reading road.'

On the way to Lincoln's Inn, Philip told her that Falkirk had been an occasional visitor to a small tavern about nine miles west of Reading, near Woolhampton. The landlord knew him as Selder, and, being slightly on the shady side of the law himself, had never questioned his comings and goings. But Falkirk always met someone else at the tavern, a seafaring man, who had come along the Bath Road from the west.

'From Bristol?'

'It sounds like it, Rosa.'

'Do we know the second man's name?'

'Decoster. Or something like it.'

'What did the two men do? Did anything change hands, for example?'

'Clever girl! The innkeeper always thought it was gold. Selder was being paid.'

'Bristol, seafarer, gold... Did Selder give the man anything in return?'

'Not obviously. Information, perhaps? But what information would Selder have to sell?'

'Philip! John Kingsley worked for Lloyds!'

'Good God! Shipping information? And Bristol has a bad record for pirate activities.'

They stared at each other. 'Philip, if Falkirk was passing on information about ships—that's a hanging offence! What if Stephen got some kind of evidence from Kingsley?'

'Falkirk would indeed be desperate to get hold of that. But what did Stephen do with it?'

'I don't know!'

'I'll get the men on to it. But here we are. Now, remember, it's your clothes you want to collect. There's no need to mention anything else. What did you say the lawyer's name was?'

'His name is Keetham. And I'm not a fool, Philip!'

Once Mr Keetham had recovered from his surprise at seeing Mrs Ordway he was very helpful. 'Of course, of course. We are not at present in touch with Colonel Stanton, but I am quite sure that he would not object to your collecting a few of your belongings. I'll have my clerk find the keys right away.'

'Keys, Mr Keetham? Isn't there a caretaker in the building? Surely he could let us in.'

'Ah! There's a slight difficulty there, I'm afraid. It is most unfortunate, but the house has temporarily lost its caretaker. He had an accident a few days ago, and we

are having difficulty in replacing him. We fully expect to
engage someone tomorrow—or very soon after.
Meanwhile, my men made sure that the house was well
locked and the front door is bolted—you'll have to go in
through the mews at the back. Most unfortunate—but a
temporary state of affairs, I assure you. It would have
been ready for you if I had known you were back in
town, Mrs Ordway.'

He gave a few instructions to his clerk, then invited
Mr Winbolt and Mrs Ordway to take a seat, and a glass
of Madeira. His professional air of discretion could not
quite hide his curiosity about their relationship, though
the Winbolt name was enough to ensure his willingness
to help, and Philip, as the future Lord Winbolt, was particularly desirable as a potential client.

'I hope Lord Winbolt is in better health than when I
last heard, sir? We were all sorry to hear of his illness.'
Philip reassured him. The lawyer then turned to
Rosabelle. 'Mrs Ordway, since we last saw you, there
have been a few changes in matters affecting the Ordway
estate. Would you…would you like to hear about them
now? Or…?' He cast a look at Philip.

'Mr Winbolt has my full confidence, sir. You may, if
you wish, speak quite freely before him.'

'Mrs Ordway has agreed to marry me, Mr Keetham.'
But when Mr Keetham started to express his pleasure at
the news, Philip cut him short. 'Thank you. I am grateful
for your good wishes, but I hope you will keep the news
to yourself for the time being. And we are a little pressed
for time at this particular moment.'

'Of course, of course!' He went to the door of his
office and opened it. 'Bennett! Have you found those
keys yet?'

'Coming, Mr Keetham, sir!'

Mr Keetham returned to his desk. 'I shall hope to see you again quite soon, Mrs Ordway. I think you will find that your affairs are in better order now that Colonel Stanton has taken charge. Though there will be new arrangements, of course, since you are contemplating marrying again.' He beamed on them both, then turned with a start as the clerk came in. 'Ah, the keys! Would you like my man to come with you?'

Refusing his offer of assistance and promising to return the keys as soon as they had finished with them, they extricated themselves, not without difficulty, from the lawyer's effusions and made their way back to Piccadilly and thence to Upper Brook Street. By this time it was past four o'clock and the light was beginning to fade.

'Damn that lawyer! It's too late to do very much tonight, Rosa. We'll have to come back tomorrow. And if the house is completely empty I should prefer to take a few precautions. I don't like the sound of that accident to the caretaker.'

'Can't we just fetch one dress, Philip? I should like to wear it at the ball tonight. I really haven't anything else that will do.'

'I suppose so. After all, it's what we told the lawyer we were going to do! But don't waste any time in there. It will be dark quite soon. Come!'

Since the front doors would be heavily bolted they were taken round to the mews at the back of the house and, after telling Philip's coachman to wait in Grosvenor Square for a quarter of an hour, they let themselves in. They went up the back stairs, emerging through a servant's door on to the landing at the top of the main staircase. Here they turned towards the bedrooms, but Philip suddenly stopped and grasped Rosabelle's arm. He put his hand over her mouth and pointed downstairs. Unlike the floor they were on, the lower floors were all shuttered, but they could see a flickering light on the landing below.

A voice came floating up out of the darkness. 'There's no one here,' it said.

Philip drew Rosabelle silently back against the wall.

'I tell you, Burrows, I heard something! Have you got your gun?' This voice was horribly, hatefully familiar and Rosabelle stiffened. But she nodded at Philip's warning look and made no sound.

'Look in the dining room,' the voice continued.

'Mebbe it was a rat?'

'Here?' The voice was full of contempt for the other's ignorance.

'Even the best houses get rats if there's no one to get rid of them. How long has this place been shut up?'

'Go and look in the dining room, Burrows. If you see a rat, leave it alone. We don't want to make a lot of noise for the sake of a rat, do we? But if it's anything else— one of the rest of the crowd, for example—then deal with him. I'll keep guard here in case the visitor is somewhere else.'

Footsteps were heard descending the stairs to the hall, then crossing the hall. Then silence for a moment. Suddenly a chair was knocked over and the footsteps came running out. 'I told you! It was a rat. It's gone now. I knew it wasn't anything else. We know the Ordway lot aren't back yet—we've kept a watch out for them. And no one else would dare come here. Besides, none of the others would be interested in a load of old papers.'

'They would if they knew what was in them. They wouldn't want to be transported any more than you or I do.'

'Transported!'

'Or hanged. I should have killed Stephen Ordway.'

'You did.'

'Before he got hold of Kingsley's confession, and my letter. That doxy must know where it is! I was soft with her sister, but by God I won't waste time on courtesies with the Ordway woman. She'll tell me, before she's much older.'

'You've got to find her first.'

'I will.' The deep, husky voice was full of menace. 'And when I do…'

'We'd better go.' Burrows was getting nervous. 'It's getting dark and the light from these lamps will be seen from outside through the shutters. I've had enough of this. We can't bribe a second caretaker to say he's had an accident, and they're bound to send another round soon. Anyway, we've been looking for nearly a week now and there's no sign anywhere of any papers.'

'Stephen Ordway hid them. And Rosabelle Ordway must know where.'

'Then let's wait till we find her. But for now let's go!'

The listeners heard footsteps descending the stairs and retreating to the back regions. The lamplight faded.

'The door!' whispered Rosabelle in fright.

'I locked it again behind us. They won't notice anything. And the carriage isn't marked. If they do see it, they'll think it's just arriving.'

'Philip! I'm so frightened.'

'Don't be. Fortune seems to be on our side. That rat was a wonderful piece of luck. I have to admit that the odds were worse than I normally enjoy if it had come to a fight tonight!'

'Don't talk of it!' Rosabelle shuddered.

'Come—they've gone. Fetch your dress and we'll go, too.'

Rosabelle fumbled in the semi-darkness for her dress, and then they cautiously descended the back stairs again and let themselves out. The carriage was waiting—there was no sign of anyone else.

When they arrived back at Arlington Street they found Emily in a great state of anxiety.

'Rosa! Where have you both been? You've left very little time to get ready. Is that the dress? Give it to your maid and let her smooth it out for you.'

'My dear Emily, four hours is too long for the most demanding toilette!' said Philip. 'I intend to make sure that Rosa has something sustaining to eat before embarking on anything so energetic.' He spoke lightly but, unseen by Rosabelle, he gave his sister a significant look and nodded slightly in Rosabelle's direction.

Emily took a closer look at Rosabelle's pallor and said, 'I was just about to have something myself, Philip. But on your own head be it if we are late. I will not hurry my preparations. I refuse to be seen at Chesterfield House in anything but a state of polished perfection, I warn you. Come, Rosa. We shall have a small, luxurious collation in my room, while your maid is getting your dress ready. Philip, you may send up some champagne.' Philip smiled his approval at his quick-witted sister and promised to see to it.

There had been a certain amount of discussion over the evening's invitation to the ball at Chesterfield House. The problem of Rosabelle's identity made social appearances difficult for her, and so far she had avoided society, but Emily and Philip had between them persuaded her to risk it.

'You can go as my friend, Annabelle Kelland, and Philip will just have to exercise restraint!' Emily had said gaily. 'Please come, Rosa! It will make such a difference if I have someone else to talk to!'

So, half-dreading it and half-looking forward to an evening spent in the very highest society, Rosabelle had agreed to go.

Now, somewhat shaken by her experiences in the Upper Brook Street house, she would willingly have stayed at home that night, if she could have done so without disappointing her friends. But a peaceful half-hour with Emily, with a glass of champagne and a light supper, helped to restore her. And when Emily first of all approved wholeheartedly of her dress, then started laughing at its colour, she was able to join in. When Philip came to collect them he was puzzled to find them still giggling.

'But what is there to laugh about?' he asked. 'I have never seen you look better, Emily, and Rosabelle always looks enchanting in blue—azure, isn't it?'

'No, no…not azure, Philip,' gasped Emily. 'This time it's celestial!' And his two ladies went off into another gale of laughter. His perplexed look only made matters worse. By the time that the joke was explained and order restored, Rosabelle had quite forgotten her fears. And later, as they came into the entrance hall of Chesterfield House and slowly ascended its magnificent staircase, she looked serenely lovely. Madame Fanchon had said herself that she had never made a more beautiful dress than the one Rosabelle was wearing that night—a clear blue *peau de soie*, worn over white silk, the bodice lavishly embroidered with small pearls and beads of crystal.

They danced and talked the night away and Rosabelle found that she was enjoying herself in a manner that, three hours before, she would have said was impossible. Philip was taking care to be discreet, aware that life could become very complicated indeed, if his name was linked with that of Rosabelle Ordway's sister. He danced no more than was conventionally polite with 'Emily's friend', but all the same he used his considerable powers of dissimulation to keep an eye on her throughout the evening. Julian Falkirk was accepted everywhere, even at social events as august as this one, and Philip was taking no risks. It was as well.

Halfway through the evening Rosabelle and Emily had repaired to the cloakroom to refresh themselves before supper, having arranged to meet Philip at the door to the supper room. When Emily was delayed by an elderly dowager who wanted to talk about Lord Winbolt, Emily signed to Rosabelle to carry on. But Rosabelle had hardly gone twenty paces before she was roughly seized. A hand was placed over her mouth and she was pulled into a narrow side passage.

'Don't try anything,' said Falkirk's voice. 'Or I'll break your neck.'

When Emily rejoined Philip, he was visibly restraining his impatience. 'Where's…er Anna?' he asked.

'She should be here,' said Emily. 'I was held up by Lady Grant, and told her to go on. Hasn't she arrived?'

'Oh, my God!' said Philip. 'No, she hasn't. Where did you say she left you?'

'Near the corridor to the library. But—'

Philip interrupted impatiently. 'Emily, stay here for a bit. I'll have to look for her.'

'But why—'

'Stay here, I tell you!' And with that he plunged into the crowd. He made his way back to the spot where Emily had last seen Rosabelle, then retraced her steps, looking for a likely place where she might have gone astray—or been abducted. He soon found the narrow side passage and hurried down it...

Rosabelle had no illusions about her plight. Falkirk's words that afternoon had painted a picture which had chilled her soul, and now it was harsh reality. But her faith in Philip kept her spirits up. She kicked and struggled as Falkirk dragged her along the passage, delaying their progress to the door at the far end which led into the garden. There, she knew, Falkirk would be able to do what he wished with her. His hand bruised her mouth, and his arm was so tight round her body that she felt her ribs would crack, every breath was agony, but still she fought, driven by a furious determination to survive.

'Be still, you little termagant! I don't intend to kill you, unless you make me. I need you!'

They had reached the door. Rosabelle was very nearly exhausted. When Falkirk slammed her up against the wall and held her by the throat with one hand, while he opened the door with the other, she had no strength to pull away.

'I'm...I'm—' she croaked.

'I don't give a damn who you are, you wildcat! Ordway or Kelland, it's all one to me. I'm going to keep you in my hands until I have the other one, too. Then we'll see who will talk!'

The door was open and Falkirk pushed her outside, and began to propel her along the path. Rosabelle asked herself frantically where all the servants, the waiters, the maids, the lamp attendants—where had they all gone? But Falkirk had chosen his spot cleverly. This was a dark part of the garden which was seldom used by anyone, a path leading to a disused mews block. There was no one in sight. She began to despair.

'Turn round, Falkirk!' The voice, icy, commanding, and crackling with menace, came from behind.

Falkirk jumped round, releasing Rosabelle as he did so.

'Run, Rosa! Run!' said Philip, keeping his eyes firmly on his opponent. It was as well. Falkirk leapt on him with a roar. Rosabelle screamed and put her hands over her eyes. It was happening! Her worst fears were about to be realised! Philip would be beaten, kicked, left to die, just as Stephen had been left. Oh God, she would not be able to bear it!

There were sounds of men breathing heavily, fighting, the crunch as blows met their target, a snarling sound from Falkirk. Suddenly Rosa took her hands away. She must not stand aside helplessly while Falkirk did his worst—Philip needed her help! She ran to the man standing over the recumbent body on the ground and rained blows on him, shouting and kicking…

'Rosa! Hey, Rosa! Wait! That hurts!' It was Philip's voice. Rosabelle froze.

'Can this be my gentle, ladylike Rosabelle? I don't believe it!' Philip's arms were restraining her, Philip's face was close to hers, Philip's eyes were gazing into hers with that well-loved, quizzical look. She glanced down. At her feet Falkirk was lying on the ground, groaning.

'Philip! It's you! Oh, I thought…I thought….' Rosabelle burst into tears.

'I know. You thought me too much of a gentleman to know how to fight a cur like Falkirk. I told you—I've lived a full life, Rosa. Not all of it has been among gentlemen. Calm down, my love, calm down! There's no need for this. Come, let me take you to Emily. I'll find someone to look after this *canaille* till I come back.'

Together they walked back along the corridor. Philip caught a passing footman and said calmly, 'There's someone lying outside in the garden back there. He...he has clearly met with some accident. Stay with him while I see that this lady is safe, will you? But...don't let him get away!'

The footman took note of Rosabelle's torn dress and disturbed state, Philip's ruffled hair and the rip in his coat and for a moment his impassive countenance showed a certain amount of emotion. Then he said calmly, 'Certainly, Mr Winbolt. Where did you say the gentleman was?'

Philip then sent another servant to fetch Emily, and when she arrived he delivered Rosabelle into her sympathetic hands. 'Take her back to the cloakroom, and do what you can with her dress. She has had a shock, but she'll be all right. I have some business to complete, then I'll take you both home.'

He went back along the passage, but when he went outside he found the footman somewhat painfully getting off his knees.

'You didn't tell me 'e was a bloody prize fighter!' he said resentfully. 'I 'adn't 'ardly got out 'ere when 'e clocked me one. Then 'e was over the wall and orf, before I could 'oller for 'elp! Beggin' your pardon, Mr Winbolt.'

Philip was furious, but not with the footman—the fault was his. 'I should have made sure he was properly out before I left him,' he said grimly. 'What's your name?'

'Jenkins, sir.' The footman had now recovered enough to be apprehensive about Philip's reaction to what had happened.

'Well, Jenkins, I'm sorry to have let you in for all that. I hope you'll forgive and, if possible, forget what happened tonight. Here, this might help.' He pressed a coin into Jenkins's hand.

'Cor! Thank you, sir!'

'Not a word about the lady, Jenkins. Remember!'

'Not a word about nothing, sir. Not h'ever. Thank you, sir.'

Philip went back into the house, followed by Jenkins. He was amused to see Jenkins about his work again later, looking as immaculate and as impassive as if the events in the garden had never taken place.

He soon found his two ladies again. Rosabelle was looking quite cheerful, and her dress showed no obvious signs of her struggle. Emily was the one who looked shattered. 'That man,' she said. 'Falkirk. What has happened to him?'

'Nothing,' said Philip. 'He got away.'

There was a shocked silence. Then Philip added, 'On reflection, I think that's just as well. It could have involved Rosa in a major scandal and, at the moment, that is the last thing we want.'

'But, Philip,' said Rosabelle, looking worried, 'Falkirk won't rest until he has taken revenge for the humiliation he suffered tonight at your hands. And you know now how vicious he can be.'

'Exactly, Rosa, darling. I am better prepared. And if I've beaten him once I can beat him again.'

'Not if he has company.'

'You're right. But you may rest easy, my love. I shall make sure you are safe—and I shan't risk my own neck, either. Emily, you look tired. Shall we go back to Arlington Street?'

'No,' said Emily slowly. 'I won't let that scoundrel spoil our evening. If Rosa agrees, we shall stay and have some supper. Then if there is any speculation later on about tonight, no one will be able to claim that the Winbolts—I include you in them, Rosa—looked as if they had been involved. What do you say?'

'I agree,' said Rosabelle firmly. 'As long as the pins in my dress hold together.'

Laughing, the three of them went in to supper. It would have seemed to the polite world at Lord Chesterfield's ball that Mr Winbolt and the two ladies with him hadn't a care in the world.

The polite world would have been surprised if it had followed Mr Winbolt on an errand he undertook the next morning before the ladies were up. His destination was certainly not one usually sought out by gentlemen of the *ton*. And when he left Bow Street to go back to his grandfather's house, he was accompanied by an undistinguished ferrety-looking individual, with a habit of looking round him with bright, keen eyes wherever he went. The ferret's name was Barnaby Stokes.

Chapter Fourteen

Barnaby Stokes made a better bodyguard than he did a spare groom or footman—the two roles he was ostensibly to play in the Winbolt household. When dressed in Lord Winbolt's livery he looked the part well enough. But he was woefully inept at handling carriage doors and steps, and his bow-legged gait and aggressive demeanour added nothing to the style of a lady's progress through town. Nor did his habit of bundling her parcels inelegantly under his arm, or hanging them round his neck, add to her consequence.

Any remonstrance brought forth the reply, 'Well, ma'm, I arsk yer! 'Ow am I to save yer, if me 'ands is full of bits and bobs? I trained with the Bow Street Runners, not with a bloomin' domestic agency, beggin' yer pardon, and no offence meant.'

After one or two minor disasters, Philip negotiated with Lord Chesterfield for a temporary loan of one of his footmen, and thereafter Barnaby Stokes acted as Philip's groom, or merely followed the ladies at a discreet distance if they were out on foot. But whenever they went out of the house Miss Winbolt and her friend, Miss

Kelland, were always accompanied by their new footman, Jenkins by name.

Jenkins and Barnaby Stokes got on remarkably well, and each learned a lot from the other. They were eager to do the job they had really been engaged for—that is, to protect their employers from harm—for they were both in complete agreement that Mr Winbolt was a true gent— a pleasant cove to work for, and generous with it. And the two young ladies were as nice a couple of gentry-morts as they'd ever come across.

Protected by their two guardians, Philip and Rosabelle had searched the Upper Brook Street house, in likely and unlikely places, for anything that might be the papers Falkirk wanted, but they found nothing. Whatever Stephen had done with them, he had hidden them too well for anyone else to find. So, when the new caretaker came to take up his post in the house, they returned the keys to Mr Keetham and resigned themselves to defeat.

'I had such hopes,' mourned Rosabelle. 'I thought we might be rid of Falkirk and his threats, that our minds could be set at rest. But now...'

'Don't despair. Stephen can't have been the only one with a grudge against Falkirk. Tell me as many names of Stephen's associates as you can remember.'

'Falkirk, Burrows, John Kingsley... There was a man called...North?...Neath? No, Nairn! Samuel Nairn. And there was another—a man called Fraser, I think, though I never saw him.'

Philip had been writing busily. 'And I've got Decoster's name down already. Rosa, I have some work for Stokes and Jenkins for the rest of the day. You won't want to go out, will you?'

'No, Emily and I had planned to look at the latest *Ladies' Almanack*. She might be inspired to want to go

out to Harding Howells to look at the new silks and mus-
lins tomorrow, however…' They both smiled. Rosabelle
went on, 'Why? What are you planning to do, Philip?'

'I shall send Jenkins and Stokes out on a fishing expedition. I want to know more about those men.'

However, when Philip showed Stokes his list, Stokes
pronounced that he knew one name at least.

'Samuel Nairn to my own knowledge is in Newgate at
this very moment. A friend o' mine put 'im there 'imself
not a month since.'

'For what?'

'Pore devil was in debt up to 'is ears. All gone on
drink and the poppy merchants.'

'Can you go to see him? Is he…is he still *compos
mentis*?'

'I think 'e is. Course I don't know wot Newgate 'as
done to'im. Terrible 'ard, Newgate, on a man. But I c'n
go and see 'im. I'll soon tell!'

'Well, then, I want you to see Mr Nairn and, if you
can, ask him some questions for me. I'll write them down
for you. If Mr Nairn can help me, I might be able to do
something for him in return, tell him.'

'Mr Winbolt, sir!'

'What is it, Jenkins?'

'Mr Kingsley's dead, sir, but I know his former manservant, sir. I'll have a chat with him, shall I, Mr
Winbolt?'

'Right! Find out, if you can, what happened the night
Mr Kingsley died, and anything else that might be of use.
Now, what about Burrows? Do either of you know any-
thing about him? Or Decoster, or Fraser?'

They both shook their heads. But Barnaby Stokes offered to ask some friends in Bow Street about them, and

Jenkins promised to make enquiries in The Footman's Friend and The Running Dog, and other places where valets and footmen congregated for gossip and relaxation.

The result of their labours was quite promising. Samuel Nairn was not only perfectly, one might say miraculously, still in his right mind. He was also ready to accept assistance from Mr Winbolt in return for information about Falkirk—to be specific, he was ready to swear that Falkirk had boasted to him of murdering John Kingsley. He would sign a document to that effect. Philip set that process in motion straight away.

John Kingsley's valet, after some persuasion, was now ready to swear that on the night Mr Kingsley had died, he had heard a quarrel between his master and another gentleman, though he had not seen the gentleman concerned. Mr Kingsley had called him 'Selly'. He had heard this 'Selly' threatening his master, and the following morning he had found Mr Kingsley dead. He had been too frightened to say anything at the time. But he had continued to mourn his dead master, and time had somewhat reduced his fear of 'Selly'. When pressed, he admitted that 'Selly's' voice was easy to recognise, and was remarkably similar to that of a certain Mr Julian Falkirk.

'I 'ave to say, Mr Winbolt, that the h'evidence of servants and convicted debtors is not going to go down well in a court of law. Not at all well. Especially if you're trying to say that this ''Selly'' is really Mr Falkirk, wot is about to become a lord.'

'That's 'oo it was! In the garden the other night!' Jenkins was so excited that he interrupted them. 'I've been wonderin' where I see'd 'im before. Well, I'm blowed! Mr Falkirk!'

'I'm aware of the problem, Stokes,' said Philip. 'And a court of law is not my immediate aim. But if I can get enough to persuade Burrows that it would be better to save his own neck by talking, then I'm sure we could persuade a magistrate to act.'

'So Burrows is the one you want, is he?'

'He is Falkirk's right-hand man.'

'Right, governor. We'll find 'im for you.'

After some days, during which Rosabelle and Emily had spent quite a bit of time exercising in the garden, or reading indoors, Philip had gathered a fair amount of information. He had Samuel Nairn's deposition, and Nairn was now in the process of being released from Newgate. He also had a signed statement from Kingsley's valet. Bow Street knew nothing of any Decoster, but one man remembered seeing something about a Da Costa who had been involved with privateers in Bristol.

Burrows had been traced to an ill-kept tavern the other side of Leicester Square, and Philip himself had learned about the last name on the list. Fraser came of a good family and had been a well-known member of Society. Then rumours had started circulating about his treatment of his servants and others, and he had disappeared for a while. He had recently reappeared, but not in any circles recognised in good society. As for Falkirk, he seemed to have vanished from sight, and Philip was still debating what his next step should be when an unforeseen complication forced him to think again...

At the end of that week, London was in the grip of one of its periodical November fogs. It had been a miserable day—dark and cold—and the evening was no better. After one look out of his bedchamber window in the morning, Lord Winbolt had announced that he would spend the day in his room, and his grandchildren had not seen him. Philip had been out on business and the two young ladies had spent the day reading before the fire in the saloon. Now they were lingering over dinner, enjoying the convivial warmth of a good fire and the soft light of the branched candlesticks on the dining table. There were just three of them at the table—Lord Winbolt had remained in his room.

By common consent they had left aside their present problems and the talk was of books and the theatre, of travel and art. Suddenly, this agreeable moment of relaxation was interrupted by thunderous knocking at the front doors. It was not a time for casual visitors, and they waited with some curiosity to hear who or what it could be. Voices were heard in the hall and Maynard soon appeared at the door of the dining room.

'A Colonel Stanton, sir. He wishes to speak to you. I told him you were at dinner, but he was very insistent.'

'Giles!' Philip and Rosabelle spoke in unison as they both got up.

Maynard was brushed aside as Giles Stanton entered the room, saying, 'Excuse me for breaking in on you like this, Philip—' He stopped dead. 'Rosabelle!' he exclaimed. 'So you *are* here! What the devil do you think you've been doing? Oh, this goes beyond everything! To see you here without a care in the world while I...we've been sick with worry over you!'

He was clearly in a fury. He went over to Rosabelle and shook her. 'How dare you put Aunt Laura through all this distress! I thought you had given up your tormenting, ill-considered ways, but I see I was wrong...'

'Er...Giles, old fellow! Take your hands off my betrothed. Or I shall have to hit you, and that's the last thing I would wish for.' Philip spoke gently, but there

was steel in his voice. He moved over and stood by
Rosabelle.

Giles Stanton looked astounded. 'Philip! I… Am I
mad? How can she possibly be going to marry you? It's
her sister you're going to marry—Annabelle Kelland!'

'This is Rosabelle Ordway. But it's the girl I am going
to marry.'

Rosabelle had gone very pale. 'Are you saying that
you've brought my sister to London, Giles? Oh, how
could you? After all my warnings and letters…'

'Giles, is she right?' asked Philip sharply. 'Is Miss
Kelland in London?'

Giles Stanton looked from one to the other as if they
had gone mad. 'I don't understand what the devil you're
both talking about! You brought her sister to London! I
haven't seen her sister! And this can't possibly be your
betrothed, Philip, how can it be?' He turned to Rosabelle.
'Tell him, Rosa! Tell him about Annabelle's letters, how
you and Aunt Laura hoped she would marry Winbolt
here!'

Rosabelle tried to say something but found it impossible to speak. Confusion and anxiety for her sister were
keeping her silent.

Giles exclaimed in exasperation and turned back to
Philip. 'I'm beginning to believe you're all drunk,' he
said, glancing at the wine on the table. 'Rosabelle
Ordway—that is to say, this lady here—' he pointed at
Rosabelle '—has been the bane of my life for the last six
months. In all that time she has never once indicated that
she had any kind of special interest in you, Winbolt.
Indeed, she was delighted that you were going to marry
her sister!' He turned again to Rosabelle, angry once
again. 'Tell me why on earth you didn't wait for us at
Temperley, Rosabelle!'

'Us?' asked Philip.

'Aunt Laura and me. We arrived at Temperley this morning. We stayed last night at Wallingford, and this morning Aunt Laura wasn't well enough to travel straight away. Rosabelle was very anxious to see her sister, so she went on ahead. But when we arrived at Temperley we heard she had already left again.' He turned to Rosabelle again. 'I'll have something to say to Goss about this. Where is he?'

Philip intervened. 'Giles, I...I don't know how to tell you this. I can see you have been as deceived as I was. You obviously don't know that the Kelland sisters are identical twins. This is Rosabelle Ordway, who changed places with her sister at Easter, and has been in Berkshire and London ever since. The lady with you in the North was Annabelle Kelland.'

Giles Stanton sank into a chair. He looked from one to the other. 'I've spent all day trying to get here—the fog is everywhere. And when I walked into this room I thought it had all been worth while. Rosa was here, safe and sound. Are you trying to tell me that this isn't Rosabelle, after all?' As he stared at Rosabelle, his face changed, and, for the first time he seemed to take in what Philip had said. He looked from one to the other. 'Does Aunt Laura know, too?'

'Yes. I'm sorry, Giles. We shouldn't have done it. But I was at the end of my tether...'

'I've been played like a fish,' said Giles bitterly. But after a moment he sat up and said, *'But in that case, where is Annabelle now?'*

Philip said gravely, 'If she's not at Temperley, and not here—'

Maynard came into the room, looking agitated. 'Forgive me, sir, but there's an individual at the back demanding to see Colonel Stanton. I thought it best to let you know straight away. He has ridden from Berkshire, sir.'

'It's Goss!' said Giles. 'Thank God! He'll know where she is.'

But it was John Bostock who came in. 'Colonel Stanton, sir, they found Goss, your man. He's been wounded. He says that he and Miss Belle were set upon shortly after they left Temperley by two men They shot Goss, and…and they carried Miss Belle off with them.'

'Falkirk's work!' They gazed at one another, stunned. Giles got up. 'I must go.'

'Wait, Giles! This needs planning.'

Giles would have argued, but he was brought to see the sense of this. Emily took John Bostock out to the kitchen to find food and a bed, and Stokes and Jenkins and Giles's groom were despatched to find reinforcements. While they waited Giles was also fed. But when the men returned the news was negative. Falkirk had not been seen in London for a while. Giles sat down and put his head in his hands.

'Giles, this isn't any good,' Philip said softly. 'Unless we alarm Falkirk unduly, I am sure Annabelle is safe for the moment.'

'But she's been in his hands since this morning! I'll go mad if I don't *do* something, Philip!'

'Remember what you told me at Badajoz? You have to know the terrain before you attack. It was good advice then and it's good advice now. Believe me, Giles, Annabelle is safe for tonight. Though Falkirk has searched the house in Upper Brook Street, he has failed to find his papers. He's desperate to have them in his hands, and his only hope is to get Annabelle to show him where they are. She's safe for tonight.'

'But Annabelle doesn't know anything about the papers, damn you!'

'We know that. But he doesn't.'

Giles turned to Rosabelle. 'Did Stephen say *nothing* before he died?'

'He was delirious,' she said miserably. 'He could only think of money. He said again and again that his bank account had failed him, after all. He said it over and over.'

'No, no!' Giles exclaimed. 'It's where he hid the papers. Why didn't I think of it before?'

'But—' said Rosabelle.

'Where?' said Philip.

'I'll show you. Tomorrow. But first we must find Falkirk. I'll swear he's somewhere in London.'

'I think I could flush him out,' said Rosabelle. 'They keep an eye on this house, I know they do. If I were to take a walk out in the open street, it's very likely Falkirk would have me followed. I feel certain that he keeps a watch on us all, and he wants both Anna and me—he said so.'

'No!' said Philip. 'It's too dangerous.'

'Why not? I put Anna into this mess. It's up to me to get her out of it.'

'No, Rosa. I can't let you take the risk.'

'The risk wouldn't be all that great, if you and Giles were at hand. And it would be by far the quickest means of getting Falkirk to show himself. Let me do it, Philip! I can't...I can't bear to think of Anna in Falkirk's hands for a moment longer than necessary.'

'I'm sorry. I understand your feelings, of course I do, Rosa darling. But so many things could go wrong. No!'

'He's right,' said Giles decisively. 'There must be another way.'

Rosabelle looked from one to the other. Two strong, determined men, knowing what was best. Anna would have argued further with them and even enjoyed it, she knew. But that was not her way, she was not clever with arguments and noise. Being Rosa, and knowing that she would not win, she said no more.

'Burrows! Burrows will know where Falkirk can be found, and I think I can put my hand on Burrows.'

'I'd like to put my hands on Burrows,' said Giles grimly. 'Both of them. Round his throat.'

'We'll go in search of him first thing tomorrow, Giles. But leave him alive long enough for him to lead us to Falkirk.'

A most unaccustomed spirit of rebellion stirred within Rosabelle. It might take a day or more to find Burrows and persuade him to betray Falkirk. Her idea would have been far more effective. Could she possibly carry it out alone? The thought was petrifying, but, in the circumstances, very tempting.

'What are Stokes and Jenkins doing at the moment?' she asked meekly.

'They can look after you,' said Philip. 'Giles and I together are more than a match for anything Falkirk can do—wouldn't you agree, Giles?'

'I'll say—remember that time at Almeida?'

'With the French on one side and the guerillas on the other? And that bandit Villanteo—'

'No, Villanteo was at Talavera...'

Rosabelle stood up. 'I'm sure you'll excuse me. I'll leave you two gentlemen to talk over old times, shall I?' The slight acid in her tone was lost on Philip and Giles. They were deep in reminiscence.

'Goodnight, my dear,' said Philip, looking up and rising to escort her to the foot of the stairs. 'Try not to worry. You'll be safer indoors. And we shall find Annabelle for you.' He kissed her hand, and presented her with her candle.

'Goodnight, my dear. Goodnight, Giles.' She started up the stairs. 'Safer indoors!' she muttered to herself. 'Safer indoors, not worrying about Anna in the hands of that villain while they take heaven knows how long looking for him! I think not, Philip, my dear. I may not be able to argue, but I am not a spineless idiot, either...! And Barnaby Stokes will help.'

The next morning the two gentlemen set out early on their quest for news of Burrows and Falkirk. Rosabelle watched them go, then found Emily.

'Emily, are you planning to go out today?'

'I don't think so. If it clears up I might want to pay a visit to Harding Howells again this afternoon, perhaps. Why?'

'I'd like to make use of Barnaby Stokes. I have to go out on an errand.'

'What are you up to, Rosa?'

'Nothing dangerous,' said Rosabelle, crossing her fingers. 'But I'd prefer to have Barnaby with me. Don't ask me any more, Emily. I can't tell you, and I'd rather not lie.'

Emily was not at all happy, but she eventually gave in. 'But I shall tell Philip the minute he gets in,' she warned.

'Pray do!' said Rosabelle blithely. She donned her heaviest pelisse, and the warmest of her new shawls. She paid particular care in selecting the right muff. It was not only warm—it had a slender pocket inside. Into this she slipped a wickedly sharp paper knife which usually rested on the desk in the library. Philip had only recently warned her about it. She hoped it was as dangerous as he had said it was—it could be useful.

She found Barnaby Stokes waiting for her. 'Now, Barnaby—I don't want you to carry any parcels, or help with crossing the road. Indeed, I very definitely want you to follow me a good few paces behind. I must appear to be on my own. Understand?'

'I understand what you say, miss. I'm not at all sure it's what Mr Winbolt would wish.'

'Mr Winbolt is not here, Barnaby. He has gone out looking for Mr Burrows.'

'Then why amn't I with 'im?'

'Because I need you, and Mr Winbolt doesn't—he has Colonel Stanton to keep him company. Now, are you going to do what I ask? Or shall I take Jenkins? I am going out in either case.'

'I'd better do it, then.'

'There's one more thing, and it is extremely important! If anything should happen to me, do not attempt to rescue me, but find Mr Winbolt, or Colonel Stanton, and tell him that I shall bring Mr Falkirk to Upper Brook Street within the hour. Within the hour—have you got that?'

'And what if I can't find either of the gents in that time?'

Rosabelle stopped to think. 'I think you will—you know where they are likely to be, you told them where Burrows was to be found yourself. But if you cannot trace them within the time, then you must send Jenkins after them and come to Upper Brook Street on your own. You…you mustn't fail me, Barnaby.'

'Wait a minute! I'm not sure I'm doin' right to let you go, at all!'

'You cannot stop me, Mr Stokes! Come!'

Rosabelle made her way on to Arlington Street and

thence into Piccadilly. The fog had still not cleared—visibility was limited to fifty paces or less. She walked purposefully in the direction of Grosvenor Square. If Falkirk were as anxious as he had said to get hold of both Kelland twins, he would be keeping watch for her. She was very nervous, but the thought of Anna in Falkirk's hands kept her walking steadily on. A curricle loomed up out of the murk and she tensed. But no, it went on its way towards St James's. A couple of horsemen, another curricle…

Someone tapped her elbow. Rosabelle turned and looked down. A small boy, looking half-starved, dressed in rags and blue with cold, was holding out his hand. She fumbled for some coins. Suddenly her arms were gripped from behind, and the coins fell to the ground. A gag was thrust into her mouth, she was bundled swiftly into a closed carriage which had drawn up close by and it set off with a jerk. She fell on to the seat.

She was sore, she was frightened, but at the same time she rejoiced. Her plan had succeeded sooner than she could have hoped! Falkirk had surfaced and she would soon see Anna again. She tried to suppress any sign of triumph as she turned her head to look at him—and saw a complete stranger regarding her.

'Well, well!' he drawled removing the gag, 'I was told what to expect, but I would never have believed it! Not one, but two pieces of prime fare, and both exactly the same. What a sight!'

Rosabelle took a deep breath. She did not have to act a part. She was very frightened. 'Who are you, sir? And wh…what do you want with me?'

'Don't worry, girl. Mr Falkirk would have my skin if I harmed you before he has a chance to question you himself.'

'Falkirk?' She pretended to make for the window of the carriage. He pulled her back so roughly that her cry of terror was perfectly genuine.

'If you try that again, I'll forget Falkirk's orders and teach you to behave.' The voice was as smooth, but his eyes were cold. He had enjoyed hurting her.

'Who are you?' asked Rosabelle, her teeth chattering. It had been easy to be brave when drawing up her plan the night before. The reality was so much worse than she had imagined. 'And where are you taking me?'

'To join your sister, what else?' he said. 'Mr Falkirk wants to ask you a few questions. I do hope you have some answers. Mr Falkirk is getting rather desperate. There's no knowing what he might do. He might even hand you over to me.'

The carriage drew up. Rosabelle was bundled out, and she saw that they were in a sort of yard at the back of an inn. The gates were shut behind them and her captor took cruel hold of her wrist and dragged her inside. They went along a passage and into a dingy room.

'Thank you, Fraser. You've delivered Rosabelle Ordway number two, I see!' Falkirk was standing at the side of the room. In a far corner sat Annabelle, pale, dishevelled, but defiant. There was an ugly bruise on her temple, and her hands were tied behind her back.

'You've hurt her!' Rosabelle wrenched herself free, ran over to her sister and knelt down beside her. 'Anna! Are you all right?'

'I've felt better,' said Annabelle, trying to smile. 'But all things considered...'

'Oh, Anna! I'm so sorry...'

'Now, this is most enlightening,' said Falkirk. 'We seem at last to have solved the mystery. I gather that our latest arrival is the real Widow Ordway. So she's the one who can tell us where to look. Isn't that so?'

Rosabelle stood up. 'I told you, I was Rosabelle Ordway, but you wouldn't believe me. I'm not going to ask for any mercy, for I know you are without it—I saw what you did to Stephen. But there is no point in keeping my sister here, sir. Surely now you know which of us is which, you can release her?'

'Well, that depends a bit on what you're going to do for me, Ro-sa-belle,' said Falkirk. 'If I was going to do you a favour like that, I'd like one in return.' His manner changed, and he came over and hauled her to her feet. 'You've wasted my time for long enough!' he snarled, putting his face close to hers. 'You're going to tell me where your snake of a husband hid those papers, Rosabelle Ordway, or you'll say goodbye to your sister for good.'

'I...I...can't.'

Falkirk had himself in hand again. 'I hope that isn't true,' he said calmly. 'Oh, I do so hope it isn't true! The world will lose two of its loveliest stars if it is. Don't be cozened into believing I wouldn't do it, my dears. I've killed so many—two more deaths will make little difference. Men or women—they're all one to me.'

There was a tap on the door. Fraser talked to someone, then came over to Falkirk and whispered something in his ear. Falkirk nodded, then spoke briskly to the girls. His businesslike tone was somehow more frightening than anything else. It was clear that he now regarded them as objects, hindrances in his way, which he would remove without a moment's thought.

'You've got ten minutes for reflection. I don't propose to let either of you go until I know where to find those papers. If you really don't know, Rosabelle, then God help both of you!' He went out, taking Fraser with him.

Chapter Fifteen

'Anna! What happened?' Rosabelle spoke in a whisper. 'How did you come to fall into Falkirk's hands?'

'He had men watching Temperley.'

'We heard. John Bostock came to tell us.'

'What about Goss? Oh, Rosa, is Goss dead?'

'No, he's alive. But we have to think about what we're going to do.' She dropped her voice even lower and put her lips close to Annabelle's ear. 'Anna, I have to tell you. I don't know where the papers are.'

'I thought as much,' Annabelle whispered back. 'But I don't think Falkirk believes that.'

'No, and he mustn't. He'd kill us here and now, if he did. We must persuade him that I know, but that it's too complicated for me to explain. I have to show him.'

Annabelle nodded.

Rosabelle went on whispering, 'Philip and Giles will be at Upper Brook Street in about half an hour. We have to get Falkirk there, but not too soon. We must stay to-gether—tell him that we can't remember without each other. Pretend to be frightened.'

'I don't have to!' said Anna with feeling.

There were sounds of the men returning. Rosabelle put

her arm round her sister and, as Falkirk entered, Annabelle gave a dry sob.

'Well? Have you decided? Tell me quickly—I haven't any time to waste.'

'I don't have to decide, sir. You misunderstood when I said I couldn't tell you.'

'I thought I must have,' Falkirk said with a sardonic smile. 'So where are they?'

'In the drawing room.' Rosabelle hesitated.

'Come on, come on! That's not enough!'

'I'm trying to remember!' cried Rosabelle, desperation in her voice.

'You have to, Rosa!' Annabelle said, convincingly desperate herself. 'Didn't you…didn't you say something about the mantelpiece?'

'Oh, yes! The mantelpiece. Did I say mantelpiece, Anna?'

'You said there was a knob, or a piece of wood which was carved in a strange way…'

'Whereabouts?' demanded Falkirk.

'In the drawing room,' Rosabelle said, looking a little puzzled.

'Good God! I know it's the drawing room, you featherhead! Where, on the mantelpiece, in the fireplace in the drawing room?'

'Yes,' said Rosabelle.

'Where, where, where?'

'I think Mr Falkirk means in what part of the carving on the mantelpiece, Rosa. Please, please try to remember, dear,' said Annabelle.

'Oh!' Rosabelle wrinkled her brow in a well-simulated effort to remember. 'It's been so long since I was there…' she said, and put her hand to her head. 'I think it was on the…right.'

'Good, good.'

'Or was it the left?' She extended her right hand, then her left. 'The left, I think.' She took one look at Falkirk's darkening countenance and faltered, 'I always get confused between my right and my left.'

'This is useless!' exclaimed Falkirk. He went to the door. 'Fraser!' he yelled. 'Get the coach ready!' He came back to the sisters. 'I'm taking you to Upper Brook Street. If we're stopped, you can tell them you've come to collect something. Meanwhile, your sister will stay here.'

'No!' cried Rosabelle in a panic. 'If Anna isn't with me I won't be able to remember anything at all! She has always helped me. I'm not leaving her here. I won't, I won't!'

It was clear that Falkirk was pressed for time. Whatever he had been told outside had created a crisis. 'She'll come. But she'll be tied up,' he said. 'Come on!'

'I won't go unless Anna is in the carriage with me. I'm too frightened—and I don't trust you, Falkirk.'

'You'd better produce those papers pretty quickly, you little shrew, or neither of you will live to go anywhere.'

'I've said I will, but I can't find where Stephen hid them if I'm not there to see the place,' stammered Rosabelle. 'I'm not very good at remembering if things aren't in front of me. And even then I won't be able to think straight unless Anna is with me.'

'That's right, sir,' said Anna, sounding eager to please. 'We have always been very dependent on each other— twins are, you know.'

Falkirk pushed both of them before him out of the room. Fraser produced a length of cord and Anna was bound up, feet as well as wrists, and put into the carriage. Rosabelle joined her, followed by Falkirk. Fraser sat outside. When Rosabelle sat down she felt something on the seat. It was her muff! She had left it in the carriage when they had arrived. While Falkirk was busy with seating himself close to Anna, she quietly slipped the paper knife out of its pocket and put it in her sleeve. She just managed it in time—Falkirk was turning to her.

'In case either of you decides to try anything, Mrs Ordway,' said Falkirk, 'we'll keep this on view.' 'This' was a short stiletto, and it was held to Anna's throat. A faint trace of blood, a graze, appeared on Anna's skin.

The next half hour was a nightmare. The road was rough, and each time the carriage lurched to a halt as something loomed out of the fog and crossed its path, the stiletto touched Anna's throat, and one more tiny drop of blood appeared. There was only one good thing about the journey. It was so slow that there should have been plenty of time for Philip and Giles to reach Upper Brook Street before them.

By the end of that journey Rosabelle had been tense for so long that when she got out of the carriage her legs would hardly support her. The fog swirled around them— there was no chance that they would be seen. Fraser slipped down off the box at the entrance to the mews and disappeared. A few minutes later the front door opened. So much for Mr Keetham's security measures!

They went straight upstairs into the drawing room, Rosabelle first, then Falkirk and the driver of the carriage half-carrying Anna between them. Here they paused a moment. The shutters were closed and there was very little light in the room. The place looked ghostly in the gloom, the mirrors reflecting the pale shapes of furniture shrouded in holland covers. Anna was dumped on to a

chair, and then Falkirk sent the driver out again to stand
guard.

'I…I can't see,' said Rosabelle loudly.

'Open the shutters, Fraser.'

'Is that wise?'

'She's an Ordway, isn't she? She has every right to be
here. Open them.'

Then, when Fraser fumbled with the unfamiliar
catches, Falkirk said impatiently, 'I'm beset by fools!'
and went over to help him.

Rosabelle was standing next to her sister, and had the
paper knife out before Falkirk had even reached the window. In seconds she had slit through the ropes which
bound Anna's wrists, and put the knife down on a table
next to her sister. Anna resumed her former uncomfortable position.

'Now!' said Falkirk. 'The mantelpiece.'

Rosabelle went slowly over to the fireplace. Where
were Philip and Giles? Had Barnaby Stokes failed to find
them? Had he got lost in the fog? Her blood ran cold at
the thought of what might happen if they didn't arrive.
Quite soon. But at least Anna had her hands free, and
she would be able to cut the rope round her ankles as
soon as Falkirk's attention was elsewhere. There might
be a chance to run… No, she must have faith, she did
have faith. Philip would come.

'Er…let me see…' she said. 'The right console…'

'You said it was the left one,' Falkirk said in a hard
voice.

'So I did! But now I'm here, I'm sure it was the right
one.' Her gaze moved frantically over the carved wood.
That cherub looked likely. Where, oh, *where* were Philip
and Giles? She uttered a desperate prayer. Please God,
let him come soon! Then she took a deep breath and said,

'I think this might be it.' Falkirk pushed her out of the way roughly and peered at the carving.

'Which?' he asked.

'That cherub there. His head turns,' said Rosabelle, trying to sound convincing.

Falkirk pressed frantically, pulling this way and that. Nothing happened. He regarded her murderously. 'If you are trying to hoax me...' he said.

Rosabelle's knees were trembling. 'You have to press it in a certain way,' she said. 'It's no good hammering it.'

'You do it!'

Rosabelle put her hand out and touched the cherub's face. It shifted. She gasped and jumped back.

Falkirk and Fraser pushed her away so hard this time that she stumbled, and Anna leapt up to save her. Falkirk paid no attention. He and Fraser were bending forward to examine the carving, their heads almost touching the bracket...

The door from the anteroom burst open and Philip and Giles came hurtling in. Their rush took them right up to the fireplace where they slammed Fraser and Falkirk against the ornate mantelpiece. There was a howl from Falkirk, but he turned like a tiger and threw Philip off. Fraser was struggling with Giles. All four men were powerful, and Falkirk and Fraser were fighting for their survival. They went back and forth, sending tables flying, ripping covers off the furniture to throw them over their attackers, hurling chairs wildly in an effort to trip them up. No trick was too low, no hold was barred. The fight was ferocious. The twins stayed in a corner watching the violence in horror, till they saw the driver of the carriage appear at the door.

'Quickly!' cried Annabelle, but her sister was already

at the door. Together they threw themselves at it, and
slammed it shut. A howl from outside suggested that the
unfortunate man had not quite got his fingers out in time.
'Lock it!' panted Annabelle. After a struggle they got the
key turned, and then they turned to survey the scene.

Fraser was lying unconscious on the floor. Philip was
standing behind Falkirk, holding the latter's arm up behind his back. From the look on Falkirk's face, the grip
was excruciating.

'Right!' said Giles, breathing rather fast. 'We'll get
Burrows in.' As if it had been prearranged, Jenkins and
Barnaby Stokes came in, with Burrows between them.

Falkirk's lips drew back in a snarl. 'You!' he said,
staring malevolently at Burrows. 'I heard about you. So
you told them all about me, did you...' And a string of
curses issued from his mouth.

'That's enough!' said Philip. 'Move! You're going to
the magistrates.'

Giles had taken a gun out, and was holding it on
Falkirk. 'Search him for weapons.' Jenkins came over
and examined Falkirk. The stiletto was produced and
Falkirk released from Philip's grip.

'I should have used that thing on you, when I had the
chance,' said Falkirk viciously, feeling his arm.

'Instead of on a woman who was bound hand and
foot,' said Rosabelle scornfully.

'What do you mean?' Philip asked.

'He held it to Anna's throat in the carriage on the way
here. He drew blood.'

'*What?*' For a moment Giles's attention was on Anna.
Now that the excitement had died down she was sitting
sideways on a chair, holding on to its back. She was very
pale, and the bruise on her head was very prominent.
'Anna!'

'Watch out!' Philip's cry came too late. Falkirk had taken the opportunity of Giles's lapse of attention to rush forward. He bent down to pick something off the floor and almost in the same gesture plunged it into Burrows's throat.

Burrows uttered a gurgling cry and fell forward. Rosabelle cried out. Barnaby Stokes and Philip threw themselves on Falkirk, and once again overpowered him. Falkirk offered little resistance. He stood between them, looking like a wild animal at bay, teeth bared. He nodded towards Burrows's body. 'He won't be able to tell tales about me now!' he said with satisfaction.

Giles had been bending over Annabelle, but now he went over to Burrows and examined him. He shook his head and straightened up. There was a cold, deadly calm about him. 'It's a pity there are so many witnesses here, Falkirk. I'd be glad to despatch you the same way Burrows went. You're two of a kind, you...'

Barnaby Stokes intervened. 'That's no way to talk, sir, if you'll pardon my saying so. It's best to let the law take its proper course.' He faced Falkirk. 'Julian Falkirk, also known as Selder, in the name of the Law I arrest you for the wilful murder of George Burrows. I require you to come with me...'

Rosabelle left Stokes to his work. She knelt down and gazed anxiously at her sister. 'Anna?'

'I'm all right. Truly. I'd like to go somewhere where it's more peaceful, though. My head aches.'

'We'll go back to Arlington Street. I'm sure that's what Philip would want.'

Philip had heard. He said, 'As soon as Jenkins comes back we'll send him for the carriage. He's fetching as-sistance for Stokes at the moment. Of course you must stay with us! I'll get Jenkins to warn Emily to have a bed for you.'

Giles was with Anna again, looking at her in silence. Rosabelle went back to join Philip. 'Is Fraser…is he dead, too?' she asked nervously.

Philip poked the recumbent Fraser with the toe of his boot. 'Unfortunately not. He'll have to be carried off when the men come for Falkirk. He might even be conscious by then. What I can't understand is how Jenkins came to miss Falkirk's other knife!'

'It…it wasn't his,' said Rosabelle nervously. 'I brought it. It's yours.'

'Mine!'

'Your paper knife. I took it in case I needed it. It must have fallen on the floor in the fight.'

'I'm glad to hear that you took some protection,' said Philip evenly. 'Though what you thought you might do with only my paper knife to protect you I cannot imagine.'

Annabelle roused herself. 'Don't! She cut my ropes with it so that we could join together to keep Falkirk's coachman out of the room. You'd have been outnumbered otherwise. Don't talk to Rosabelle like that!'

'Annabelle, you must save your voice!' said Giles, putting his hand over her lips. 'The sooner you can rest, the better.'

'I want to know something first,' she protested. 'What and where are these wretched papers?'

Giles went over to the merry little cherub on the right hand side of the mantelpiece. He pressed something and slid it to one side. When his hand reappeared it held a slender packet of papers.

'Here,' he said. 'Stephen's bank account. He used…he used to keep his pocket money here when he was a child.'

'But that was the very place I... Oh, heavens!' said Rosabelle.

'Exactly so,' said Philip curtly. 'You took an enormous risk, Rosa. How long do you think you would have lived after Falkirk got his papers?'

'I shall go mad,' said Annabelle suddenly. 'I've been chased, carried off, frightened half to death, rescued, beaten on the head and imprisoned, had my throat cut—'

'Anna!'

'Well, nearly—and all for the sake of that wretched bundle of papers. What are they?'

'You mustn't talk, Annabelle,' said Giles.

'Really? Well, silence me by telling me what I want to know.'

'It seems to be a confession signed by Kingsley.'

'Kingsley?'

'Ah! And here's a letter signed by Falkirk, thanking Kingsley for his information, and telling him it will be put to good use. He even calls himself Selder in it! Exactly what we wanted. It would have been enough to deliver Falkirk into the hands of the authorities.'

'Stephen's revenge,' said Rosa sadly. 'And his death warrant.'

'They would have been your death warrant, too,' said Philip. 'Thank God we turned up when we did!'

'But I *sent* for you, Philip!' said Rosabelle.

'Yes. So you did. Well, we'll leave that discussion for another time. I can hear a carriage drawing up.'

'I'll carry Anna,' said Giles.

'And I'll bring Fraser,' said Philip. Fraser was still lying on the floor. Philip took him by the heels and dragged him into the hall.

They made their way out down the stairs in a little procession, passing Barnaby Stokes and his prisoner on the way. Falkirk was standing in the hall next to his jailer, hands tied behind him, his face as if carved in stone. He ignored them as they passed. As they emerged through the front door, several men drew back and waited for them. Then the little band went inside to assist Barnaby Stokes with his prisoners.

The Arlington Street house was in a bustle when they arrived, but Anna's room was ready for her. Rosabelle noticed that Giles seemed remarkably reluctant to relinquish his burden. He brought her in, and brushed aside any offers of help in carrying her up the stairs. Annabelle's own protests he ignored, merely telling her to be quiet and rest her throat.

Philip smiled at the expression on Rosabelle's face. 'Leave them. They have some sorting out to do,' he said.

'I can't stand aside while my sister is carried off by a bully like Giles Stanton,' she said indignantly. 'Anna has more spirit than I have, but she's not well. He'll walk all over her! I've some experience of Colonel Stanton's ways. And from the way he talked to me last night when he thought I was Annabelle, time has not improved him.'

'You really think not? You're wrong. The boot is far more probably on the other foot! And, I assure you, you may safely leave Emily to see that they observe the proprieties. Forget them for the moment, Rosa. I want to talk to you.'

He led her into the library. 'I've lost my paper knife,' he said idly. 'It's been taken as part of the evidence. Why did you do it?'

'Take the paper knife?' she asked, disingenuously.

'Don't play with me. The paper knife is the least of the matter. You knew you were taking a dreadful risk when you embarked on that escapade this morning.

Falkirk is a ruthless killer—you knew that. Not many days ago, you could hardly bring yourself to talk about him, he had frightened you so much. But this morning you deliberately threw yourself into his path, although you knew that I would have stopped you if I could. Didn't you care what it would have done to me, if I had lost you? How much I would have blamed myself? How impossible I would have found it to *live* with myself? Why did you do it?'

Rosabelle saw that she had seriously hurt him. She remembered Emily's words to her—that Philip regarded the safety of all those connected with him as his personal reponsibility. She went over to him and put her arms round him. He stiffened.

'I'd like an answer to my question first, Rosa.' He gently put her arms down from him, and walked several paces away.

'Philip!'

'Oh, don't think I no longer love you as much as I did! The temptation to take you in my arms and kiss the life out of you, right now, is very strong! And it's very tempting, too, to gloss things over with kisses, and put what happened this morning behind us. But it wouldn't solve anything in the long term.'

'I don't understand…?'

'I thought I had your trust. It was a shock to find that I hadn't, after all.'

'That's not so! I do trust you! I put absolute trust in you when I let myself be captured by Falkirk. No one could have had more faith in any other person, than I had in you this morning.'

'But not last night.'

'Ah!' Rosabelle paused, then she said slowly, 'Philip, you're talking now of judgement, not faith.'

'In what way?'

'You and Giles Stanton are both accustomed to making decisions which affect the lives of others—quick decisions, made in wartime conditions. About soldiers. Men.'

'Yes, but I fail to see—'

'Wait a little, I am still working it out. You decided last night that Anna, my sister, my twin sister, could wait until you had first of all found Burrows, had then persuaded him to cooperate with you, then have him take you to Falkirk, then work out a way of rescuing Anna. You didn't consult me, you didn't let me take part, you expected me to sit back and do nothing! Philip, I *could not* sit back and do nothing while such a lengthy process was unwinding! Anna needed my help. She was only in Falkirk's hands because she had recognised my need for help this spring—long before I met you. I would have gone mad sitting here in Arlington Street, wondering what was happening. And…I'm sorry if this offends you…I thought you were wrong not to let me assist you.'

Rosabelle paused, but there was no reaction. She went on, 'I'm not a child, not a doll. I love my sister. This was the quickest way to rescue her, so I set about doing it. But to say that I didn't trust you is foolish. I put my whole life, and Anna's, too, in your hands… Can't you see that?'

She waited again, and this time when he didn't speak she went over to him. 'I love you, Philip. And six months ago I could not have done what I did this morning. I was too weak, too cowardly. You have given me the confidence I need, the trust in another human being, which is as necessary to me as breath. I'm not brave like Anna. I haven't her initiative. I need someone to love me…perhaps have faith in me… Then I can do anything, even…even use my own judgement. Don't deprive me of that—it's your greatest gift to me. Apart from your love.' Her voice broke on these words.

Philip gathered her into his arms. 'Rosa, Rosa, Rosa! Don't! You don't have to say any more! You're right! I'm an unfeeling monster. I should have realised what a bond there is between you and Anna. I was wrong. I promise, I don't regard you as a child—or as a doll. And I never will. To me you're a lovely, passionate woman— my treasure, my friend, my counsellor…and my adored wife. If you will still have me?'

'Oh, yes, Philip! Please!'

'When?'

At this point the door handle rattled and Emily came into the room. 'Colonel Stanton has left,' she said calmly, 'and your sister has been bathed and bandaged and is now asleep, I hope. I thought you must have had time to settle your quarrel by now, and I am come to play propriety. You've been alone long enough. Besides, I shall *die* of curiosity if someone doesn't tell me soon what happened today! But don't start yet! I've had some food put out in the dining room, and we can talk in there. Grandpapa is there already.'

When they had gathered in the dining room, Philip said, 'Before I begin, Grandfather, I want to tell you that Rosa and I are now at liberty to publish our engagement. I hope she will agree to marry me as soon as we can arrange a date.'

Lord Winbolt was delighted and supported this scheme with all his heart. Emily pulled the bell and Maynard came in with a bottle of champagne. 'I thought we might be needing it,' said Emily with a satisfied smile. 'But you must not think of marrying before next Easter!'

'Easter!' Philip was appalled.

'It would be just one year since you met. And if you

think an important wedding such as yours can be arranged in a day or two—or even a month or two—you are very much mistaken! What about the bride clothes and all the other preparations?' Emily regarded the expression of outrage on her brother's face with some amusement. She turned to Rosabelle. 'Rosa will agree with me, I am sure.'

Having noticed the twinkle in Emily's eye, Rosabelle was emboldened to reply, 'I should think Easter would be almost too soon…'

'Oh, no!' said Philip with decision. 'I might, I just might, wait till Twelfth Night. But not a week longer. Don't tempt me too far, or I shall take you up before me on my stallion and whistle you off to Gretna tomorrow!'

'You're all talking a great deal of nonsense!' said Lord Winbolt irritably. 'Rosa must decide a time to suit the greatest number of people. I take it that the wedding will take place in Berkshire?'

'I would like that,' said Rosabelle.

'Very well. It looks as if I shall be seeing Shearings again before I die, after all. But I can't promise to wait too long. I may get a more pressing invitation.'

'The weather is always worse in January or February, Rosa,' said Philip persuasively. 'I think Grandfather should come down, at his leisure, but as soon as possible.'

'Christmas would be nice…' said Rosabelle pensively.

'Rosa!' shrieked Emily. 'Your clothes!'

'She only needs one dress in which to marry,' said Philip. 'It can't take long to make one dress.'

The issue was never seriously in doubt. It was soon settled that the wedding of Rosabelle Ordway to Lord Winbolt's heir would take place at Christmas, or very soon after.

'I shall tell Anna as soon as she wakes up,' said Rosabelle happily.

Annabelle swore that the news was the one thing to cause her to forget headache, bruise, sore throat and all the rest. For the rest of the day, she, Rosabelle and Emily spent a very happy time planning the celebrations.

'Rosa! What a wonderful Christmas Temperley will have once more! We must consult Becky. She can remember all the things our parents and grandparents did! Oh, it will be exciting beyond anything! A wedding at Christmas!'

Emily went off to arrange for more samples to be sent from Harding Howells, and to gather together all the copies of *The Ladies Magazine*, *La Belle Assemblée*, *The Cabinet of Fashion*, and others that she could find. The sisters were left alone.

They talked for a while of life at Temperley and Shearings, then Rosabelle asked, somewhat hesitantly, 'And what about you, Anna? Might there be another wedding at Christmas?'

The colour rose in Annabelle's cheeks, but she said composedly enough, 'I very much doubt it. I should need a husband, for a start.'

'And what about Giles Stanton?'

'Most unlikely! We seem to fall out with shocking regularity.'

'He seemed quite attentive yesterday.'

'Was he?' The colour in Annabelle's cheeks increased. 'But no! Let's just say that I shall be your bridesmaid, and hold your bouquet for you. Perhaps Philip will mistake me for you, and I shall have a rich husband after all!'

Annabelle refused to allow her sister to question her further on her relationship with Giles Stanton.

Indeed, the next day it appeared that there was more than one gentleman in London eager to pursue the lovely 'Mrs Ordway'.

When the first bouquet arrived, Rosa was excited and flattered—until she read the note attached to it.

'Who on earth is Peter Wainwright?' she asked. 'I seem to have made something of a hit with him, but I have no idea where!'

'He'd better take care!' said Philip. 'His admiration is natural, I understand it perfectly well. But he must learn to keep his flowers and his feelings to himself! Or find another object of his admiration.'

'Er…in fact, I think that the flowers are intended for me,' said Annabelle, in a little embarrassment. 'Colonel Wainwright was quite attentive before we went to Buxton. He must have learned I am in London again.'

Philip and Rosabelle exchanged a look. 'I see,' said Rosa slowly.

When a second floral tribute for Mrs Ordway arrrived, Rosabelle was better prepared. 'Colonel Wainwright appears to have a rival,' she said. 'Does ''Richard Pettifer'' mean anything to you, Anna?'

'Oh, yes! Captain Pettifer was very flattering. I think he was the one who compared my eyes with bluebells— or was that Major Dabney?'

'Annabelle! Were you a flirt?'

'Of course not! I was a ''success'', that's all. And you have no idea how very pleasant it was to be in demand, to wear beautiful clothes, to be complimented on my appearance or the grace of my dancing! Most of it sheerest flattery, of course, but a welcome change from a life in obscurity at Temperley, listening to compliments on the yields of my tenants' fields, or the good condition of the fences—or otherwise,' she added with a sly look at Philip.

'Oh, those fences!' Rosabelle exclaimed in horror. 'If you only knew how much trouble I had over those fences!'

But a more serious contender for Annabelle's favours appeared later in the day. Lord Monteith called, a most eligible young man, the son of an Earl and heir to handsome estates in the West Country. But Annabelle refused to see him, pleading that she was not strong enough for visitors. Emily dealt with him, and he eventually left, but he was not happy. It isn't often that such an important young man is denied access to the lady of his choice. But Annabelle appeared indifferent. She seemed to be waiting for someone else.

Chapter Sixteen

It was perhaps unfortunate that Colonel Stanton should appear just as Lord Monteith was taking his leave. However, Maynard took in the situation and showed the new caller into the library until his lordship departed. Giles was then taken to the small parlour where Annabelle was waiting...

When Rosabelle came into the parlour some time later she found the air bristling with hostility. 'Oh,' she said blankly, 'I thought I'd find Philip and Emily here. Forgive me.' And she made to go out again.

'Pray do not feel you have to go, Rosa,' said Annabelle in a high, brittle voice, quite unlike her usual tones. 'Colonel Stanton was just leaving.'

Giles Stanton's countenance grew even more forbidding. 'Annabelle—' he began.

'If you do not leave this room, sir, then I will!'

'In that case there is no more to be said,' he said furiously. 'Goodbye, Miss Kelland.' He turned and gave a brief bow in Rosabelle's direction, 'Rosabelle,' and strode out. There was complete silence in the room for a moment or two.

Then Rosabelle asked, 'May I…dare I ask what that was all about?'

Annabelle, twin flags of anger flying in her cheeks, exploded. 'Giles Stanton is an unfeeling, arrogant oaf! And I hope never to see him again!'

'Anna, he—'

'I refuse to discuss him, or anything connected with him, Rosa! If you wish to please me, you will not even mention his name. I do not wish to hear it.'

And Annabelle continued to be adamant. When Rosabelle, Philip, or anyone else brought the name of Giles Stanton into the conversation Annabelle simply fell silent until the discussion was over.

The rest of November was spent in London in a flurry of mantua-makers, drapers' shops, haberdashery stores, shoemakers, grocery supplies—three months' work crammed into three weeks. Rosabelle was in a happy daze for most of the time. She stood in a dream while Madame Fanchon or one of her assistants fitted and pinned and pulled. It was fortunate that she had Annabelle and Emily to keep her feet somewhere near the ground, for the wedding clothes would otherwise never have been finished.

Because of sundry delays, it was the second week in December before they got away, though there had been much to-ing and fro-ing between London and Berkshire in the meantime. They travelled in convoy down the Bath Road, with a large escort of grooms and postilions to see to their safety and comfort, and took the journey at a leisurely pace, spending a night on the way, so that Lord Winbolt should not get overtired. They were fortunate with the weather—the fog had completely disappeared,

and though the days were cold, they were crisp and
bright. As a result the roads were dry and travel easy.
But though the sun sparkled on the traces of frost on the
trees and on the waters of the rivers they crossed, nothing
could rival the sparkle of eyes, laughter and wit as the
wedding party made its way to Temperley and Shearings.

At Temperley Becky was waiting with jugs of mulled
ale and spiced wine for everyone. Mr Kelland was downstairs with Aunt Laura, and the house fairly buzzed with
excitement and activity. As the little convoy wound its
way up the drive, children of the workers from both estates ran alongside, waving streamers and branches of
evergreen.

'Papa! Aunt Laura! Becky!' There were scenes of confused laughter, and many embraces, as both sisters were
welcomed back to Temperley. Philip waited with the second carriage, until some of the tumult had subsided, then
he gave a sign to one of the grooms to assist Emily and
Lord Winbolt out, and the three Winbolts walked forward. Some complicated introductions followed, then the
family party repaired to the large parlour, which was so
vast that it was hardly ever used. But Becky had seen to
it that the room was warm with huge fires burning at each
end, the flames bathing the panelled walls, plaster ceiling
and heavy furniture in a mellow glow.

'Now this is something!' said Lord Winbolt. 'None of
your fingle-fangling decoration here. Good honest wood
and plasterwork.' He sat down with a sigh of satisfaction
on a large armchair, made to accommodate the more
elaborate clothes of the previous century.

Philip smiled at Rosabelle. 'I can see he is going to be
hard on me for the alterations we've had done at
Shearings!'

'I like them. Oh, Philip, we're home at last! I can't tell you how content I am!'

'Well, I'm not! Not yet. There's still the little matter of our wedding. And then I'll take you home. To our home.' He raised her hand to his lips and kissed it, his eyes never leaving hers.

'I can't help it,' said Lady Ordway, raising a handkerchief to her eyes. 'It's so lovely to see two young people so much in love.'

'Yes,' said Mr Kelland briskly. 'But do not, I pray, let us get sentimental. There is far too much to think of. Can anyone tell me exactly when the wedding is to be? Or is that asking too much?'

'I would marry your daughter tomorrow, sir. I have the licence.'

'I wish you would, Winbolt—it would save a lot of fuss. But I doubt we'll get away with that.'

'We shall be married during the twelve days of Christmas, Papa.'

'Well then, why not start the New Year together? Have the wedding on the thirty-first of December. That gives you all three weeks to settle in after your journey, send off invitations and announcements and there will still be time to enjoy Christmas. I'm assuming the licence is a special one, Winbolt, and that you can choose your own day.'

This idea met with general approval, and they began to discuss who else was to be invited.

Eventually the Winbolts set off to complete their journey to Shearings, and the Kelland family party were left alone.

'Is there…is there anyone else you would wish to invite, Anna?' asked Rosabelle.

'I don't think so,' her sister replied, listlessly. 'You've

mentioned all the local people who should come. And there certainly isn't anyone else.'

Rosabelle looked at her in concern. For days Annabelle had joked and laughed with the rest, teasing Philip, conversing with Lady Ordway with whom she appeared to have a very good relationship, and adding to the general gaiety. But she had been unable to hide her unhappiness from her twin. Rosabelle wondered whether the rough treatment Annabelle had suffered at the hands of Falkirk and his gang was having a belated effect, and asked if her sister was well, but Anna replied, 'Of course I am! Pray don't worry about me, Rosa. I shall soon come about.'

Busy as Rosabelle was exchanging visits with neighbours, spending time at Shearings with Philip planning the household there, and, of course, working with Annabelle, Becky and the rest at Temperley, she still found time to keep a close watch on Annabelle. Annabelle did not seem to her to be 'coming about'. She talked to Philip about it.

'It's Giles Stanton, Philip, I'm sure of it.'

'So am I. What is more, I'm positive that Giles is as unhappy as your sister.'

'Then why don't they make it up?'

'How can they? They never meet. And unless something is done about it, pride and obstinacy will keep them apart permanently.'

'You're speaking very plainly about my sister, Philip.'

'I admire your sister a great deal, but I'm not sure she is the soul of forgiveness and patience. And Giles has always been pig-headed, though he usually comes round in the end.' Philip gave her a look. 'Shall I leave the matter in your hands?'

'For the moment, perhaps.'

A few days later the sisters were sitting alone in the little parlour. Aunt Laura was resting, and Mr Kelland was reading, as usual. Rosabelle took a deep breath and said carefully, 'Anna, I'm sure Philip would like Giles St—'

'No!'

'My dear, I can't carry on not mentioning Giles! He is Aunt Laura's nephew, and one of Philip's best friends. Why do you dislike him so?'

'Not even Samuel Carter at his worst ever spoke to me as that man has! You have no idea how unreasonable and...and cruel he can be,' Annabelle said bitterly.

'Believe me, I have. You forget that I knew him before you! But this is the season when we should forget and forgive past insults and injuries. I can't bear to see you so unhappy. Let me invite him to the wedding—you needn't speak to him, if you really don't wish to.'

'You're mistaken, Rosa. It is Colonel Stanton who would not speak to me! On the last occasion we met, he made his opinion of me perfectly clear! I am beneath his contempt. But I can do very well without him!'

'I'm sure you could, dear. But would you really object if I sent him an invitation?'

'I've told you a hundred times, Rosa! I do not wish ever to see that monster again!' Annabelle paused, then said, 'Besides, I don't expect he would come.'

Rosabelle said nothing more, but instead asked Annabelle to enlist Becky's aid in decorating the house. This she did, and soon all Becky's memories of how the old house had been dressed for Christmas were revived and followed.

* * *

On Christmas Eve the snow began to fall, large, gentle
flakes of white, floating on to the shoulders of the singers
as they wound their way through the village and up to
Temperley.

'Do you remember last Christmas, Miss Annabelle?'
said Becky. 'We had snow then, too.'

'But this year we're having a real Christmas, Becky,
darling. Everyone is here, and the house looks just as it
should.'

Annabelle looked at the ivy, the holly, the fir branches,
sniffed the air scented with spices and the fresh tang of
the greenery. Everything was now in place. The party
from Shearings had arrived that afternoon, and would
stay till after the wedding. The larders were piled high
with food for the feast, and fires were lit in every room.
The sound of church bells wafted in through the snow-
laden air.

She smiled as she observed Rosabelle and Philip, about
to come downstairs after an hour with her father. They
stood framed in an arch of greenery at the top of the
staircase, pausing for a moment, lost to the world. She
sighed and turned away. Such moments were private, not
to be stared at, not to have their glory diminished by
sadness or envy.

Christmas Eve passed in a flurry of activity, and
Christmas Day was already an hour old when the church
party returned to Temperley. Lady Ordway, Lord
Winbolt and Mr Kelland had elected to stay behind in
the house, but Philip had escorted the three girls through
the snow to the late night service. Though it had stopped
snowing several hours before, the paths and lanes were
covered, and the four young people had slipped and slith-
ered back to the house. There was much laughter and

high spirits when they came into the hall, until they remembered that the older generation had probably retired.

'I'm quite tired, too,' said Rosabelle. 'There's a great deal to do tomorrow.'

'I'll see you to your room,' said Philip.

As they went up the stairs, Philip said, 'I was wrong, it appears. Giles is implacable.'

'I did write. But he won't come now. And the snow has made it impossible, anyway,' Rosa said sadly.

'You did your best, my heart. Don't be sad. There's so much to be happy about. It's less than a week now, then I won't have to say goodnight at your door.' He bent his head. Then lifted it as a sound of coughing came up the stairs. He looked at Rosabelle and said ruefully, 'Sisters! Poor Emily is afflicted with her cough again. If she doesn't see about it soon, I will! Goodnight, my love.'

'You haven't long to wait now, Philip, dear,' said Emily behind them. 'Someone has to see that you behave—we can't have Rosa falling by the wayside at this late stage!'

'Sometimes, Emily, you go too far! I was merely kissing, yes, kissing my betrothed goodnight. And with three of you all sleeping in the same bedroom, seduction would be well nigh impossible! I know my limitations.'

'Spare your bride's blushes and go to bed! Goodnight, Philip, dear.' She kissed him and, raising an eyebrow at Rosabelle, went on into the bedroom.

Philip kissed Rosabelle tenderly and dragged himself away. The house grew quiet again.

Annabelle slowly mounted the stairs. It was all just as she had pictured it exactly one year ago. The stairs were wound with holly and ivy, and there was mistletoe in the hall. Tonight there had been the sounds of footsteps and suppressed laughter on the landing as the others had bade each other goodnight, and now here at the top of the stairs she could hear whispers and the rustle of silk and taffeta. Even the scents of perfume and lavender, honey and beeswax were as she had imagined them.

But hall and stairs were empty of any tall, dark-haired beau to be King to her Queen of the Revels. There was still no one to come in through the door, to tell her how lovely she looked, to invite her to a ball or some other revelry in the neighbourhood. And now there never would be. Her own foolish, self-willed behaviour had seen to that. She turned slowly towards the bedchamber...

There was suddenly a thunderous knocking at the door. Becky and John Bostock came hurrying through from the kitchen. When they saw Annabelle at the top of the stairs Becky paused and asked, 'What shall I do, Miss Belle?'

'You'd better open it, Becky. It's late, but it's no night to leave a traveller outside.'

Annabelle waited halfway down the stairs, her heart in her mouth as Becky opened the door, and she heard a deep voice say, 'Miss Kelland?'

* * * * *

You don't have to wait!
Annabelle's story is also out this month
in "Christmas Belles" *Part Two*

MILLS & BOON®

Makes any time special

**Enjoy a romantic novel from
Mills & Boon®**

Presents™ *Enchanted*™ *Temptation*®

Historical Romance™ *Medical Romance*™

MILLS & BOON®

Next Month's Romance Titles

Each month you can choose from a wide variety of romance novels from Mills & Boon®. Below are the new titles to look out for next month from the Presents™ and Enchanted™ series.

Presents™

TO WOO A WIFE	Carole Mortimer
CONTRACT BABY	Lynne Graham
IN BED WITH THE BOSS	Susan Napier
SURRENDER TO SEDUCTION	Robyn Donald
OUTBACK MISTRESS	Lindsay Armstrong
THE SECRET DAUGHTER	Catherine Spencer
THE MARRIAGE ASSIGNMENT	Alison Kelly
WIFE BY AGREEMENT	Kim Lawrence

Enchanted™

BE MY GIRL!	Lucy Gordon
LONESOME COWBOY	Debbie Macomber
A SUITABLE GROOM	Liz Fielding
NEW YEAR...NEW FAMILY	Grace Green
OUTBACK HUSBAND	Jessica Hart
MAKE-BELIEVE MOTHER	Pamela Bauer & Judy Kaye
OH, BABY!	Lauryn Chandler
FOLLOW THAT GROOM!	Christie Ridgway

On sale from 8th January 1999

H1 9812

Available at most branches of WH Smith, Tesco, Asda, Martins, Borders and all good paperback bookshops

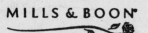

We are giving away a year's supply of Mills & Boon® books to the five lucky winners of our latest competition. Simply match the six film stars to the films in which they appeared, complete the coupon overleaf and send this entire page to us by 30th June 1999. The first five correct entries will each win a year's subscription to the Mills & Boon series of their choice. What could be easier?

CABARET	__	GONE WITH THE WIND	__
ROCKY	__	SMOKEY & THE BANDIT	__
PRETTY WOMAN	__	GHOST	

C8L

Please turn over for details of how to enter ➜

HOW TO ENTER

There are six famous faces and a list of six films overleaf. Each of the famous faces starred in one of the films listed and all you have to do is match them up!

As you match each one, write the number of the actor or actress who starred in each film in the space provided. When you have matched them all, fill in the coupon below, pop this page in an envelope and post it today. Don't forget you could win a year's supply of Mills & Boon® books—you don't even need to pay for a stamp!

Mills & Boon Hollywood Heroes Competition
FREEPOST CN81, Croydon, Surrey, CR9 3WZ
EIRE readers: (please affix stamp) PO Box 4546, Dublin 24.

Please tick the series you would like to receive if you
are one of the lucky winners

Presents™ ❏   Enchanted™ ❏ Historical Romance™ ❏

Medical Romance™ ❏ Temptation® ❏

Are you a Reader Service™ subscriber?   Yes ❏   No ❏

Ms/Mrs/Miss/Mr ....Initials ....
(BLOCK CAPITALS PLEASE)

Surname...

Address ....

....

.................................Postcode............................

(I am over 18 years of age)   C8L

Closing date for entries is 30th June 1999. One entry per household. Free subscriptions are for four books per month. Competition open to residents of the UK and Ireland only. As a result of this application, you may receive further offers from Harlequin Mills & Boon and other carefully selected companies. If you would prefer not to share in this opportunity please write to The Data Manager at the address shown above.

Mills & Boon is a registered trademark of
Harlequin Mills & Boon Ltd.